I0612138

THE TRUMPETER SWAN

MORE WILDSIDE CLASSICS

Dacobra, or The White Priests of Ahriman, by Harris Burland
The Nabob, by Alphonse Daudet
Out of the Wreck, by Captain A. E. Dingle
The Elm-Tree on the Mall, by Anatole France
The Lance of Kanana, by Harry W. French
Amazon Nights, by Arthur O. Friel
Caught in the Net, by Emile Gaboriau
The Gentle Grafter, by O. Henry
Raffles, by E. W. Hornung
Gates of Empire, by Robert E. Howard
Tom Brown's School Days, by Thomas Hughes
The Opium Ship, by H. Bedford Jones
The Miracles of Antichrist, by Selma Lagerlof
Arsène Lupin, by Maurice LeBlanc
A Phantom Lover, by Vernon Lee
The Iron Heel, by Jack London
The Witness for the Defence, by A.E.W. Mason
The Spider Strain and Other Tales, by Johnston McCulley
Tales of Thubway Tham, by Johnston McCulley
The Prince of Graustark, by George McCutcheon
Bull-Dog Drummond, by Cyril McNeile
The Moon Pool, by A. Merritt
The Red House Mystery, by A. A. Milne
Blix, by Frank Norris
Wings over Tomorrow, by Philip Francis Nowlan
The Devil's Paw, by E. Phillips Oppenheim
Satan's Daughter and Other Tales, by E. Hoffmann Price
The Insidious Dr. Fu Manchu, by Sax Rohmer
Mauprat, by George Sand
The Slayer and Other Tales, by H. de Vere Stacpoole
Penrod (Gordon Grant Illustrated Edition), by Booth Tarkington
The Gilded Age, by Mark Twain
The Blockade Runners, by Jules Verne
The Gadfly, by E.L. Voynich

Please see www.wildsidepress.com for a complete list!

THE TRUMPETER SWAN

SWAN

TEMPLE BAILEY

WILDSIDE PRESS

THE TRUMPETER SWAN

This edition published in 2006 by Wildside Press, LLC.
www.wildsidepress.com

CHAPTER I

A MAJOR AND TWO MINORS

I

It had rained all night, one of the summer rains that, beginning in a thunder-storm in Washington, had continued in a steaming drizzle until morning.

There were only four passengers in the sleeper, men all of them—two in adjoining sections in the middle of the car, a third in the drawing-room, a fourth an intermittent occupant of a berth at the end. They had gone to bed unaware of the estate or circumstance of their fellow-travellers, and had waked to find the train delayed by washouts, and side-tracked until more could be learned of the condition of the road.

The man in the drawing-room shone, in the few glimpses that the others had of him, with an effulgence which was dazzling. His valet, the intermittent sleeper in the end berth, was a smug little soul, with a small nose which pointed to the stars. When the door of the compartment opened to admit breakfast there was the radiance of a brocade dressing-gown, the shine of a sleek head, the staccato of an imperious voice.

Randy Paine, long and lank, in faded khaki, rose, leaned over the seat of the section in front of him and drawled, "'It is not raining rain to me—it's raining roses—down—'"

A pleasant laugh, and a deep voice, "Come around here and talk to me. You're a Virginian, aren't you?"

"By the grace of God and the discrimination of my ancestors," young Randolph, as he dropped into the seat opposite the man with the deep voice, saluted the dead and gone Paines.

"Then you know this part of it?"

"I was born here. In this county. It is bone of my bone and flesh of my flesh," there was a break in the boy's voice which robbed the words of grandiloquence.

"Hum—you love it? Yes? And I am greedy to get away. I want wider spaces—"

"California?"

"Yes. Haven't seen it for three years. I thought when the war was over I might. But I've got to be near Washington, it seems. The heat drove me out, and somebody told me it would be cool in these hills—"

"It is, at night. By day we're not strenuous."

"I like to be strenuous. I hate inaction."

He moved restlessly. There was a crutch by his side. Young Paine noticed it for the first time. "I hate it."

He had a strong frame, broad shoulders and thin hips. One placed him immediately as a man of great physical force. Yet there was the crutch. Randy had seen other men, broad-shouldered, thin-hipped, who had come to worse than crutches. He did not want to think of them. He had escaped without a scratch. He did not believe that he had lacked courage, and there was a decoration to prove that he had not. But when he thought of those other men, he had no sense of his own valor. He had given so little and they had given so much.

Yet it was not a thing to speak of. He struck, therefore, a note to which he knew the other might respond.

"If you haven't been here before, you'll like the old places."

"I am going to one of them."

"Which?"

"King's Crest."

A moment's silence. Then, "That's my home. I have lived there all my life."

The lame man gave him a sharp glance. "I heard of it in Washington—delightful atmosphere—and all that—"

"You are going as a—paying guest?"

"Yes."

A deep flush stained the younger man's face. Suddenly he broke out. "If you knew how rotten it seems to me to have my mother keeping—boarders—"

"My dear fellow, I hope you don't think it is going to be rotten to have me?"

"No. But there are other people. And I didn't know until I came back from France—She had to tell me when she knew I was coming."

"She had been doing it all the time you were away?"

"Yes. Before I went we had mortgaged things to help me through the University. I should have finished in a year if I hadn't enlisted. And Mother insisted there was enough for her. But there wasn't with the interest and everything—and she wouldn't sell an acre. I shan't let her keep on—"

"Are you going to turn me out?"

His smile was irresistible. Randy smiled back. "I suppose you think I'm a fool—?"

"Yes. For being ashamed of it."

Randy's head went up. "I'm not ashamed of the boarding-house. I am ashamed to have my mother work."

"So," said the lame man, softly, "that's it? And your name is Paine?"

"Randolph Paine of King's Crest. There have been a lot of us—and not a piker in the lot."

"I am Mark Prime."

"Major Prime of the 135th?"

The other nodded. "The wonderful 135th—God, what men they were—" his eyes shone.

Randy made his little gesture of salute. "They were that. I don't wonder you are proud of them."

"It was worth all the rest," the Major said, "to have known my men."

He looked out of the window at the drizzle of rain. "How quiet the world seems after it all—"

Then like the snap of bullets came the staccato voice through the open door of the compartment.

"Find out why we are stopping in this beastly hole, Kemp, and get me something cold to drink."

Kemp, sailing down the aisle, like a Lilliputian drum major, tripped over Randy's foot.

"Beg pardon, sir," he said, and sailed on.

Randy looked after him. "'His Master's voice—'"

"And to think," Prime remarked, "that the coldest thing he can get on this train is ginger ale."

Kemp, coming back with a golden bottle, with cracked ice in a tall glass, with a crisp curl of lemon peel, ready for an innocuous libation, brought his nose down from the heights to look for the foot, found that it no longer barred the way, and marched on to hidden music.

"Leave the door open, leave it open," snapped the voice, "isn't there an electric fan? Well, put it on, put it on   "

"He drinks nectar and complains to the gods," said the Major softly, "why can't we, too, drink?"

They had theirs on a table which the porter set between them. The train moved on before they had finished. "We'll be in Charlottesville in less than an hour," the conductor announced.

"Is that where we get off, Paine?"

"One mile beyond. Are they going to meet you?"

"I'll get a station wagon."

Young Paine grinned. "There aren't any. But if Mother knows you're coming she'll send down. And anyhow she expects me."

"After a year in France—it will be a warm welcome—"

"A wet one, but I love the rain, and the red mud, every

blooming inch of it."

"Of course you do. Just as I love the dust of the desert."

They spoke, each of them, with a sort of tense calmness. One doesn't confess to a lump in one's throat.

The little man, Kemp, was brushing things in the aisle. He was hot but unconquered. Having laid out the belongings of the man he served, he took a sudden recess, and came back with a fresh collar, a wet but faultless pompadour, and a suspicion of powder on his small nose.

"All right, sir, we'll be there in fifteen minutes, sir," they heard him say, as he was swallowed up by the yawning door.

II

Fifteen minutes later when the train slowed up, there emerged from the drawing-room a man some years older than Randolph Paine, and many years younger than Major Prime. He was good-looking, well-dressed, but apparently in a very bad temper. Kemp, in an excited, Skye-terrier manner, had gotten the bags together, had a raincoat over his arm, had an umbrella handy, had apparently foreseen every contingency but one.

"Great guns, Kemp, why are we getting off here?"

"The conductor said it was nearer, sir."

Randolph Paine was already hanging on the step, ready to drop the moment the train stopped. He had given the porter an extra tip to look after Major Prime. "He isn't used to that crutch, yet. He'd hate it if I tried to help him."

The rain having drizzled for hours, condensed suddenly in a downpour. When the train moved on, the men found themselves in a small and stuffy waiting-room. Around the station platform was a sea of red mud. Misty hills shot up in a circle to the horizon. There was not a house in sight. There was not a soul in sight except the agent who knew young Paine. No one having come to meet them, he suggested the use of the telephone.

In the meantime Kemp was having a hard time of it. "Why in the name of Heaven didn't we get off at Charlottesville," his master was demanding.

"The conductor said this was nearer, sir," Kemp repeated. His response had the bounding quality of a rubber ball. "If you'll sit here and make yourself comfortable, Mr. Dalton, I'll see what I can do."

"Oh, it's a beastly hole, Kemp. How can I be comfortable?"

Randy, who had come back from the telephone with a look on his face which clutched at Major Prime's throat, caught Dalton's complaint.

"It isn't a beastly hole," he said in a ringing voice, "it's God's country—I got my mother on the phone, Major. She has sent for us and the horses are on the way."

Dalton looked him over. What a lank and shabby youth he was to carry in his voice that ring of authority. "What's the answer to our getting off here?" he asked.

"Depends upon where you are going."

"To Oscar Waterman's—"

"Never heard of him."

"Hamilton Hill," said the station agent.

Randy's neck stiffened. "Then the Hamiltons have sold it?"

"Yes. A Mr. Waterman of New York bought it."

Kemp had come back. "Mr. Waterman says he'll send the car at once. He is delighted to know that you have come, sir."

"How long must I wait?"

"Not more than ten minutes, he said, sir," Kemp's optimism seemed to ricochet against his master's hardness and come back unhurt. "He will send a closed car and will have your rooms ready for you."

"Serves me right for not wiring," said Dalton, "but who would believe there is a place in the world where a man can't get a taxi?"

Young Paine was at the door, listening for the sound of hoofs, watching with impatience. Suddenly he gave a shout, and the others looked to see a small object which came whirling like a bomb through the mist.

"Nellie, little old lady, little old lady," the boy was on his knees, the dog in his arms—an ecstatic, panting creature, the first to welcome her master home!

Before he let her go, the little dog's coat was wet with more than rain, but Randy was not ashamed of the tears in his eyes as he faced the others.

"I've had her from a pup—she's a faithful beast. Hello, there they come. Gee, Jefferson, but you've grown! You are almost as big as your name."

Jefferson was the negro boy who drove the horses. There was a great splashing of red mud as he drew up. The flaps of the surrey closed it in.

Jefferson's eyes were twinkling beads as he greeted his master. "I sure is glad to see you, Mr. Randy. Miss Caroline, she say there was another gemp'mun?"

"He's here—Major Prime. You run in there and look after his bags."

Randy unbuttoned the flaps and gave a gasp of astonishment:

"*Becky*—Becky Bannister!"

In another moment she was out on the platform, and he was holding her hands, protesting in the meantime, "You'll get wet, my dear—"

"Oh, I want to be rained on, Randy. It's so heavenly to have you home. I caught Jefferson on the way down. I didn't even wait to get my hat."

She did not need a hat. It would have hidden her hair. George Dalton, watching her from the door, decided that he had never seen such hair, bronze, parted on the side, with a thick wave across the forehead, it shaded eyes which were clear wells of light.

She was a little thing with a quality in her youth which made one think of the year at the spring, of the day at morn, of Botticelli's Simonetta, of Shelley's lark, of Wordsworth's daffodils, of Keats' Eve of St. Agnes—of all the lovely radiant things of which the poets of the world have sung—

Of course Dalton did not think of her in quite that way. He knew something of Browning and little of Keats, but he had at least the wit to discern the rareness of her type.

As for the rest, she wore faded blue, which melted into the blue of the mists, stubbed and shabby russet shoes and an air of absorption in her returned soldier. This absorption Dalton found himself subconsciously resenting. Following an instinctive urge, he emerged, therefore, from his chrysalis of ill-temper, and smiled upon a transformed universe.

"My raincoat, Kemp," he said, and strode forth across the platform, a creature as shining and splendid as ever trod its boards.

Becky, beholding him, asked, "Is that Major Prime?"

"No, thank Heaven."

Jefferson, steering the Major expertly, came up at this moment. Then, splashing down the red road whirled the gorgeous limousine. There were two men on the box. Kemp, who had been fluttering around Dalton with an umbrella, darted into the waiting-room for the bags. The door of the limousine was opened by the footman, who also had an umbrella ready. Dalton hesitated, his eyes on that shabby group by the mud-stained surrey. He made up his mind suddenly and approached young Paine.

"We can take one of you in here. You'll be crowded with all of those bags."

"Not a bit. We'll manage perfectly, thank you," Randy's voice dismissed him.

He went, with a lingering glance backward. Becky, catching

that glance, waked suddenly to the fact that he was very good-looking. "It was kind of him to offer, Randy."

"Was it?"

Nothing more was said, but Becky wondered a bit as they drove on. She liked Major Prime. He was an old dear. But why had Randy thanked Heaven that the other man was not the Major?

III

The Waterman motor passed the surrey, and Dalton, straining his eyes for a glimpse of the pretty girl, was rewarded only by a view of Randy on the front seat with his back turned on the world, while he talked with someone hidden by the curtains.

Perhaps the fact that she was hidden by the curtains kept Dalton's thoughts upon her. He felt that her beauty must shine even among the shadows—he envied Major Prime, who sat next to her.

The Major was aware that his position was enviable. It was worth much to watch these two young people, eager in their reunion. "Becky Bannister, whom I have known all my life," had been Randy's presentation of the little lady with the shining hair.

"Grandfather doesn't know that I came, or Aunt Claudia. They felt that your mother ought to see you first and so did I. Until the last minute. Then I saw Jefferson driving by—I was down at the gate to wave to you, Randy—and I just came—" her gay laugh was infectious—the men laughed with her.

"You must let me out when we get to Huntersfield, and you mustn't tell—either of you. We are all to dine together to-night at your house, Randy, and when you meet me, you are to say—*Becky*'—just as you did to-day, as if I had fallen from the skies."

"Well, you did fall—straight," Randy told her. "Becky, you are too good to be true; oh, you're too pretty to be true. Isn't she, Major?"

"It is just because I am—American. Are you glad to get back to us, Randy?"

"Glad," he drew a long breath. Nellie, who had wedged herself in tightly between her master and Jefferson, wriggled and licked his hand. He looked down at her, tried to say something, broke a little on it, and ended abruptly, "It's Heaven."

"And you weren't hurt?"

"Not a scratch, worse luck."

She turned to Major Prime and did the wise thing and the thing he liked. "You were," she said, simply, "but I am not going to be sorry for you, shall I?"

"No," he said, "I am not sorry for—myself—"

For a moment there was silence, then Becky carried the conversation into lighter currents. "Everybody is here for the Horse Show next week. Your mother's house is full, and those awful Waterman people have guests."

"One of them came down with us."

"The good-looking man who offered us a ride?"

"Oh, of course if you like that kind of looks, he's the kind of man you'd like," said Randy, "but coming down he seemed rather out of tune with the universe."

"How out of tune?"

"Well, it was hot and he was hot—"

"It *is* hot, Randy, and perhaps he isn't used to it."

"Are you making excuses for him?"

"I don't even know him."

Major Prime interposed. "His man was a corking little chap, never turned a hair, as cool as a cucumber, with everybody else sizzling."

They were ascending a hill, and the horse went slowly. Ahead of them was a buggy without a top. In the buggy were a man and a woman. The woman had an umbrella over her, and a child in her arms.

"It's Mary Flippin and her father. See if you can't overtake them, Jefferson. I want you to see Fiddle Flippin, Randy."

"Who is Fiddle Flippin?"

"Mary's little girl. Mary is a war bride. She was in Petersburg teaching school when the war broke out, and she married a man named Branch. Then she came home—and she called the baby Fidelity."

"I hope he was a good husband."

"Nobody has seen him, he was ordered away at once. But she is very proud of him. And the baby is a darling. Just beginning to walk and talk."

"Stop a minute, Jefferson, while I speak to them."

Mr. Flippin pulled up his fat horse. He was black-haired, ruddy, and wide of girth. "Well, well," he said, with a big laugh, "it is cert'n'y good to see you."

Mary Flippin was slender and delicate and her eyes were blue. Her hair was thick and dark. There was Scotch-Irish blood in the Flippins, and Mary's charm was in that of duskiness of hair and blueness of eye. "Oh, Randy Paine," she said, with her cheeks flaming, "when did you get back?"

"Ten minutes ago. Mary, if you'll hand me that corking kid, I'll kiss her."

Fiddle was handed over. She was rosy and round with her mother's blue eyes. She wore a little buttoned hat of white piqué, with strings tied under her chin.

"So," said Randy, after a moist kiss, "you are Fiddle-dee-dee?"

"Ess—"

"Who gave you that name?"

"It is her own way of saying Fidelity," Mary explained.

"Isn't she rather young to say anything?"

"Oh, Randy, she's a year and a half," Becky protested. "Your mother says that you talked in your cradle."

Randy laughed, "Oh, if you listen to Mother—"

"I'm glad you're in time for the Horse Show," Mr. Flippin interposed, "I've got a couple of prize hawgs—an' when you see them, you'll say they ain't anything like them on the other side."

"Oh, Father—"

"Well, they ain't. I reckon Virginia's good enough for you to come back to, ain't it, Mr. Randy—?"

"It is good enough for me to stay in now that I'm here."

"So you're back for good?"

"Yes."

"Well, we're mighty glad to have you."

Fiddle Flippin, dancing and doubling up on Randy's knee like a very soft doll, suddenly held out her arms to her mother.

As Mary leaned forward to take her, Randy was aware of the change in her. In the old days Mary had been a gay little thing, with an impertinent tongue. She was not gay now. She was a Madonna, tender-eyed, brooding over her child.

"She has changed a lot," Randy said, as they drove on.

"Why shouldn't she change?" Becky demanded.

"Wouldn't any woman change if she had loved a man and had let him go to France?"

IV

It was still raining hard when the surrey stopped at a high and rusty iron gate flanked by brick pillars overgrown with Virginia creeper.

"Becky," said young Paine, "you can't walk up to the house. It's pouring."

"I don't see any house," said Major Prime.

"Well, you never do from the road in this part of the country. We put our houses on the tops of hills, and have acres to the right of us, and acres to the left, and acres in front, and acres behind, and you can never visit your neighbors without going miles, and nobody ever walks except little Becky Bannister when she runs away."

"And I am going to run now," said Becky. "Randy, there's a raincoat under that seat. I'll put it on if you will hand it out to me."

"You are going to ride up, my dear child. Drive on, Jefferson."

"Randy, *please*, your mother is waiting. She didn't come down to the station because she said that if she wept on your shoulder, she would not do it before the whole world. But she is *waiting*—And it isn't fair for me to hold you back a minute."

He yielded at last reluctantly. "Remember, you are to act as if you had never met me," she said to Major Prime as she gave him her hand at parting, "when you see me to-night."

"Becky," Randy asked, in a sudden panic, "are the boarders to be drawn up in ranks to welcome me?"

"No, your mother has given you and Major Prime each two rooms in the Schoolhouse, and we are to dine out there, in your sitting-room—our families and the Major. And there won't be a soul to see you until morning, and then you can show yourself off by inches."

"Until to-night then," said Randy, and opened the gate for her.

"Until to-night," she watched them and waved her hand as they drove off.

"A beautiful child," the Major remarked from the shadow of the back seat.

"She's more than beautiful," said Randy, glowing, "oh, you wait till you really know her, Major."

V

The Schoolhouse at King's Crest had been built years before by one of the Paines for two sons and their tutor. It was separated from the old brick mansion by a wide expanse of unmowed lawn, thick now in midsummer with fluttering poppies. There was a flagged stone walk, and an orchard at the left, beyond the orchard were rolling fields, and in the distance one caught a glimpse of the shining river.

On the lower floor of the Schoolhouse were two ample sitting-rooms with bedrooms above, one of which was reached by outside stairs, and the other by an enclosed stairway. Baths had been added when Mrs. Paine had come as a widow to King's Crest with her small son, and had chosen the Schoolhouse as a quiet haven. Later, on the death of his grandparents, Randy had inherited the estate, and he and his mother had moved into the mansion. But he had kept his rooms in the Schoolhouse, and was glad to know that he could go back to them.

Major Prime had the west sitting-room. It was lined with low bookcases, full of old, old books. There was a fireplace, a winged chair, a broad couch, a big desk of dark seasoned mahogany, and over the mantel a steel engraving of Robert E. Lee. The low windows at the back looked out upon the wooded green of the ascending hill; at the front was a porch which gave a view of the valley.

Randolph's arrival had had something of the effect of a triumphal entry. Jefferson had driven him straight to the Schoolhouse, but on the way they had encountered old Susie, Jefferson's mother, who cooked, and old Bob, who acted as butler, and the new maid who waited on the table. These had followed the surrey as a sort of ecstatic convoy. Not a boarder was in sight but behind the windows of the big house one was aware of watching eyes.

"They are all crazy to meet you," Randy's mother had told him, as they came into the Major's sitting-room after those first sacred moments when the doors had been shut against the world, "they are all crazy to meet you, but you needn't come over to lunch unless you really care to do it. Jefferson can serve you here."

"What do you want me to do?"

"My dear, I'm so proud of you, I'd like to show you to the whole world."

"But there are so many of us, Mother."

"There's only one of you—"

"And we haven't come back to be put on pedestals."

"You were put on pedestals before you went away."

"I'll be spoiled if you talk to me like that."

"I shall talk as I please, Randy. Major Prime, isn't he as handsome as a—rose?"

"*Mother*—"

"Well, you are   "

"Mother, if you talk like this to the boarders, I'll go back and get shot up—"

She clung to him. "Randy, don't say such a thing. He mustn't talk like that, must he, Major?"

"He doesn't mean it. Paine, this looks to me like the Promised Land—"

"I'm glad you like it," said Mrs. Paine, "and now if you don't mind, I'll run along and kill the fatted calf—"

She kissed her son, and under a huge umbrella made her way through the poppies that starred the grass—

"*On Flanders field—where poppies blow*"—the Major drew a sudden quick breath—He wished there were no poppies at King's

Crest.

"I hate this hero stuff," Randy was saying, "don't you?"

"I am not so sure that I do. Down deep we'd resent it if we were not applauded, shouldn't we?"

Randy laughed. "I believe we should."

"I fancy that when we've been home for a time, we may feel somewhat bitter if we find that our pedestals are knocked from under us. Our people don't worship long. They have too much to think of. They'll put up some arches, and a few statues and build tribute houses in a lot of towns, and then they'll go on about their business, and we who have fought will feel a bit blank."

Randy laughed, "You haven't any illusions about it, have you?"

"No, but you and I know that it's all right however it goes."

Randy, standing very straight, looked out over the valley where the river showed through the rain like a silver thread. "Well, we didn't do it for praise, did we?"

"No, thank God."

Their eyes were seeing other things than these quiet hills. Things they wanted to forget. But they did not want to forget the high exaltation which had sent them over, or the quiet conviction of right which had helped them to carry on. What the people at home might do or think did not matter. What mattered was their own adjustment to the things which were to follow.

Randy went up-stairs, took off his uniform, bathed and came down in the garments of peace.

"Glad to get out of your uniform?" the Major asked.

"I believe I am. Perhaps if I'd been an officer, I shouldn't."

"Everybody couldn't be. I've no doubt you deserved it."

"I could have pulled wires, of course, before I went over, but I wouldn't."

From somewhere within the big house came the reverberation of a Japanese gong.

Randy rose. "I'm going over to lunch. I'd rather face guns, but Mother will like it. You can have yours here."

"Not if I know it," the Major rose, "I'm going to share the fatted calf."

VI

It was late that night when the Major went to bed. The feast in Randy's honor had lasted until ten. There had been the shine of candles, and the laughter of the women, the old Judge's genial humor. Through the windows had come the fragrance of honeysuckle and of late roses. Becky had sung for them, standing between two straight white candles.

"In the beauty of the lilies, Christ was born across the sea,
With the glory in his bosom which transfigures you and me.
As he died to make men holy, let us die to make men free
While God is marching on—"

The last time the Major had heard a woman sing that song had been in a little French town just after the United States had gone into the war. She was of his own country, red-haired and in uniform. She had stood on the steps of a stone house and weary men had clustered about her—French, English, Scotch, a few Americans. Tired and spent, they had gazed up at her as if they drank her in. To them she was more than a singing woman. She was the daughter of a nation of dreamers, *the daughter of a nation which made its dreams come true*! Behind her stood a steadfast people, and—God was marching on—!

He had had his leg then, and after that there had been dreadful fighting, and sometimes in the midst of it the voice of the singing woman had come back to him, stiffening him to his task.

And here, miles away from that war-swept land, another woman sang. And there was honeysuckle outside, and late roses—and poppies, and there was Peace. And the world which had not fought would forget. But the men who had fought would remember.

He heard Randy's voice, sharp with nerves. "Sing something else, Becky. We've had enough of war—"

The Major leaned across the table. "When did you last hear that song, Paine?"

"On the other side, a red-haired woman—whose lover had been killed. I never want to hear it again—"

"Nor I—"

It was as if they were alone at the table, seeing the things which they had left behind. What did these people know who had stayed at home? The words were sacred—not to be sung; to be whispered—over the graves of—France.

CHAPTER II

STUFFED BIRDS

I

The Country Club was, as Judge Bannister had been the first to declare, "an excrescence."

Under the old régime, there had been no need for country clubs. The houses on the great estates had been thrown open for the county families and their friends. There had been meat and drink for man and beast.

The servant problem had, however, in these latter days, put a curb on generous impulse. There were no more niggers underfoot, and hospitality was necessarily curtailed. The people who at the time of the August Horse Show had once packed great hampers with delicious foods, and who had feasted under the trees amid all the loveliness of mellow-tinted hills, now ordered by telephone a luncheon of cut-and-dried courses, and motored down to eat it. After that, they looked at the horses, and with the feeling upon them of the futility of such shows yawned a bit. In due season, they held, the horse would be as extinct as the Dodo, and as mythical as the Centaur.

The Judge argued hotly for the things which had been. Love of the horse was bred in the bone of Old Dominion men. He swore by all the gods that when he had to part with his bays and ride behind gasoline, he would be ready to die.

Becky agreed with her grandfather. She adored the old traditions, and she adored the Judge. She spent two months of every year with him in his square brick house in Albemarle surrounded by unprofitable acres. The remaining two months of her vacation were given to her mother's father, Admiral Meredith, whose fortune had come down to him from whale-hunting ancestors. The Admiral lived also in a square brick house, but it had no acres, for it was on the Main Street of Nantucket town, with a Captain's walk on top, and a spiral staircase piercing its middle.

The other eight months of the year Becky had spent at school in an old convent in Georgetown. She was a Protestant and a Presbyterian; the Nantucket grandfather was a Unitarian of Quaker stock, Judge Bannister was High Church, and it was his wife's Presbyterianism which had been handed down to Becky. Religion had therefore nothing to do with her residence at the school. A great many of the Bannister girls had been educated at convents, and when a Bannister had done a thing once it was apt to be done again.

Becky was nineteen, and her school days were just over. She knew nothing of men, she knew nothing indeed of life. The world was to her an open sea, to sail its trackless wastes she had only a cockle-shell of dreams.

"If anybody," said Judge Bannister, on the first day of the Horse Show, "thinks I am going to eat dabs of things at the club when I can have Mandy to cook for me, they think wrong."

He gave orders, therefore, which belonged to more opulent days, when his father's estate had swarmed with blacks. There was now in the Judge's household only Mandy, the cook, and Calvin, her husband. Mandy sat up half the night to bake a cake, and Calvin killed chickens at dawn, and dressed them, and pounded the dough for biscuits on a marble slab, and helped his wife with the mayonnaise.

When at last the luncheon was packed there was coffee in the thermos bottle. Prohibition was an assured fact, and the Judge would not break the laws. The flowing glass must go into the discard with other picturesque customs of the South. His own estate that had once been sold by John Randolph to Thomas Jefferson for a bowl of arrack punch—! Old times, old manners! The Judge drank his coffee with the air of one who accepts a good thing regretfully. He stood staunchly by the Administration. If the President had asked the sacrifice of his head, he would have offered it on the platter of political allegiance.

So on this August morning, an aristocrat by inheritance, and a democrat by assumption, he drove his bays proudly. Calvin, in a worn blue coat, sat beside him with his arms folded.

Becky was on the back seat with Aunt Claudia. Aunt Claudia was a widow and wore black. She was small and slight, and the black was made smart by touches of white crepe. Aunt Claudia had not forgotten that she had been a belle in Richmond. She was a stately little woman with a firm conviction of the necessity of maintaining dignified standards of living. She was in no sense a snob. But she held that women of birth and breeding must preserve the fastidiousness of their ideals, lest there be social chaos.

"There would be no ladies left in the world," she often told Becky, "if we older women went at the modern pace."

Becky, in contrast to Aunt Claudia's smartness, showed up rather ingloriously. She wore the stubbed russet shoes, a not too fresh cotton frock of pale yellow, and a brown straw sailor.

"You might at least have stopped to change your shoes," Aunt Claudia told her, as they left the house behind.

"I was out with Randy and the dogs. It was heavenly, Aunt Claudia."

"My dear, if a walk with Randy is heavenly, what will you call Heaven when you get to it?"

They drove through the first gate, and Calvin climbed down to open it. Beyond the gate the road descended gradually through an open pasture, where sheep grazed on the hillside or lay at rest in the shade. The bells of the leaders tinkled faintly, the ewes and the lambs were calling. Beyond the big gate, the highroad was washed with the recent rains. From the gate to the club was a matter of five miles, and the bays ate up the distance easily.

The people on the porch of the Country Club were very gay and gorgeous, so that Becky in her careless frock and shabby shoes would have been a pitiful contrast if she had cared in the least what the people on the porch thought of her. But she did not care. She nodded and smiled to a friend or two as the Judge stopped for a moment in the crush of motors.

George Dalton was on the porch. When he saw Becky he leaned forward for a good look at her.

"Some girl," he said to Waterman, as the surrey moved on, "the one in the sailor hat. Who is she?"

Oscar Waterman was a newcomer in Albemarle. He had bought a thousand acres, with an idea of grafting on to Southern environment his own ideas of luxurious living. The county families had not called, but he was not yet aware of his social isolation. He was rich, and most of the county families were poor—from his point of view the odds were in his favor—and it was never hard to get guests. He could always motor up to Washington and New York, and bring a crowd back with him. His cellars were well stocked, and his hospitality undiscriminating.

"I don't know the girl," he told Dalton, "but the old man is Judge Bannister. He's one of the natives—no money and oodles of pride."

In calling Judge Bannister a "native," Oscar showed a lack of proportion. A native, in the sense that he used the word, is a South Sea Islander, indigenous but negligible. Oscar was fooled, you see, by the Judge's old-fashioned clothes, and the high surrey, and the horses with the flowing tails. His ideas of life had to do with motor cars and mansions, and with everybody very much dressed up. He felt that the only thing in the world that really counted was money. If you had enough of it the world was yours!

II

Year after year the Bannisters of Huntersfield had eaten their

Horse Show luncheon under a clump of old oaks beneath which the horses now stopped. The big trees were dropping golden leaves in the dryness. From the rise of the hill one looked down on the grandstand and the crowd as from the seats of an amphitheater.

Judge Bannister remembered when the women of the crowd had worn hoops and waterfalls. Aunt Claudia's memory went back to bustles and bonnets. There were deeper memories, too, than of clothes—of old friends and young faces—there was always a moment of pensive retrospect when the Bannisters stopped under the old oak on the hill.

Randolph Paine, his mother and Major Prime were to join them at luncheon. Separate plans had been made by the boarders who had packed themselves into various cars and carriages, and had their own boxes and baskets.

"Caroline Paine is always late," the Judge said with some impatience; "if we don't eat on time, we shall have to hurry. I have never hurried in my life and I don't want to begin now."

Claudia Beaufort was accustomed to impatience in men, and she was inflexible as a hostess. "Well, of course, we couldn't begin without them, could we?" she asked. "There they come now, Father. William, you'd better help Major Prime."

Randy was driving the fat mare, Rosalind. Nellie Custis, Randolph's wiry hound, loped along with flapping ears in the rear of the low-seated carriage. Major Prime was on the back seat with Mrs. Paine.

"My dear Judge," he said, as the old gentleman came to the side of the carriage, "I can't tell you how honored I am to be included in your party. This is about the best thing that has happened to me in a long time."

"I wanted you to get the old atmosphere. You can't get it at the Country Club. We Bannisters have lunched up here for sixty years—older than you are, eh?"

"Twenty years—"

"We used to call it the races, but now they tack on the Horse Show. It was different, of course, when all the old places were owned by the old families. But they can't change the oaks and the sweep of the hills, and the mettle of the horses, thank God."

"I am sorry I was late," said Caroline Paine, as they settled themselves under the trees, "but I went to town to have my hair waved."

"I wish you wouldn't, Caroline," Mrs. Beaufort told her, "your hair is nice enough without it."

Caroline Paine took off her hat, "I couldn't get it up to look like this, could I?"

The Judge surveyed the undulations critically. "Caroline," he said, "you are too pretty to need it."

"I want to keep young for Randolph's sake," Mrs. Paine told him, "then he'll like me better than any other girl."

"You needn't think you have to get your hair curled to make me love you," said her tall son; "you are ducky enough as you are."

Major Prime, delighting in their lack of self-consciousness, made a diplomatic contribution. "Why quarrel with such a charming coiffure?"

Mrs. Paine smiled at him, comfortably. "I feel much better," she said; "they are always trying to hold me back."

She was a woman of ample proportions and of leisurely habit. Life had of late hurried her a bit, but she still gave the effect of restful calm. She was of the same generation as Aunt Claudia, and a widow. But she wore her widowhood with a difference. She had on to-day a purple hat. Her hair was white, her dress was white, and her shoes. She was prettier than Aunt Claudia but she lacked her distinction of manner and of carriage.

"They always want to hold me back when I try to be up-to-date," she repeated.

Randy threw an acorn at her. "Nobody can hold you back, Mother," he said, "when you get your mind on a thing. Aunt Claudia, what do you hear from Truxton?"

"A letter came this morning," said Mrs. Beaufort, lighting up with the thought of it. "I hadn't heard for days before that. And I was worried."

"Truxton hasn't killed himself writing letters since he went over," the Judge asserted. "Claudia, can't we have lunch?"

"William is unpacking the hamper now, Father. And I think Truxton has done very well. It isn't easy for the boys to find time."

"Randy wrote to me every week."

"Now, Mother—"

"Well, you did."

"But I'm that kind. I have to get things off my mind. Truxton isn't. And I'll bet when Aunt Claudia does get his letters that they are worth reading."

Mrs. Beaufort nodded. "They are lovely letters. I have the last one with me; would you like to hear it?"

"Not before lunch, Claudia," the Judge urged.

"I will read it while the rest of you eat." There were red spots in Mrs. Beaufort's cheeks. She adored her son. She could not understand her father's critical attitude. Had she searched for motives, however, she might have found them in the Judge's jealousy.

It was while she was reading Truxton's letter that the Flippins came by—Mr. Flippin and his wife, Mary, and little Fidelity. A slender mulatto woman followed with a basket.

The Flippins were one of the "second families." Between them and the Paines of King's Crest and the Bannisters of Huntersfield stretched a deep chasm of social prejudice. Three generations of Flippins had been small farmers on rented lands. They had no coats-of-arms or family trees. They were never asked to dine with the Paines or Bannisters, but there had been always an interchange of small hospitalities, and much neighborliness, and as children Mary Flippin, Randy and Becky and Truxton had played together and had been great friends.

So it was now as they stopped to speak to the Judge's party that Mrs. Beaufort said graciously, "I am reading a letter from Truxton. Would you like to hear it?"

Mary, speaking with a sort of tense eagerness, said, "Yes."

So the Flippins sat down, and Mrs. Beaufort read in her pleasant voice the letter from France.

Randy, lying on his back under the old oak, listened. Truxton gave a joyous diary of the days—little details of the towns through which he passed, of the houses where he was billeted, jokes of the men, of the food they ate, of his hope of coming home.

"He seems very happy," said Mrs. Beaufort, as she finished.

"He is and he isn't—"

"You might make yourself a little clearer, Randolph," said the Judge.

"He is happy because France in summer is a pleasant sort of Paradise—with the cabbages stuck up on the brown hillsides like rosettes—and the minnows flashing in the little brooks and the old mills turning—and he isn't happy—because he is homesick."

Randy raised himself on his elbow and smiled at his listening audience—and as he smiled he was aware of a change in Mary Flippin. The brooding look was gone. She was leaning forward, lips parted—"Then you think that he is—homesick?"

"I don't *think*. I know. Why, over there, my bones actually ached for Virginia."

The Judge raised his coffee cup. "Virginia, God bless her," he murmured, and drank it down!

The Flippins moved on presently—the slender mulatto trailing after them.

"If the Flippins don't send that Daisy back to Washington," Mrs. Paine remarked, "she'll spoil all the negroes on the place."

Mrs. Beaufort agreed, "I don't know what we are coming to. Did you see her high heels and tight skirt?"

"Once upon a time," the Judge declaimed, "black wenches like that wore red handkerchiefs on their heads and went barefoot. But the world moves, and some day when we have white servants wished on us, we'll pray to God to send our black ones back."

Calvin was passing things expertly. Randy smiled at Becky as he filled her plate.

"Hungry?"

"Ravenous."

"You don't look it."

"Don't I?"

"No. You're not a bread and butter sort of person."

"What kind am I?"

"Sugar and spice and everything nice."

"Did you learn to say such things in France?"

"Haven't I always said them?"

"Not in quite the same way. You've grown up, Randy. You seem *years* older."

"Do you like me—older?"

"Of course." There was warmth in her voice but no coquetry. "What a silly thing to ask, Randy."

Calvin, having served the lunch, ate his own particular feast of chicken backs and necks under the surrey from a pasteboard box cover. Having thus separated himself as it were from those he served, he was at his ease. He knew his place and was happy in it.

Mary Flippin also knew her place. But she was not happy. She sat higher up on the hill with her child asleep in her arms, and looked down on the Judge's party. Except for an accident of birth, she might be sitting now among them. Would she ever sit among them? Would her little daughter, Fidelity?

III

"We are the only one of the old families who are eating lunch out of a basket," said Caroline Paine; "next year we shall have to go to the Country Club with the rest of them."

"I shall never go to the Country Club," said Judge Bannister, "as long as there is a nigger to fry chicken for me."

"We may have to swim with the tide."

"Don't tell me that you'd rather be up there than here, Caroline."

"I'd like it for some things," Mrs. Paine admitted frankly; "you should see the clothes that those Waterman women are wearing."

"What do you care what they wear. You don't want to be like them, do you?"

"I may not care to be like them, but I want to look like them. I got the pattern of this sweater I am knitting from one of my boarders. Do you want it, Claudia?"

Mrs. Beaufort winced at the word "boarders." She hated to think that Caroline must—"I never wear sweaters, Caroline. They are not my style. But I am knitting one for Becky."

"Is it blue?" Randy asked. "Becky ought always to wear blue, except when she wears pale yellow. That was a heavenly thing you had on at dinner the night we arrived, wasn't it, Major?"

"Everything was heavenly. I felt like one who expecting a barren plain sees—Paradise."

It was not flattery and they knew it. They were hospitable souls, and in a week he had become, as it were, one of them.

Randy, returning to the subject in hand, asked, "Will you wear the blue if I come up to-night, Becky?"

"I will not." Becky was making herself a chaplet of yellow leaves, and her bronze hair caught the light. "I will not. I shall probably put on my old white if I dress for dinner."

"Of course you'll dress," said Mrs. Beaufort; "there are certain things which we must always demand of ourselves—"

Caroline Paine agreed. "That's what I tell Randy when he says he doesn't want to finish his law course. His father was a lawyer and his grandfather. He owes it to them to live up to their standards."

Randy was again flat on his back with his hands under his head. "If I stay at the University, it means no money for either of us except what you earn, Mother."

The war had taken its toll of Caroline Paine. Things had not been easy since her son had left her. They would not be easy now. "I know," she said, "but you wouldn't want your father to be ashamed of you."

Randy sat up. "It isn't that—but I ought to make some money—"

The word was a challenge to the Judge. "Don't run with the mob, my boy. The world is money-mad."

"I'm not money-mad," said Randy; "I know what I should like to do if my life was my own. But it isn't. And I'm not going to have Mother twist and turn as she has twisted and turned for the last fifteen years in order to get me educated up to the family standard."

"If you don't mind I shouldn't." Caroline Paine was setting her feet to a rocky path, but she did not falter. "You shouldn't mind if I don't."

Becky laid down the chaplet of leaves. She knew some of the things Caroline Paine had sacrificed and she was thrilled by them. "Randy," she admonished, with youthful severity, "it would be a shame to disappoint your mother."

Randolph flushed beneath his dark skin. The Paines had an Indian strain in them—Pocahontas was responsible for it, or some of the other princesses who had mixed red blood with blue in the days when Virginia belonged to the King. Randy showed signs of it in his square-set jaw, the high lift of his head, his long easy stride, the straightness of his black hair. He showed it, too, in a certain stoical impassiveness which might have been taken for indifference. His world was, for the moment, against him; he would attempt no argument.

"I am afraid this doesn't interest Major Prime," he said.

"It interests me very much," said the Major. "It is only another case of the fighting man's adjustment to life after his return. We all have to face it in one way or another." His eyes went out over the hills. They were gray eyes, deep set, and, at this moment, kindly. They could blaze, however, in stress of fighting, like bits of steel. "We all have to face it in one way or another. And the future of America depends largely on our seeing things straight."

"Well, there's only one way for Randy to face it," said Caroline Paine, firmly, "and that is to do as his fathers did before him."

"If I do," Randy flared, "it will be three years before I can make a living, and I'll be twenty-five."

Becky put on the chaplet of leaves. It fitted like a cap. She might have been a dryad, escaped for a moment from the old oak. "Three years isn't long."

"Suppose I should want to marry—"

"Oh, you—Randy—"

"But why shouldn't I?"

"I don't want you to get married," she told him; "when I come down we couldn't have our nice times together. You'd always be thinking about your wife."

IV

From the porch of the Country Club, George Dalton had seen the Judge's party at luncheon. According to George's lexicon no one who could afford to go to the club would eat out of a basket.

He rather blushed for Becky that she must sit there in the sight of everybody and share a feast with a shabby old Judge, a lean and lank stripling with straight hair, a lame duck of an officer, and two middle-aged women, who made spots of black and purple on the landscape. Like Oscar, George's ideas of life had to do largely with motor cars and yachts, and estates on Long Island, palaces at Newport and Len ox and Palm Beach. During the war he had served rather comfortably in a becoming uniform in the Quartermaster's Department in Washington. Now that the war was over, he regretted the becomings of the uniform. He felt to-day, however, that there were compensations in his hunting pink. He was slightly bronzed and had blue eyes. He was extremely popular with the women of the Waterman set, but was held to be the especial property of Madge MacVeigh.

Madge had observed his interest in the party on the hill.

"George," she said, "what are you looking at?"

"I am looking at those people who are picnicking. They probably have ants in the salad and spiders in their coffee."

"They are getting more out of it than you and I," said Madge.

"How getting more?"

"We are tired of things, Georgie-Porgie."

"Speak for yourself, Madge."

"I am speaking for both of us. You are tired of me, for example."

"My dear girl, I am not."

"You are. And I am tired of you. It's not your fault, and it's not mine. It is the fault of any house-party. People see too much of each other. I am glad I am going away to-morrow, and you'll be glad. And when we have been separated a month, you will rush up to see me, and say you couldn't live without me."

She dissected him coolly. Madge had a modern way of looking at things. She was not in the least sentimental. But she had big moments of feeling. It was because of this deep current which swept her away now and then from the shallows that she held Dalton's interest. He never knew in what mood he should find her, and it added spice to their friendship.

"I didn't know you were going to-morrow."

"Neither did I till this morning, but I am bored to death, Georgie."

She did not look it. She was long-limbed, slender, with heavy burned-gold hair, a skin which was pale gold after a July by the sea. The mauve of her dress and hat emphasized the gold of hair and skin. Some one had said that Madge MacVeigh at the end of a summer gave the effect of a statue cast in new bronze. Dalton in the early days of their friendship had called her his "Golden Girl." The name had stuck to her. She had laughed at it but had liked it. "I should hate it," she had said, "if I were rich. Perhaps some day some millionaire will turn me into gold and make it true."

"Just because you are bored to death," Dalton told her, "is no reason why you should accuse me of it."

"It isn't accusation. It's condolence. I am sorry for both of us, George, that we can't sit there under the trees and eat out of a basket and have spiders and ants in things and not mind it. Here we are in the land of Smithfield hams and spoon-bread and we ate canned lobster for lunch, and alligator pear salad."

"Baked ham and spoon-bread—for our sins?"

"It is because you and I have missed the baked ham and spoon-bread atmosphere, that we are bored to death, Georgie. Everything in our lives is the same wherever we go. When we are in Virginia we ought to do as the Virginians do, and instead Oscar Waterman brings a little old New York with him. It's Rome for the Romans, Georgie, lobsters in New England, avocados in Los Angeles, hog and hominy here."

There were others listening now, and she was aware of her amused audience.

"If you don't like my little old New York," Waterman said, "I'll change it."

"No, I am going back to the real thing, Oscar. To my sky-scrapers and subways. You can't give us those down here—not yet. Perhaps some day there will be a system of camouflage by which no matter where we are—in desert or mountain, we can open our windows to the Woolworth Building on the skyline or the Metropolitan Tower, or to Diana shooting at the stars,—and have some little cars in tunnels to run us around your estate."

"By Jove, Jefferson nearly did it," said Waterman; "you should see the subterranean passages at Monticello for the servants, so that the guests could look over the grounds without a woolly head in sight."

"Great old boob, Jefferson," said Waterman's wife, Flora.

"No," Madge's eyes went out over the hills to where Monticello brooded over great memories, "he was not a boob. He was so big that little people like us can't focus him, Flora."

She came down from her perch. "I adore great men," she said; "when I go back, I shall make a pilgrimage to Oyster Bay. I wonder how many of us who weep over Great heart's grave would have voted for him if he had lived. In a sense we crucified him."

"Madge is serious," said Flora Waterman, "now what do you think of that?"

"I have to be serious sometimes, Flora, to balance the rest of you. You can be as gay as you please when I am gone, and if you perish, you perish."

George walked beside her as the party moved towards the grandstand. "I've half a mind to go to New York with you, Madge. I came down on your account."

"It's because you followed me that I'm tired of you, Georgie. If you go, I'll stay."

She was smiling as she said it. But he did not smile. "Just as you wish, of course. But you mustn't expect me to come running when you crook your finger."

"I never expect things, but you'll come."

Perhaps she would not have been so sure if she could have looked into his mind. The day that Becky had ridden away, hidden by the flaps of the old surrey, the spark of his somewhat fickle interest had been lighted, and the glimpse that he had had of her this morning had fanned the spark into a flame.

"Did you say the old man's name is Bannister?" he asked Oscar as the Judge's party passed them later on their way to their seats.

"Yes. Judge Bannister. I tried to buy his place before I decided on Hamilton Hill. But he wouldn't sell. He said he wouldn't have any place for his stuffed birds."

"Stuffed birds?"

"His hobby is the game birds of Virginia. He has a whole room of them. I offered him a good price, but I suppose he'd rather starve than take it."

The Judge's box was just above Oscar Waterman's. Becky, looking up, saw Dalton's eyes upon her.

"It's the man who came with you on the train," she told Randy.

"What's he wearing a pink coat for?" Randy demanded. "He isn't riding."

"He probably knows that he looks well in it."

"That isn't a reason."

Becky took another look. "He has a head like the bust of Apollo in our study hall."

"I'd hate to have a head like that."

"Well, you haven't," she told him; "you may hug that thought to yourself if it is any consolation, Randy."

V

Caroline Paine's boarders sat high up on the grandstand. If the boarders seem in this book to be spoken of collectively, like the Chorus in a Greek play, or the sisters and aunts and cousins in "Pinafore," it is not because they are not individually interesting. It is because, *en Massey* only, have they any meaning in this history.

Now as they sat on the grandstand, they discerned Mrs. Paine in the Judge's box. They waved at her, and they waved at Randy, they waved also at Major Prime. They demanded recognition—some of the more enthusiastic detached themselves finally from the main group and came down to visit Caroline. The overflow straggled along the steps to the edge of the Waterman box. One genial gentleman was forced finally to sit on the rail, so that his elbow stuck straight into the middle of the back of George's huntsman's pink.

George moved impatiently. "Can't you find any other place to sit?"

The genial gentleman beamed on him. "I have a seat over there. But we came down to see Mrs. Paine. She is in Judge Bannister's box and we board with her—at King's Crest. And say, she's a corker!"

George, surveying Becky with increasing interest, decided that she was a bit above her surroundings. She sat as it were with—Publicans. George may not have used the Scriptural phrase, but he had the feeling. He was Pharisaic ally thankful that he was not as that conglomerate group in the Bannister box. A cheap crowd was his estimate. It would be rather nice to give the little girl a good time!

Filled, therefore, with a high sense of his philanthropic purpose, he planned a meeting. With his blue eyes on the flying horses, with his staccato voice making quick comments, he had Becky in the back of his mind. He found a moment, when the crowd went mad as the county favorite came in, to write a line on the back of an envelope, and hand it to Kemp, who hovered in the background, giving him quiet instructions.

"Yes, sir," said Kemp guardedly, and stood at attention until the races were over, and the crowd began to move, and then he handed the note to Judge Bannister.

The Judge put on his glasses and read it. "Where is he?" he asked Kemp.

"In the other box, sir. The one above."

"Tell him to come down."

"Yes, sir, thank you, sir."

The Judge was as pleased as Punch. "That man up there in Waterman's box has heard of my collection," he explained to his party. "He wants me to settle a point about the Virginia partridge."

"Which man?" Randy's tone was ominous.

Dalton's arrival saved the Judge an answer. In his hunting pink, with his Apollo head, Dalton was upon them. The Judge, passing him around to the members of his party, came at last to Becky.

"My granddaughter, Becky Bannister."

With George's sparkling gaze bent full upon her, Becky blushed.

Randy saw the blush. "Oh, Lord," he said, under his breath, and stuck his hands in his pockets.

"I've always called it a quail," Dalton was saying.

"You would if you come from the North. To be exact, it isn't either, it's an American Bob-white. I'd be glad to have you come up and look at my collection. There is every kind of bird that has been shot in Virginia fields or Virginia waters. I've got a Trumpeter Swan. The last one was seen in the Chesapeake in sixty-nine. Mine was killed and stuffed in the forties. He is in a perfect state of preservation, and in the original glass case."

"I'd like to come," George told him. "Could I—to-night? I don't know just how long I shall be staying down."

"Any time—any time. To-night, of course. There's nothing I like better than to talk about my birds, unless it is to eat them. Isn't that so, Claudia?"

"Yes, Father." Mrs. Beaufort was studying Dalton closely. His manner was perfect. It was, indeed, she decided, too perfect. "He is thinking too much of the way he does it." The one sin in Aunt Claudia's mind was social self-consciousness. People who thought all of the time about manners hadn't been brought up to them. They must have them without thinking. George was not, she decided, a gentleman in the Old Dominion sense. Dalton would have been amazed could he have looked into Aunt Claudia's mind and have seen himself a—Publican.

"Father," she said, after Dalton had left them, "did I hear you invite him to dinner?"

"Yes, my dear, but he could not come—"

"I'm glad he couldn't."

"Why?"

"I'm not sure that he's—our kind—"

"Nonsense, he's a very fine fellow."

"How do you know?"

"Well, I know this," testily, "that I am not to be instructed as to the sort of person I can ask to my house."

"Oh, Father, I didn't mean that. Of course you can do as you please."

"Of course I shall, Claudia."

"I think he is charming," said Mrs. Paine. "He has lovely eyes."

"Hasn't he?" said little Becky.

CHAPTER III

THE WOLF IN THE FOREST

I

The Bird Room at Judge Bannister's was back of the library. It was a big room lined with glass cases. There hung about it always the faint odor of preservatives. The Trumpeter Swan had a case to himself over the mantel. He had been rather stiffly posed on a bed of artificial moss, but nothing could spoil the beauty of him—the white of his plumage, the elegance of his lines. He was one of a dying race—the descendants of the men who had once killed for food had killed later to gratify the vanity of women who must have swans down to set off their beauty, puffs to powder their noses. No more did great flocks wing an exalted flight, high in the heavens, or rest like a blanket of snow on river banks. The old kings were dead—the glassy eyes of the Trumpeter looked out upon a world which knew his kind no more.

In the other cases were the little birds and big ones—ducks, swimming on crystal pools, canvas-backs and redheads, mallards and teal; Bob-whites, single and in coveys; sandpipers, tip-ups and peeps, those little ghosts of the seashore, shadows on the sand; there were soar and other rails, robins and blackbirds, larks and sparrows, wild turkeys and wild geese, all the toll which the hunter takes from field and stream and forest.

It was in a sense a tragic room, but it had never seemed that to Becky. She came of a race of men who had hunted from instinct but with a sense of honor. The Judge and those of his kind hated wanton killing. Their guns would never have swept away the feathered tribes of tree and sky. It was the trappers and the pot-hunters who had done that. There had motored once to the Judge's mansion a man and his wife who had raged at the brutes who hunted for sport. They had worn fur coats and there had been a bird's breast on the woman's hat.

The Judge, holding on to his temper, had exploded finally. "If you were consistent," he had flung at them, "you would not be decked in the bodies of birds and beasts."

Becky loved the birds in the glass cases, the peeps and the tip-ups, the old owl who did not belong among the game birds, but who, with the great eagle with the outstretched wings, had been admitted because they had been shot within the environs of the estate. She loved the little nests of tinted eggs, the ducks on the crystal pools.

But most of all she loved the Trumpeter. Years ago the Judge had told her of the wild swans who flew so high that no eye could see them. Yet the sound of their trumpets might be heard. It was like the fairy tale of "The Seven Brothers," who were princes, and who were turned into swans and wore gold crowns on their heads. She was prepared to believe anything of the Trumpeter. She had often tiptoed down in the night, expecting to see his case empty, and to hear his trumpet sounding high up near the moon.

There was a moon to-night. Dinner was always late at Huntersfield. In the old days three o'clock had been the fashionable hour for dining in the county, with a hot supper at eight. Aunt Claudia, keeping up with the times, had decided that instead of dining and supping, they must lunch and dine. The Judge had agreed, stipulating that there should be no change in the evening hour. "Serve it in courses, if you like, and call it dinner. But don't have it before candle-light."

So the moon was up when Becky came down in her blue dress. She had not expected to wear the blue. In spite of the fact that Randy and his mother and Major Prime had come back with them for dinner, she had planned to wear her old white, which had been washed and laid out on the bed by Mandy. But the blue was more becoming, and the man with the Apollo head had eyes to see.

She came into the Bird Room with a candle in her hand. There was a lamp high up, but she could not reach it, so she always carried a candle. She set it down on the case where the Bob-whites were cuddled in brown groups. She whistled a note, and listened to catch the answer. It had been a trick of hers as a child, and she had heard them whistle in response. She had been so sure that she heard them—a far-off silvery call—

Well, why not? Might not their little souls be fluttering close? "You darlings," she said aloud.

Randy, arriving at that moment on the threshold, heard her. "You are playing the old game," he said.

"Oh, yes," she caught her breath, "do you remember?"

He came into the room. "I remembered a thousand times when I was in France. I thought of this room and of the Trumpeter Swan, and of how you and I used to listen on still nights and think we heard him. There was one night after an awful day—with a moon like this over the battlefield, and across the moon came a black, thin streak—and a bugle sounded—far away. I was half asleep, and I said, 'Becky, there's the swan,' and the fellow next to me poked his elbow in my ribs, and said, 'You're dreaming.' But I wasn't—quite, for the thin black streak was a Zeppelin—"

She came up close to him and laid her hand on his arm. He towered above her. "Randy," she asked, "was the war very dreadful?"

"Yes," he said, "it was. More dreadful than you people at home can ever grasp. But I want you to know this, Becky, that there isn't one of us who wouldn't go through it again in the same cause."

There was no swagger in his statement, just simple earnestness. The room was very still for a moment.

Then Becky said, "Well, it's awfully nice to have you home again," and Randy, looking down at the little hand on his arm, had to hold on to himself not to put his own over it.

But she was too dear and precious—! So he just said, gently, "And I'm glad to be at home, my dear," and they walked to the window together, and stood looking out at the moon. Behind them the old eagle watched with outstretched wings, the great free bird which we stamp on American silver, backed with "In God We Trust." It is not a bad combination, and things in this country might, perhaps, have been less chaotic if we had taught newcomers to link love of God with love of liberty.

"Mr. Dalton is coming to see the birds," said Becky, and in a moment she had spoiled everything for Randy.

"Is that why you put on your blue dress?"

She was honest. "I am not sure. Perhaps."

"Yet you thought the old white one was good enough for me."

"Well, don't you like me just as well in my old white as in this?"

"Yes, of course."

"Well, then," Becky was triumphant, "why should I bother to change for you, Randy, when you like me just as well in anything?"

The argument was unanswerable, but Randy was not satisfied. "It is a mistake," he said, "not to be as nice to old friends as new ones."

"But I am nice. You said so yourself this afternoon. That I was sugar and spice and everything—nice—"

He laughed. "You are, of course. And I didn't come all the way from France to quarrel with you—"

"We've always quarreled, Randy."

"I wonder why?"

"Sister Loretta says that people only argue when they like each other. Otherwise they wouldn't want to convince."

"Do you quarrel with Sister Loretta?"

"Of course not. Nuns don't. But she writes notes when she

doesn't agree with me—little sermons—and pins them on my pillow. She's a great dear. She hates to have me leave the school. She has the feeling that the world is a dark forest, and that I am Red Riding Hood, and that the Wolf will get me."

II

Dalton found them all at dinner when he reached Huntersfield. He was not in the least prepared for the scene which met his eyes—shining mahogany, old silver and Sheffield, tall white candles, Calvin in a snowy jacket, Mrs. Beaufort and Mrs. Paine in low-necked gowns, the Judge and Randy in dinner coats somewhat the worse for wear, Becky in thin, delicate blue, with a string of pearls which seemed to George an excellent imitation of the real thing.

He had thought that the trail of Mrs. Paine's boarding-house might be over it all. He had known boarding-houses as a boy, before his father made his money. There had been basement dining-rooms, catsup bottles, and people passing everything to everybody else!

"I'm afraid I'm early," he said in his quick voice.

"Not a bit. Calvin, place a chair for Mr. Dalton."

There were fruit and nuts and raisins in a great silver Pegeen, with fat cupids making love among garlands. There was coffee in Severus cups.

Back among the shadows twinkled a priceless mirror; shutting off Calvin's serving table was a painted screen worth its weight in gold. It was a far cry from the catsup bottles and squalid service of George's early days. The Bannisters of Huntersfield wore their poverty like a plume!

The Judge carried Dalton off presently to the Bird Boom. George went with reluctance. This was not what he had come for. Becky, slim and small, with her hair peaked up to a topknot, Becky in pale blue, Becky as fair as her string of imitation pearls, Becky in the golden haze of the softly illumined room, Becky, Becky Bannister—the name chimed in his ears.

Dalton had had some difficulty in getting away from Hamilton Hill.

"It's my last night," Madge had said; "shall we go out in the garden and watch the moon rise?"

"Sorry," George had told her, "but I've promised Flora to take a fourth hand at bridge."

"And after that?" asked Madge softly.

"What do you mean?"

"Who is the new—little girl?"

It was useless to pretend. "She's a beauty, rather, isn't she?"

"Oh, Georgie-Porgie, I wish you wouldn't."

"Wouldn't what?"

"Kiss the girls—and make them—cry—"

"You've never cried—"

She laughed at that. "If I haven't it is because I know that afterwards you always—run away."

He admitted it. "One can't marry them all."

"I wonder if you are ever serious," she told him, her chin in her hand.

"I am always serious. That's what makes it—interesting—"

"But the poor little—hearts?"

"Some one has to teach, them," said George, "that it's a pretty game—"

"Will it be always a game—to you—Georgie?"

"Who knows?" he said. "So far I've held trumps—"

"Your conceit is colossal, but somehow you seem to get away with it." She smiled and stood up. "I'm going to bed early. I have been losing my beauty sleep lately, Georgie."

He chose to be gallant. "You are not losing your beauty, if that's what you mean."

Her dinner gown was of the same shade of mauve that she had worn in the afternoon. But it was of a material so sheer that the gold of her skin seemed to shine through.

"Good-night, Golden Girl," said Dalton, and kissed the tips of her fingers as she stood on the stairs. Then he went off to join the others.

Madge did not go to bed. She went out alone and watched the moon rise. Oscar Waterman's house was on a hill which gave a view of the whole valley. Gradually under the moon the houses of Charlottesville showed the outlines of the University, and far beyond the shadowy sweep of the Blue Ridge. What a world it had been in the old days—great men had ridden over these red roads in swaying carriages, Jefferson, Lafayette, Washington himself.

If she could only meet men like that. Men to whom life was more than a game—a carnival. From the stone bench where she sat she had a view through the long French windows of the three tables of bridge—there were slender, restless girls, eager, elegant youths. "Perhaps they are no worse than those who lived here before them," Madge's sense of justice told her. "But isn't there something better?"

From her window later, she saw Dalton's car flash out into the road. The light wound down and down, and appeared at last upon the highway. It was not the first time that George had played the game with another girl. But he had always come back to her. She had often wondered why she let him come. "Why do I let him?" she asked the moon.

III

It really was a great moon. It shone through the windows of the Bird Room at Huntersfield, wooing George out into the fragrant night. He could hear voices on the lawn—young Paine's laugh—Becky's. Once when he looked he saw them on the ridge, silhouetted against the golden sky. They were dancing, and Randy's clear whistle, piping a modern tune, came up to him, tantalizing him.

But the Judge held him. It took him nearly an hour to get through with the Bob-whites and the sandpipers, the wild turkeys, the ducks and the wild geese. And long before that time George was bored to extinction. He had little imagination. To him the Trumpeter was just a stuffed old bird. He could not picture him as blowing his trumpet beside the moon, or wearing a golden crown as in "The Seven Brothers." He had never heard of "The Seven Brothers," and nobody in the world wore crowns except kings. As for the old eagle, it is doubtful whether George had ever felt the symbolism of his presence on a silver coin, or that he had ever linked him in his heart with God.

Then, suddenly, the whole world changed. Becky appeared on the threshold.

"Grandfather," she said, "Aunt Claudia says there is lemonade on the lawn."

"In a moment, my dear."

George rose hastily. "Don't let me keep you, Judge—"

Becky advanced into the room. "Aren't the birds wonderful?"

"They are," said George, seeing them wonderful for the first time.

"I always feel," she said, "as if some time they will flap their wings and fly away—on a night like this—the swans going first, and then the ducks and geese, and last of all the little birds, trailing across the moon—" Her hands fluttered to show them trailing. Becky used her hands a great deal when she talked. Aunt Claudia deplored it as indicating too little repose. The nuns, she felt, should have corrected the habit. But the nuns had loved Becky's descriptive hands, poking, emphasizing, and had let her alone.

The three of them, the Judge and Becky and Dalton, went out together. The little group which sat in the wide moonlighted space in front of the house was dwarfed by the great trees which hung in masses of black against the brilliant night. The white dresses of the women seemed touched with silver.

The lemonade was delicious, and Aunt Claudia forced herself to be gracious. Caroline Paine was gracious without an effort. She liked Dalton. Not in the same way, perhaps, that she liked Major Prime, but he was undoubtedly handsome, and of a world which wore lovely clothes and did not have to count its pennies.

Major Prime had little to say. He was content to sit there in the fragrant night and listen to the rest. A year ago he had been jolted over rough roads in an ambulance. There had been a moon and men groaning. There had seemed to him something sinister about that white night with its spectral shadows, and with the trenches of the enemy wriggling like great serpents underground. The trail of the serpent was still over the world. He had been caught but not killed. There was still poison in his fangs!

He spoke sharply, therefore, when Dalton said, "It was a great adventure for a lot of fellows who went over—"

"Don't," said the Major, and sat up. "Does it matter what took them? *The thing that matters is how they came back—*"

"What do you mean?"

"A thousand reasons took them over. Some of them went because they had to, some of them because they wanted to. Some of them dramatized themselves as heroes and hoped for an opportunity to demonstrate their courage. Some of them were scared stiff, but went because of their consciences, some of them wanted to fight and some of them didn't, but whatever the reason, *they went*. And now they are back, and it is much more important to know what they think now about war than what they thought about it when they were enlisted or drafted. If their baptism of fire has made them hate cruelty and injustice, if it has opened their eyes to the dangers of a dreaming idealism which refuses to see evil until evil has had its way, if it has made them swear to purge America of the things which has made Germany the slimy crawling enemy of the universe, if they have come back feeling that God is in His Heaven but that things can't be right with the world until we come to think in terms of personal as well as of national righteousness—if they have come back thus illumined, then we can concede to them their great adventure. But if they have come back to forget that democracy is on trial, that we have talked of it to other nations and do not know it ourselves, if they have come back to let injustice or ignorance rule—then they had better have died on the fields of France—"

He stopped suddenly amid a startled silence. Not a sound

from any of them.

"I beg your pardon," he laughed a bit awkwardly, "I didn't mean to preach a sermon."

"Don't spoil it, *please*," Aunt Claudia begged brokenly; "I wish more men would speak out."

"May I say this, then, before I stop? The future of our country is in the hands of the men who fought in France. On them must descend the mantles of our great men, Washington, Lincoln, Roosevelt—we must walk with these spirits if we love America—"

"Do you wonder," Randy said, under his breath to Becky, "that his men fought, and that they died for him?"

She found her little handkerchief and wiped her eyes. "He's a—perfect—darling," she whispered, and could say no more.

Dalton was for the time eclipsed. He knew it and was not at ease. He was glad when Mrs. Paine stood up. "I am sorry to tear myself away. But I must. I can't be sure that Susie has made up the morning rolls. There's a camp-meeting at Jessica, and she's lost the little mind that she usually puts on her cooking."

Randy and the Major went with her in the low carriage, with Rosalind making good time towards the home stable, and with Nellie Custis following with flapping ears.

Dalton stayed on. The Judge urged him. "It's too lovely to go in," he said; "what's your hurry?"

Aunt Claudia, who was inexpressibly weary, felt that her father was exceeding the bounds of necessary hospitality. She felt, too, that the length of Dalton's first call was inexcusable. But she did not go to bed. As long as Becky was there, she should stay to chaperon her. With a sense of martyrdom upon her, Mrs. Beaufort sat stiffly in her chair.

The Judge was talkative and brilliant, glad of a new and apparently attentive listener. Becky had little to say. She sat with her small feet set primly on the ground. Her hands were folded in her lap. Dalton was used to girls who lounged or who hung fatuously on his words, as if they had set themselves to please him.

But Becky had no arts. She was frank and unaffected, and apparently not unconscious of Dalton's charms. The whole thing was, he felt, going to be rather stimulating.

When at last he left them, he asked the Judge if he might come again. "I'd like to look at those birds by daylight."

Becky, giving him her hand, hoped that he might come. She had been all the evening in a sort of waking dream. Even when Dalton had been silent, she had been intensely aware of his presence, and when he had talked, he had seemed to speak to her alone, although his words were for others.

"I saw you dancing," he said, before he dropped her hand.

"Oh, did you?"

"Yes."

Back of the house the dogs barked.

"Will you dance some time with me?"

"Oh, could I?"

"Why not?"

A moment later he was gone. The light of his motor flashed down the hills like a falling star.

"I wonder what made the dogs bark," the Judge said as they went in.

"They probably thought it was morning," was Mrs. Beaufort's retort, as she preceded Becky up the stairs.

IV

The dogs had barked because Randy after a quick drive home had walked back to Huntersfield.

"Look here," he burst out as he and the Major had stood on the steps of the Schoolhouse, "do you like him?"

"Who? Dalton?"

"Yes."

"He's not a man's man," the Major said, "and he doesn't care in the least what you and I think of him."

"Doesn't he?"

"No, and he doesn't care for—stuffed birds—and he doesn't care for the Judge, and he doesn't care for Mrs. Beaufort—"

"Oh, you needn't rub it in. I know what he's after."

"Do you?"

"Yes—"

The Major whistled softly a lilting tune. He had been called "The Whistling Major" by his men and they had liked his clear piping.

He stopped abruptly. "Well, you can't build fences around lovely little ladies—"

"I wish I could. I'd like to shut her up in a tower—"

They left it there. It was really not a thing to be talked about. They both knew it, and stopped in time.

Randy, climbing the outside stairs, presently, to his bedroom, turned at the upper landing to survey the scene spread out before him. The hills were steeped in silence. The world was black and gold—the fragrance of the honeysuckle came up from the hedge below. On such a night as this one could not sleep. He felt himself restless, emotionally keyed up. He descended the stairs. Then, suddenly, he found himself taking the trail back towards Huntersfield.

He walked easily, following the path which led across the hills. The distance was not great, and he had often walked it. He loved a night like this. As he came to a stretch of woodland, he went under the trees with the thrill of one who enters an enchanted forest.

An owl hooted overhead. A whip-poor-will in a distant swamp sounded his plaintive call.

Randy could not have analyzed the instinct which sent him back to Becky. It was not in the least to spy upon her, nor upon Dalton. He only knew that he could not sleep, that something drew him on and on, as Romeo was drawn perchance to Capulet's orchard.

He came out from under the trees to other hills. He was still on his own land. These acres had belonged to his father, his grandfather, his great-grandfather, and back of that to a certain gallant gentleman who had come to Virginia with grants from the King. There had been, too, a great chief, whose blood was in his veins, and who had roamed through this land before Europe knew it. Powhatan was a rare old name to link with one's own, and Randy had a Virginian's pride in his savage strain.

So, as he went along, he saw canoes upon the shining river. He saw tall forms with feathers blowing. He saw fires on the heights.

The hill in front of him dipped to a little stream. He and Becky had once waded in that stream together. How white her feet had been on the brown stones. His life, as he thought of it, was bound up in memories of Becky. She had come down from school for blissful week-ends and holidays, and she and Randy had tramped over the hills and through the pine woods, finding wild-flowers in the spring, arbutus, flushing to beauty in its hidden bed, blood-root, hepatica, wind-flowers, violets in a purple glory; finding in the summer wild roses, dewberries, blackberries, bees and butter-flies, the cool shade of the little groves, the shine and shimmer of the streams; finding in the fall a golden stillness and the redness of Virginia Creeper. They had ridden on horseback over the clay roads, they had roamed the stubble with a pack of wiry hounds at their heels, they had gathered Christmas greens, they had sung carols, they had watched the Old Year out and the New Year in, and their souls had been knit in a comradeship which had been a very fine thing indeed for a boy like Randy and a girl like Becky.

There had been, too, about their friendship a rather engaging seriousness. They had talked a great deal of futures. They had dreamed together very great dreams. Their dreams had, of course, changed from time to time. There had been that dream of Becky's when she first went to the convent, that she wanted some day to be a nun like Sister Loretto. The fact that it would involve a change of faith was thrashed over flamingly by Randy. "It is all very well for an old woman, Becky. But you'd hate it."

Becky had been sure that she would not hate it. "You don't know how lovely she looks in the chapel."

"Well, there are other ways to look lovely."

"But it would be nice to be—good."

"You are good enough."

"I am not really, Randy. Sister Loretto says her prayers all day—"

"How often do you say yours?"

"Oh, at night. And in the mornings—sometimes—"

"That's enough for anybody. If you say them hard enough once, what more can the Lord ask?"

He had been a rather fierce figure as he had flung his questions, but he had not swerved her in the least from her thought of herself as a novice in a white veil, and later as a full-fledged sister, with beads and a black head-dress.

This dream had, in time, been supplanted by one imposed upon her by the ambitions of a much-admired classmate.

"Maude and I are going to be doctors," Becky had announced as she and Randy had walked over the fields with the hounds at their heels. "It's a great opportunity for women, Randy, and we shall study in Philadelphia."

"Shall you like cutting people up?" he had demanded brutally.

She had shuddered. "I shan't have to cut them up very much, shall I?"

"You'll have to cut them up a lot. All doctors do, and sometimes they are dead."

She had argued a bit shakily after that, and that night she had slept badly. The next morning they had gone over it again. "You fainted when the kitten's paw was crushed in the door."

"It was dreadful—"

"And you cried when I cut my foot with the hatchet and we were out in the woods. And if you are going to be a doctor you'll have to look at people who are crushed and cut—"

"Oh, please, Randy—"

Three days of such intensive argument had settled it. Becky decided that it was, after all, better to be an authoress. "There was Louisa Alcott, you know, Randy."

He was scornful. "Women weren't made for that—to sit in an

attic and write. Why do you keep talking about doing things, Becky? You'll get married when you grow up and that will be the end of it."

"I am not going to get married, Randy."

"Well, of course you will, and I shall marry and be a lawyer like my father, and perhaps I'll go to Congress."

Later he had a leaning towards the ministry. "If I preached I could make the world better, Becky."

That was the time when she had come down for Hallowe'en, and it was on Sunday evening that they had talked it over in the Bird Room at Huntersfield. There had been a smouldering fire on the wide hearth, and the Trumpeter Swan had stared down at them with shining eyes. They had been to church that morning and the text had been, "The harvest is past, the summer is ended, and we are not saved."

"I want to make the world better, Becky," Randy had said in the still twilight, and Becky had answered in an awed tone, "It would be so splendid to see you in the pulpit, Randy, wearing a gown like Dr. Hodge."

But the pulpit to Randy had meant more than that. And the next day when they walked through the deserted mill town, he had said, "Everybody is dead who lived here, and once they were alive like us."

She had shivered, "I don't like to think of it."

"It's a thing we've all got to think of. I like to remember that Thomas Jefferson came riding through and stopped at the mill and talked to the miller."

"How dreadful to know that they are—dead."

"Mother says that men like Jefferson never die. Their souls go marching on."

The stream which ground the county's corn was at their feet. "But what about the miller?" Becky had asked; "does his soul march, too?"

Randy, with the burden of yesterday's sermon upon him, hoped that the miller was saved.

He smiled now as he thought of the rigidness of his boyish theology. To him in those days Heaven was Heaven and Hell was Hell.

The years at school had brought doubt—apostasy. Then on the fields of France, Randy's God had come back to him—the Christ who bound up wounds, who gave a cup of cold water, who fought with flaming sword against the battalions of brutality, who led up and up that white company who gave their lives for a glorious Cause. Here, indeed, was a God of righteousness and of justice, of tenderness and purity. To other men than Randy, Christ had in a very personal and specific sense been born across the sea.

It was in France, too, that the dream had come to him of a future of creative purpose. He had always wanted to write. Looking back over his University days, he was aware of a formative process which had led towards this end. It was there he had communed with the spirit of a tragic muse. There had been all the traditions of Poe and his tempestuous youth—and Randy, passing the door which had once opened and closed on that dark figure, had felt the thrill of a living personality—of one who spoke still in lines of ineffable beauty—"*Banners yellow, glorious, golden, On its roof did float and flow—*" and again "*A dirge for her the doubly dead, in that she died so young—*" with the gayety and gloom and grandeur of those chiming, rhyming, tolling bells—"*Keeping time, time, time, In a sort of Runic rhyme—*" and that "*grim and ancient Raven wandering from the Nightly shore—*"

"Do you think I could write?" Randy had asked one of his teachers, coming verse-saturated to the question.

The man had looked at him with somber eyes. "You have an ear for it—and an eye—But genius pays a price."

"What do you mean?"

"It shows its heart to the world, dissects its sacred thoughts, has no secrets—"

"But think of leaving a thing behind you like—'To Helen—'"

"Do you think the knowledge that he had written a few bits of incomparable verse helped Poe to live? If he had invented a pill or a headache powder, he would have slept on down and have dined from gold dishes."

"I'd rather write 'Ulalume' than dine from gold dishes."

"You think that now. But in twenty years you will sigh for a—feather bed—"

"You don't believe that."

There had come a lighting of the somber eyes. "My dear fellow, if you, by the grace of God, have it in you to write, what I believe won't have anything to do with it. You will crucify yourself for the sake of a line—starve for the love of a rhythm."

Randy had not yet starved for love of a rhythm, but he had lost sleep during those nights in France, trying to put into words the things that gripped his soul. There had been beauty as well as horror in those days. What a world it had been, a world of men—a striving, eager group, raised for the moment above sordidness, above self—

He had not found verse his medium, although he had drunk eagerly of the golden cups which others had to offer him. But his prose had gained because of his belief in beauty of structure and of singing lovely words. As yet he had nothing to show for his pains, but practice had given strength to his pen—he felt that some day with the right theme he might do—wonders—

The trees had again closed in about him. A shadow flitted by—a fox, unafraid and in search of a belated meal. Randy remembered the days when he and Becky had thought that there might be wolves in the forest. He laughed a little, recalling Becky's words. "Sister Loretto has the feeling that the world is a dark forest, and that I am Red Riding Hood." Was it that which had brought him back? Was there, indeed, a Wolf?

When he reached Huntersfield, and the dogs barked, he had feared for the moment discovery. He was saved, however, by the friendly silence which followed that first note of alarm. The dogs knew him and followed him with wagging tails as he skirted the lawn and came at last to the gate which had closed a few minutes before on Dalton's car. He saw the Judge go in, Aunt Claudia, Becky—shadowy figures between the white pillars.

Then, after a moment, a room on the second floor was illumined. The shade was up and he saw the interior as one sees the scene of a play. There was the outline of a rose-colored canopy, the gleam of a mirror, the shine of polished wood, and in the center, Becky in pale blue, with a candle in her hand.

And as he saw her there, Randolph knew why he had come. To worship at a shrine. That was where Becky belonged—high above him. The flame of the candle was a sacred fire.

CHAPTER IV

RAIN AND RANDY'S SOUL

I

Madge came down the next morning dressed for her journey. "Oscar and Flora are going to take me as far as Washington in their car. They want you to make a fourth, Georgie."

Dalton was eating alone. Breakfast was served at small tables on the west terrace. There was a flagged stone space with wide awnings overhead. Except that it overlooked a formal garden instead of streets, one might have been in a Parisian café. The idea was Oscar's. Dalton had laughed at him. "You'll be a *boulevardier*, Oscar, until you die."

Oscar had been sulky. "Well, how do you want me to do it?"

"Breakfast in bed—or in a breakfast room with things hot on the sideboard, luncheon, out here on the terrace when the weather permits, tea in the garden, dinner in great state in the big dining-room."

"I suppose you think you know all about it. But the thing that I am always asking myself is, were you born to it, Dalton?"

"I've been around a lot," Dalton evaded. "Of course if you don't want me to be perfectly frank with you, I won't."

"Be as frank as you please," Oscar had said, "but it's your air of knowing everything that gets me."

Dalton's breakfast was a hearty one—bacon and two eggs, and a pile of buttered toast. There had been a melon to begin with, and there was a pot of coffee. He was eating with an appetite when Madge came down.

"I had mine in bed," Madge said, as George rose and pulled out a chair for her. "Isn't this the beastliest fashion, having little tables?"

"That's what I told Oscar."

"Oscar and Flora will never have too much of restaurants. They belong to the class which finds all that it wants in a jazz band and scrambled eggs at Jack's at one o'clock in the morning. Georgie, in my next incarnation, I hope there won't be any dansants or night frolics. I'd like a May-pole in the sunshine and a lot of plump and rosy women and bluff and hearty men for my friends—with a fine old farmhouse and myself in the dairy making butter—"

George smiled at her. "I should have fancied you an Egyptian princess, with twin serpents above your forehead instead of that turban."

"Heavens, no. I want no ardours and no Anthonys. Tell me about the new little girl, Georgie."

"How do you know there is a—new little girl?"

"I know your tricks and your manners, and the way you managed to meet her at the Horse Show. And you saw her last night."

"How do you know?"

"By the light in your eyes."

"Do I show it like that? Well, she's rather—not to be talked about, Madge—"

She was not in the least affronted. "So that's it? You always begin that way—putting them on a pedestal—If you'd only keep one of us there it might do you good."

"Which one—you?" he leaned a little forward.

"No." Indignation stirred within her. How easy it was for him to play the game. And last night she had lain long awake, listening for the sound of his motor. She had seen the moon set, and spectral dawn steal into the garden. "No, I'm running away. I am tired of drifting always on the tides of other people's inclination. We have stayed down here where it is hot because Oscar and Flora like it, yet there's all the coolness of the North Shore waiting for us—"

She rose and walked to the edge of the terrace. The garden was splashed now with clear color, purple and rose and gold. The air was oppressive, with a gathering haze back of the hills.

"I'm tired of it. Some day I'm going to flap my wings and fly away where you won't be able to find me, Georgie. I'd rather be a wild gull to the wind-swept sky, than a tame pigeon—to eat from your hand—" She said it lightly; this was not a moment for plaintiveness.

There was a dancing light in his eyes. "You're a golden pheasant—and you'll never fly so far that I shan't find you."

Oscar arriving at this moment saved a retort. "Flora's not well. We can't motor up, Madge."

"I am sorry but I can take a train."

"There's one at three. I don't see why you are going," irritably; "Flora won't stay here long after you leave."

"I am not as necessary as you think, Oscar. There are plenty of others, and I must go—"

"Oh, very well. Andrews will drive you down."

"I'll drive her myself," said Dalton.

II

Aunt Claudia was going to Washington also on the three o'clock train. She had had a wireless from Truxton who had sailed from Brest and would arrive at New York within the week.

"Of course you'll go and meet him, Aunt Claudia," Becky had said; "I'll help you to get your things ready."

Aunt Claudia, quite white and inwardly shaken by the thought of the happiness which was on its way to her, murmured her thanks.

Becky, divining something of the tumult which was beneath that outward show of serenity, patted the cushions of the couch in Mrs. Beaufort's bedroom. "Lie down here, you darling dear. It was such a surprise, wasn't it?"

"Well, my knees are weak," Mrs. Beaufort admitted.

The nuns had taught Becky nice ways and useful arts, so she folded and packed under Aunt Claudia's eye and was much applauded.

"Most girls in these days," said Mrs. Beaufort, "throw things in. Last summer I stayed at a house where the girls sat on their trunks to shut them, and sent parcel-post packages after them of the things they had left out."

"Sister Loretto says that I am not naturally tidy, so she keeps me at it. I used to weep my eyes out when she'd send me back to my room—But crying doesn't do any good with Sister Loretto."

"Crying is never any good," said Aunt Claudia. She was of Spartan mold. "Crying only weakens. When things are so bad that you must cry, then do it where the world can't see."

Becky found herself thrilled by the thought of Aunt Claudia crying in secret. She was a martial little soul in spite of her distinctly feminine type of mind.

Aunt Claudia's lingerie, chastely French-embroidered in little scallops, with fresh white ribbons run in, was laid out on the bed in neat piles. There was also a gray corduroy dressing-gown, lined with silk.

"This will be too warm," Becky said; "please let me put in my white crepe house-coat. It will look so pretty, Aunt Claudia, when Truxton comes in the morning to kiss you—"

Aunt Claudia had been holding on to her emotions tightly. The thought of that morning kiss which for three dreadful years had been denied her—for three dreadful years she had not known whether Truxton would ever breeze into her room before breakfast with his "Mornin' Mums." She felt that if she allowed herself any softness or yielding at this moment she would spoil her spotless record of self-control and weep in maudlin fashion in Becky's arms.

So in self-defense, she spoke with coldness. "I never wear borrowed clothes, my dear."

Becky, somewhat dishevelled and warm from her exertions, sat down to argue it. "I haven't had it on. And I'd love to give it to you—"

"My dear, of course not. It's very generous of you—very—" Aunt Claudia buried her face suddenly in the pillows and sobbed stormily.

Becky stood up. "Oh, Aunt Claudia," she gasped. Then with the instinctive knowledge that silence was best, she gave her aunt a little pat on the shoulder and crept from the room.

She crept back presently and packed the crepe house-coat with the other things. Then, since Aunt Claudia made no sign, she went down-stairs to the kitchen.

Mandy, the cook, who had a complexion like an old copper cent, and who wore a white Dutch cap in place of the traditional bandana, was cutting corn from the cob for fritters.

"If you'll make a cup of tea," Becky said, "I'll take it up to Aunt Claudia. She's lying down."

"Is you goin' wid her?" Mandy asked.

"To New York? No. She'll want Truxton all to herself, Mandy."

"Well, I hopes she has him," Mandy husked an ear of corn viciously. "I ain' got my boy. He hol's his haid so high, he ain' got no time fo' his ol' Mammy."

"You know you are proud of him, Mandy."

"I ain' sayin' I is, and I ain' sayin' I isn't. But dat Daisy down the road, she ac' like she own him."

"Oh, Daisy? Is he in love with her?"

"Love," with withering scorn, "*love*? Ain' he got somefin' bettah to do than lovin' when he's jes' fit and fought fo' Uncle Sam?" She beat the eggs for her batter as if she had Daisy's head under the whip. "He fit and fought fo' Uncle Sam," she repeated, "and now he comes home and camps hisse'f on Daisy's do'-step."

Against the breeze of such high indignation, any argument would be blown away. Becky changed the subject hastily. "Mandy," she asked, "are you making corn fritters?"

"I is—"

"What else for lunch?"

"An omlec—"

"Mandy, I'm so hungry I could eat a house—"

"You look it," Mandy told her; "effen I was you, I'd eat and git fat."

"It isn't fashionable to be fat, Mandy."

"Skeletums may be in style," said Mandy, breaking eggs for the omelette, "but I ain' ever found good looks in bones."

"Don't you like *my* bones, Mandy?"

"You ain't got none, honey."

"You called me a skeleton."

The kettle boiled. "Effen I called you a skeletum," Mandy said as she placed a cup and saucer on a small napkined tray, "my min' was on dat-ar Daisy. You ain' got no bones, Miss Becky. But Daisy, she's got a neck like a picked tukkey, and her shoulder-blades stan' out like wings."

III

Becky went to the train with her aunt. George Dalton drove Madge down and passed the old surrey on the way.

Later Madge met Mrs. Beaufort and Becky on the station platform, and it was when Dalton settled her in her chair in the train that she said, "She's a darling. Keep her on a pedestal, Georgie—"

"You're a good sport," he told her; "you know you'd hate it if I did."

"I shouldn't. I'd like to think of you on your knees—"

It was time for him to leave her. She gave him her hand. "Until we meet again, Georgie."

Her eyes were cool and smiling. Yet later as she looked out on the flying hills, there was trouble in them. There had been a time when Dalton had seemed to square with her girlish dreams.

And now, there was no one to warn this other girl with dreams in her eyes. George was not a vulture, he was simply a marauding bee—!

Becky was already in the surrey when George came back, and Calvin was gathering up his reins.

"Oh, look here, I wish you'd let me drive you up, Miss Bannister," George said, sparkling; "there's no reason, is there, why you must ride alone?"

"Oh, no."

"Then you will?"

Her hesitation was slight. "I should like it."

"And can't we drive about a bit? You'll show me the old places? It is such a perfect day. I hope you haven't anything else to do."

She had not. "I'll go with Mr. Dalton, Calvin."

Calvin, who had watched over more than one generation of Bannister girls, and knew what was expected of them, made a worried protest.

"Hit's gwine rain, Miss Becky."

Dalton dismissed him with a wave of the hand. "I won't let her get wet," he lifted Becky from the surrey and walked with her to his car.

Kemp, who had come down in the house truck with Madge's trunks, stood stiff and straight by the door. Being off with Miss MacVeigh he was on with Miss Bannister. Girls might come and girls might go in his master's life, but Kemp had an air of going on forever.

When he had seated Becky, Dalton stepped back and gave hurried instructions.

"At four, Kemp," he said, "or if you are later, wait until we come."

"Very well, sir." Kemp stood statuesquely at attention until the car whirled on. Then he sat down on the station platform, and talked to the agent. He was no longer a servant but a man.

As the big car whirled up the hill, Becky, looking out upon the familiar landscape, saw it with new eyes. There was a light upon it which had never been for her on sea or land. She had not believed that in all the world there could be such singing, blossoming radiance.

They drove through the old mill town and the stream was bright under the willows. They stopped on the bridge for a moment to view the shining bend.

"There are old chimneys under the vines," Becky said; "doesn't it seem dreadful to think of all those dead houses—"

George gave a quick turn. "Why think of them? You were not made to think of dead houses, you were made to live."

On and on they went, up the hills and down into the valleys, between rail fences which were a riot of honeysuckle, and with the roads in places rough under their wheels, with the fields gold with stubble, the sky a faint blue, with that thick look on the horizon.

George talked a great deal about himself. Perhaps if he had listened instead to Becky he might have learned things which would have surprised him. But he really had very interesting things to tell, and Becky was content to sit in silence and watch his hands on the wheel. They were small hands, and for some tastes a bit too plump and well-kept, but Becky found no fault with them. She felt that she could sit there forever, and watch his hands and listen to his clear quick voice.

At last George glanced at the little clock which hung in front of him. "Look here," he said, "I told Kemp to have tea for us at a place which I found once when I walked in the woods. A sort of summer house which looks towards Monticello. Do you know it?"

"Yes. Pavilion Hill. It's on Randy Paine's plantation—King's Crest."

"Then you've been there?"

"A thousand times with Randy."

"I thought it was Waterman's. We shan't be jailed as trespassers, shall we?"

"No. But how could you tell your man to have tea for us when you didn't know that I'd be—willing?"

"But I did—know—"

A little silence, then "How?"

"Because when I put my mind on a thing I usually get my way."

She sat very still. He bent down to her. "You're not angry?"

"No." Her cheeks were flaming. She was thrilled by his masterfulness. No man had ever spoken to her like that. She was, indeed, having her first experience of ardent, impassioned pursuit. So might young Juliet have given ear to Romeo. And if Romeo had been a Georgie-Porgie, then alas, poor Juliet!

The Pavilion had been built a hundred and fifty years before of cedar logs. There had been a time when Thomas Jefferson had walked over to drink not tea, but something stronger with dead and gone Paines. Its four sides were open, but the vines formed a curtain which gave within a soft gloom. They approached it from the east side, getting out of their car and climbing the hill from the roadside. They found Kemp with everything ready. The kettle was boiling, and the tea measured into the Canton teapot which stood in its basket—

"Aren't you glad you came?" Dalton asked. "Kemp, when you've poured the tea, you can look after the car."

The wind, rising, tore the dry leaves from the trees. Kemp, exiled, as it were, from the Pavilion, sat in the big car and watched the gathering blackness. Finally he got out and put up the curtains. Everything would be ready when Dalton came. He knew better, however, than to warn his master. George was apt to be sharp when his plans were spoiled.

And now throughout the wooded slope there was the restless movement of nature disturbed in the midst of peaceful dreaming. The trees bent and whispered. The birds, flying low, called sharp warnings. A small dog, spurning the leaves, as she followed a path up the west side of the hill, stopped suddenly and looked back at the man who followed her.

"We'll make the Pavilion if we can, old girl," he told her, and as if she understood, she went up and up in a straight line, disregarding the temptation of side tours into bush and bramble.

George and Becky had finished their tea. There had been some rather delectable sweet biscuit which Kemp kept on hand for such occasions, and there was a small round box of glacé nuts, which George had insisted that Becky must keep. The box was of blue silk set off by gold lace and small pink roses.

"Blue is your color," George had said as he presented it.

"That's what Randy says."

"You are always talking of Randy."

She looked her surprise. "I've always known him."

"Is he in love with you?"

She set down the box and looked at him. "Randy is only a boy. I am very fond of him. But we aren't either of us—silly."

She brought the last sentence out with such scorn that George had a moment of startled amaze.

Then, recovering, he said with a smile, "Is being in love silly?"

"I think it's rather sacred—"

The word threw him back upon himself. Love was, you understand, to George, a game. And here was Becky acting as if it were a ritual.

Yet the novelty of her point of view made her seem more than ever adorable. In his heart he found himself saying, "Oh, you lovely, lovely little thing."

But he did not say it aloud. Indeed he, quite unaccountably, found himself unable to say anything, and while he hesitated, there charged up the west hill a panting dog with flapping ears. At the arched opening of the Pavilion she paused and wagged a tentative question.

"It's Nellie Custis—" Becky rose and ran towards her. "Where's your master, darling? *Randy—*"

In response to her call came an eerie cry—the old war cry of the Indian chiefs. Then young Paine came running up. "Becky! Here? There's going to be a storm. You better get home—"

He stopped short. Dalton was standing by the folding table.

"Hello, Paine," he said, with ease. "We're playing 'Babes in the Wood.'"

"You seem very comfortable," Randy was as stiff as a wooden tobacco sign.

"We are," Becky said. "Mr. Dalton waved his wand like the Arabian nights—"

"My man did it," said Dalton; "he's down there in the car."

Randy felt a sense of surging rage. The Pavilion was his. It was old and vine-covered, and hallowed by a thousand memories.

And here was Dalton trespassing with his tables and chairs and his Canton teapot. What right had George Dalton to bring a Canton teapot on another man's acres?

Becky was pouring tea for him. "Two lumps, Randy?"

"I don't want any tea," he said ungraciously. His eyes were appraising the flame of her cheeks, the light in her eyes. What had Dalton been saying? "I don't want any tea. And there's a storm coming."

All her life Becky had been terrified in a storm. She had cowered and shivered at the first flash of lightning, at the first rush of wind, at the first roll of thunder. And now she sat serene, while the trees waved despairing arms to a furious sky, while blackness settled over the earth, while her ears were assailed by the noise of a thousand guns.

What had come over her? More than anything else, the thing that struck against Randy's heart was this lack of fear in Becky!

IV

Of course it was Dalton who took Becky home. There had been a sharp summons to Kemp, who came running up with raincoats, a rush for the car, a hurried "Won't you come with us, Randy?" from Becky, and Randy's curt refusal, and then the final insult from Dalton.

"Kemp will get you home, Paine, when he takes the tea things."

Randy wanted to throw something after him—preferably a tomahawk—as Dalton went down the hill, triumphantly, shielding Becky from the elements.

He watched until a curtain of rain shut them out, but he heard the roar of the motor cutting through the clamor of the storm.

"Well, they're off, sir," said Kemp cheerfully.

He was packing the Canton teapot in its basket and was folding up the chairs and tables. Randy had a sense of outrage. Here he was, a Randolph Paine of King's Crest, left behind in the rain with a man who had his mind on—teapots—He stood immovable in the arched opening, his arms folded, and with the rain beating in upon him.

"You'll get wet," Kemp reminded him; "it's better on this side, sir."

"I don't mind the rain. I won't melt; I've had two years in France."

"You have, sir?" something in Kemp's voice made Randy turn and look at him. The little man had his arms full of biscuit boxes, and he was gazing at Randy with a light in his eyes which had not been for Dalton.

"I had three years myself. And the best of my life, sir."

Randy nodded. "A lot of us feel that way."

"The fighting," said Kemp, "was something awful. But it was—big—and after it things seem a bit small, sir." He drew a long breath and came back to his Canton teapot and his folding table and his plans for departure.

"I'll be glad to take you in the little car, Mr. Paine."

"No," said Randy; "no, thank you, Kemp. I'll wait here until the storm is over."

Kemp, with a black rubber cape buttoned about his shoulders and standing out over his load like a lady's hoopskirts, bobbed down the path and was gone.

Randy was glad to be alone. He was glad to get wet, he was glad of the roar and of the tumult which matched the tumult in his soul.

Somehow he had never dreamed of this—that somebody would come into Becky's life and take her away—

Nellie Custis shivered and whined. She hated thunderstorms. Randy sat down on the step and she crept close to him. He laid his hand on her head and fear left her—as fear had left Becky in the presence of Dalton.

After that the boy and the dog sat like statues, looking out, and in those tense and terrible moments a new spirit was born in Randolph Paine. Hitherto he had let life bring him what it would. He had scarcely dared hope that it would bring him Becky. But now he knew that if he lost her he would face—chaos—

Well, he would not lose her. Or if he did, it would not be to let her marry a man like Dalton. Surely she wouldn't. She *couldn't*—But there had been that light in her eyes, that flame in her cheek—that lack of fear—Dalton's air of assurance, the way she had turned to him.

"Oh, God," he said suddenly, out loud, "don't let Dalton have her."

He was shaken by an emotion which bent his head to his knees. Nellie Custis pressed close against him and whined.

"He shan't have her, Nellie. He shan't—"

He burned with the thought of Dalton's look of triumph. Dalton who had carried Becky off, and had left him with Kemp and a Canton teapot.

He recalled Kemp's words. "After it things seem a bit small, sir."

Well, it shouldn't be small for him. It had seemed so big—over there. So easy to—carry on.

If he only had a fighting chance. If he had only a half of Dalton's money. A little more time in which to get on his feet.

But in the meantime here was Dalton—with his money, his motors, and his masterfulness. And his look of triumph—

In a sudden fierce reaction he sprang to his feet. He stood in the doorway as if defying the future. "Nobody shall take her away from me," he said, "she's mine—"

His arms were folded over his chest, his wet black locks almost hid his eyes. So might some young savage have stood in the long ago, sending his challenge forth to those same hills.

CHAPTER V

LITTLE SISTER

I

It is one thing, however, to fling a challenge to the hills, and another to live up to the high moment. Looking at it afterwards in cold blood, Randy was forced to admit that his chances of beating George Dalton in a race for Becky were small.

There seemed some slight hope, however, in the fact that Becky was a Bannister and ought to know a gentleman when she saw one.

"And Dalton's a—a bounder," said Randy to Nellie Custis.

Nellie Custis, who was as blue-blooded as any Bannister, cocked a sympathetic ear. Cocking an ear with Nellie was a weighty matter. Her ears were big and unmanageable. When she got them up, she kept them there for some time. It was a rather intriguing habit, as it gave her an air of eager attention which wooed confidence.

"He's a bounder," said Randy as if that settled it.

But it did not settle it in the least. A man with an Apollo head may not be a gentleman under his skin, but how are you to prove it? The world, spurning Judy O'Grady, sanctions the Colonel's lady, and their sisterhood becomes socially negligible. Randy should have known that he could not sweep George Dalton away with a word. Perhaps he did know it, but he did not care to admit it.

He and Nellie Custis were in the garage. It had once been a barn, but the boarders had bought cars, so there was now the smell of gasoline where there had once been the sweet scent of hay. And intermittently the air was rent with puffs and snorts and shrieks which drowned the music of that living chorus which has been sung in stables for centuries.

There were three cars. Two of them have nothing to do with this story, but the third will play its part, and merits therefore description.

It was not an expensive car, but it was new and shining, and had a perky snub-nosed air of being ready for anything. It belonged to the genial gentleman who used it without mercy, and thus the little car wove back and forth over the hills like a shuttle, doing its work sturdily, coming home somewhat noisily, and even at rest, seeming to ask for something more to do.

The genial gentleman was very proud of his car. He talked a

great deal about it to Randy, and on this particular morning when he came out and found young Paine sitting on a wheelbarrow with Nellie Custis lending him a cocked ear, he grew eloquent.

"Look here, I've been thinking. There ought to be a lot of cars like this in the county."

To Randy the enthusiasms of the genial gentleman were a constant source of amazement. He was always wanting the world to be glad about something. Randy felt that at this moment any assumption of gladness would be a hollow mockery.

"Any man," said the genial gentleman, rubbing a cloth over the enamel of the little car, "any man who would start selling this machine down here would make a fortune."

Randy pricked up his ears.

"How could he make a fortune?"

"Selling cars. Why, the babies cry for them—" he chuckled and rubbed harder.

"How much could he make?" Randy found himself saying.

The genial gentleman named a sum, "Easy."

Randy got up from the wheelbarrow and came over. "Is she really as good as that?"

"Is she really? Oh, say—" the genial gentleman for the next ten minutes dealt in superlatives.

Towards the end, Randy was firing questions at him.

"Could I own a car while I was selling them?"

"Sure—they'd let you have it on installments to be paid for out of your commissions—"

"And I'd have an open field?"

"My dear boy, in a month you could have cars like this running up and down the hills like ants after sugar. They speak for themselves, and they are cheap enough for anybody."

"But it is a horse-riding country, especially back in the hills. They love horse-flesh, you know."

"Oh, they'll get the gasoline bug like the rest of us," said the genial gentleman and slapped him on the back.

Randy winced. He did not like to be slapped on the back. Not at a moment—when he was selling his soul to the devil—

For that was the way he looked at it.

"I shall have to perjure myself," he said to Major Prime later, as they talked it over in the Schoolhouse, "to go through the country telling mine own people to sell their horses and get cars."

"If you don't do it, somebody else will."

"But a man can't be convincing if he doesn't believe in a thing."

"No, of course. But you've got to look at it this way, the world moves, and horses haven't had an easy time. Perhaps it is their moment of emancipation. And just for the sake of a sentiment, a tradition, you can't afford to hold back."

"I can't afford to lose this chance if there is money in it. But it isn't what I had planned."

As he sat there on the step and hugged his knees, every drop of blood in Randy seemed to be urging "Hurry, hurry." He felt as a man might who, running a race, finds another rider neck and neck and strains towards the finish.

To sell cars in order to win Becky seemed absurd on the face of it. But he would at least be doing something towards solving the problem of self-support, and towards increasing the measure of his own self-respect.

"What had you planned?" the Major was asking.

"Well of course there is the law—And I like it, but there would be a year or two before I could earn a living—And I've wanted to write—"

"Write what? Books?"

"Anything," said Randy, explosively, "that would make the world sit up."

"Ever tried it?"

"Yes. At school. I talked to a teacher of mine once about it. He said I had better invent a—pill—"

The Major stared, "A pill?"

Randy nodded. "He didn't quite mean it, of course. But he saw the modern trend. A poet? A poor thing! But hats off to the pillmaker with his multi-millions!"

"Stop that," said the Major.

"Stop what?"

"Blaming the world for its sordidness. There is beauty enough if we look for it."

"None of us has time to look for it. We are too busy trying to sell cars to people who love horses."

II

In the end Randy got his car. And after that he, too, might have been seen running shuttlelike back and forth over the red roads. Nellie Custis was usually beside him on the front seat. She took her new honors seriously. For generations back her forbears had loped with flapping ears in the lead of a hunting pack. To be sitting thus on a leather seat and whirled through the air with no need of legs from morning until night required some readjustment on the part of Nellie Custis. But she had always followed where Randy led. And in time she grew to like it, and watched the road ahead with eager eyes, and with her ears perpetually cocked.

Now and then Becky sat beside Randy, with Nellie at her feet. The difference between a ride with Randy and one with George Dalton was, Becky felt, the difference a not unpleasant commonplace and the stuff that dreams are made of.

"It is rather a duck of a car," she had said, the first time he took her out in it.

"Yes, it is," Randy had agreed. "I am getting tremendously fond of her. I have named her 'Little Sister.'"

"Oh, Randy, you haven't."

"Yes, I have. She has such confiding ways. I never believed that cars had human qualities, Becky."

"They are not horses of course."

"Well, they have individual characteristics. You take the three cars in our barn. The Packard reminds one of that stallion we owned three years ago—blooded and off like the wind. The Franklin is a grayhound—and Little Sister is a—duck—"

"Mr. Dalton's car is a—silver ship—"

"Oh, does he call it that?" grimly.

"No—"

"Was it your own—poetic—idea?"

"Yes."

"And you called Little Sister a duck," he groaned. "And when my little duck swims in the wake of his silver ship, and he laughs, do you laugh, too?"

There was a dead silence. Then she said, "Oh, Randy—"

He made his apology like a gentleman. "That was hateful of me, Becky. I'm sorry—"

"You know I wouldn't laugh, Randy, and neither would he."

"Who?"

"Mr. Dalton."

"Wouldn't what?"

"Laugh."

He hated her defense of young Apollo—but he couldn't let the subject alone.

"You never have any time for me."

"Randy, are you going to scold me for the rest of our ride?"

"Am I scolding?"

"Yes."

"Then I'll stop it and say nice things to you or you won't want to come again."

Yet after that when he saw her in Dalton's car, her words

would return to him, and gradually he began to think of her as sailing in a silver ship farther and farther away in a future where he could not follow.

Little Sister was a great comfort in those days. She gave him occupation and she gave him an income. He was never to forget his first sale. He had not found it easy to cry his wares. The Paines of King's Crest had never asked favors of the country-folk, or if they had, they had paid generously for what they had received. To go now among them saying, "I have something to sell," carried a sting. There had been nothing practical in Randy's education. He had no equipment with which to meet the sordid questions of bargain and sale.

He had thought of this as he rode over the hills that morning to the house of a young farmer who had been suggested by the genial gentleman as a good prospect. He turned over in his mind the best method of approach. It was a queer thing, he pondered, to visualize himself as a salesman. He wondered how many of the other fellows who had come back looked at it as he did. They had dreamed such dreams of valor, their eyes had seen visions. To Randy when he had enlisted had come a singing sense that the days of chivalry were not dead. He had gone through the war with a laugh on his lips, but with a sense of the sacredness of the crusade in his heart. He had returned—still dreaming—to sell snub-nosed cars to the countryside!

Why, just a year ago—! He remembered a black night of storm, when, hooded like a falcon—he had ridden without a light on his motorcycle, carrying dispatches from the Argonne, and even as he had ridden, he had felt that high sense of heroic endeavor. On the success of his mission depended other lives, the saving of nations—victory—!

And now he, with a million others, was faced by the problem of the day's work. He wondered how the others looked at it—those gallant young knights in khaki who had followed the gleam. Were they, too, grasping at any job that would buy them bread and butter, pay their bills, keep them from living on the bounty of others?

He felt that in some way the thing was all wrong. There should have been big things for these boys to do. There seemed something insensate in a civilization which would permit a man who wore medals of honor to sell ribbon over a counter, or weigh out beef at a butcher's. Yet he supposed that many of them were doing it. Indeed he knew that some of them were. The butcher's boy, who brought the meat over every morning to King's Crest, wore two decorations, and when Randy had stopped for breakfast supplies, the hero of Belleau Woods had cut off sausages as calmly as he had once bayonetted Huns.

Randy wondered what the butcher's boy was feeling under that apparently stolid surface. Was his horizon bounded by beef and sausages, or did his soul expand with memories of the shoulder-to-shoulder march, the comradeship of the trenches, the laughter and songs? Did his pulses thrill with the thought of the big things he might yet do in these days of peace, or was he content to play safe and snip sausages?

Randy felt that he was not content. It was not that he loved war. But he loved the visions that the war had brought him. There had seemed no limit then to America's achievement. She had been a laggard—he thanked God that he had not been a party to that delay. But when she had come in, she had come in with all her might and main. And her young men had fought and the future of the whole world had been in their hands, and since peace had come the future of the world must still be reckoned in the terms of their glorious youth.

And now, something within Randy began to sing and soar. He felt that here were things to be put on paper—the questions which he flung at himself should be written for other men to read. That was what men needed—questions. Questions which demanded answers not only in words but in deeds. This was a moment for men of high thoughts and high purposes.

And he was selling cars—!

Well, some day he would write. He was writing a little now, at night. In his room at the top of the Schoolhouse. Yet the things that he had written seemed trivial as he thought of them. What he wanted was to strike a ringing note. To have the fellows say when they read it, "If it is true for him it is true for me."

Yet when one came to think of it, there were really not any "fellows." Not in the sense that it had been "over there." They were scattered to the four winds, dispersed to the seven seas—the A. E. F. was extinct—as extinct—as the Trumpeter Swan!

And now his thoughts ran fast, and faster. Here was his theme. Where was that glorious company of young men who had once sounded their trumpets to the world? Gone, as the swans were gone—leaving the memory of their whiteness—leaving the memory of their beauty—leaving the memory of their—song—

He wanted to turn back at once. To drive Little Sister at breakneck speed towards pen and paper. But some instinct drove him doggedly towards the matter on hand. One might write masterpieces, but there were cars to be sold.

He sold one—; quite strangely and unexpectedly he found that the transaction was not difficult. The man whom he had come to see was on the front porch and was glad of company. Randy explained his errand. "It is new business for me. But I've got something to offer you that you'll find you'll want—"

He found that he could say many things truthful about the merits of Little Sister. He had a convincing manner; the young farmer listened.

"Let me take you for a ride," Randy offered, and away they went along the country roads, and through the main streets of the town in less time that it takes to say—"Jack Robinson."

When they came back, the children ran out to see, and Randy took them down the road and back again. "You can carry the whole family," he said, "when you go—"

The man's wife came out. She refused to ride. She was afraid.

But Randy talked her over. "My mother felt like that. But once you are in it is different."

She climbed in, and came back with her face shining.

"I am going to buy the car," her husband said to her.

Randy's heart jumped. Somehow he had felt that it would not really happen. He had had little faith in his qualities as salesman. Yet, after all, it had happened, and he had sold his car.

Riding down the hill, he was conscious of a new sense of achievement. It was all very well to dream of writing masterpieces. But here was something tangible.

"Nellie," he said, "things are picking up."

Nellie laid her nose on his knee and looked up at him. It had been a long ride, and she was glad they were on the homeward stretch. But she wagged her tail. Nellie knew when things were going well with her master. And when his world went wrong, her sky darkened.

III

The sale of one car, however, does not make a fortune. Randy realized as the days went on that if he sold them and sold them and sold them, Dalton would still outdistance him financially.

There remained, therefore, fame, and the story in the back of his mind. If he could lay a thing like that at Becky's feet! He had the lover's urge towards some heaven-kissing act which should exalt his mistress—A book for all the world to read—a picture painted with a flaming brush, a statue carved with a magic instrument. It was for Becky that Randy would work and strive hoping that by some divine chance he might draw her to him.

He worked at night until the Major finally remonstrated.

"Do you ever go to bed?"

Randy laughed. "Sometimes."

"Are you writing?"

"Trying to."

"Hard work?"

"I like it,"—succinctly.

The Major smoked for a while in silence. Then he said, "I suppose you don't want to talk about it."

It was a starry night and a still one. The younger boarders had gone for a ride. The older boarders were in bed. The Major was stretched in his long chair. Randy sat as usual on the steps.

"Yes," he said, "I'd like to talk about it. I have a big idea, and I can't put it on paper."

He hugged his knees and talked. His young voice thrilled with the majesty of his conception. Here, he said, was the idea. Once upon a time there had been a race of wonderful swans, with plumage so white that when they rested in flocks on the river banks they made a blanket of snow. Their flight was a marvellous thing—they flew so high that the eye of man could not see them—but the sound of their trumpets could be heard. The years passed and the swans came no more to their old haunts. Men had hunted them and killed them—but there were those who held that on still nights they could be heard—sounding their trumpets—

"I want to link that up with the A. E. F. We were like the swans—a white company which flew to France—Our idealism was the song which we sounded high up. And the world listened—and caught the sound—And now, as a body we are extinct, but if men will listen, they may still hear our trumpets—sounding—!"

As he spoke the air seemed to throb with the passion of his phrases. His face was uplifted to the sky. The Major remembered a picture in the corridor of the Library of Congress—the Boy of Winander—Oh, the boys of the world—those wonderful boys who had been drawn out from among the rest, set apart for a time, and in whose hands now rested the fate of nations!

"It is epic," he said, slowly. "Take your time for it."

"It's too big," said Randy slowly, "and I am not a genius—But it is my idea, all right, and some day, perhaps, I shall make it go."

"You must make it clear to yourself. Then you can make it clear to others."

"Yes," Randy agreed, "and now you can see why I am sitting up nights."

"Yes. How did you happen to think of it, Paine?"

"I've been turning a lot of things over in my mind—; what the other fellows are doing about their jobs. There's that boy at the butcher's, and a lot of us went over to do big things. And now we have come back to the little things. Why, there's Dalton's valet—Kemp—taking orders from that—cad."

His scorn seemed to cut into the night. "And I am selling cars—I sold one to-day to an old darkey, and I felt my grandsires turn in their graves. But I like it."

The Major sat up. "Your liking it is the biggest thing about you, Paine."

"What do you mean?"

"A man who can do his day's work and not whine about it, is the man that counts. That butcher's boy may have a soul above weighing meat and wrapping sausages, but at the moment that's his job, and he is doing it well. There may be a divine discontent, but I respect the man who keeps his mouth shut until he finds a remedy or a raise.

"I don't often speak of myself," he went on, "but perhaps this is the moment. I am as thirsty for California, Paine, as a man for drink. It is the dry season out there, and the hills are brown, but I love the brown, and the purple shadows in the hollows. I have ridden over those hills for days at a time,—I shall never ride a horse over them again." He stopped and went on. "Oh, I've wanted to whine. I have wanted to curse the fate that tied me to a chair like this. I have been an active man—out-of-doors, and oh, the out-of-doors in California. There isn't anything like it—it is the sense of space, the clear-cut look of things. But I won't go back. Not till I have learned to do my day's work, and then I will let myself play a bit. I'd like to take you with me, Paine—you and a good car—and we'd go over the hills and far away—

"I haven't told you much of my life. And there's not a great deal to tell. Fifteen years ago I married a little girl and thought I loved her. But what I really loved was the thought of doing things for her. I had money and she was poor. It was pleasant to see her eyes shine when I gave her things—But money hasn't anything to do with love, Paine, and that is where we American men fall down. When we love a woman we begin to tell her of our possessions and to tempt her by them. And the thing that we should do is to show her ourselves. We should say, 'If I were stripped of all my worldly goods what would there be in me for you to like?' My little wife and I had not one thing in common. And one day she left me. She found a man who gave her love for love. I had given her cars and flowers and boxes of candy and diamonds and furs. But she wanted more than that. She died—two years ago. I think she had been happy in those last years. I never really loved her, but she taught me what love is—and it is not a question of barter and sale—"

He seemed to be thinking aloud. Randy spoke after a silence. "But a man must have something to offer a woman."

"He must have himself. Oh, we are all crooked in our values, Paine. The best that a man can give a woman is his courage, his hope, his aspiration. That's enough. I learned it too late. I don't know why I am saying all this to you, Paine."

But Randy knew. It was on such nights that men showed their souls to each other. It was on such nights that his comrades had talked to him in France. Under the moon they had seemed self-conscious. But beneath a sky of stars, the words had come to them.

As he sat at his desk later, he thought of all that the Major had said to him: that possessions had nothing to do with love; that the test must be, "What would there be in me to like if I were stripped of all my worldly goods?"

Well, he had nothing. There were only his hopes, his dreams, his aspiration—himself.

Would these weigh with any woman in the balance against George Dalton's splendid trappings?

The dawn crept in and found him still sitting at his desk. He had not written a dozen lines. But his thoughts had been the long, long thoughts of youth.

CHAPTER VI

GEORGIE-PORGIE

I

It would never have happened if Aunt Claudia had been there. Aunt Claudia would have built hedges about Becky. She would have warned the Judge. She would, as a last resort, have challenged Dalton. But Fate, which had Becky's future well in hand, had sent Aunt Claudia to meet Truxton in New York. And she was having the time of her life.

Her first letter was a revelation to her niece. "I didn't know," she told the Judge at breakfast, "that Aunt Claudia could be like this—"

"Like what?"

"So young and gay—"

"She is not old. And when she was young she was gayer than you."

"Oh, not really, Grandfather."

"Yes. And she looked like you—and had the same tricks with her hands, and her hair was bright and brown. And she was very pretty."

"She is pretty yet," said Becky, loyally, but she was quite sure that whatever might have been Aunt Claudia's likeness to herself in the past, her own charms would not in the future shrink to fit Aunt Claudia's present pattern. It was unthinkable that her pink and white should fade to paleness, her slenderness to stiffness, her youthful radiance to a sort of weary cheerfulness.

There was nothing weary in the letter, however. "Oh, my dear, my dear, you should see Truxton. He is so perfectly splendid that I am sure he is a changeling and not my son. I tell him that he can't be the bundle of cuddly sweetness that I used to carry in my arms. I wore your white house-coat that first morning, Becky, and he sent some roses, and we had breakfast together in my rooms at the hotel. I believe it is the first time in years that I have looked into a mirror to really like my looks. You were sweet, my dear, to insist on putting it in. Truxton must stay here for two weeks more, and he wants me to stay with him. Then we shall come down together. Can you get along without me? We are going to the most wonderful plays, and to smart places to eat, and I danced last night on a roof garden. Should I say 'on' or 'in' a roof garden? Truxton says that my step is as light as a girl's. I think my head is a little turned. I am very happy."

Becky laid the letter down. "Would anyone have believed that Aunt Claudia *could*—"

"You have said that before, my dear. Your Aunt Claudia wasn't born in the ark—"

"But, Grandfather, I didn't mean that."

"It sounded like it. I shall write to her to stay as long as she can. We can get along perfectly without her."

"Of course," said Becky slowly. She had a feeling that, at all costs, she ought to call Aunt Claudia back.

For Dalton, after that first ride in the rain from Pavilion Hill, had speeded his wooing. He had swept Becky along on a rushing tide. He had courted the Judge, and the Judge had pressed upon him invitation after invitation. Day and night the big motor had flashed up to Huntersfield, bringing Dalton to some tryst with Becky, or carrying her forth to some gay adventure. Her world was rose-colored. She had not dreamed of life like this. She seemed to have drunk of some new wine, which lighted her eyes and flamed in her cheeks. Her beauty shone with an almost transcendent quality. As the dove's plumage takes on in the spring an added luster, so did the bronze of Becky's hair seem to burn with a brighter sheen.

Yet the Judge noticed nothing.

"Did you ask him to dine with us?" he had demanded, when Dalton had called Becky up on the morning of the receipt of Aunt Claudia's letter.

"No, Grandfather."

"Then I'll do it," and he had gone to the telephone, and had urged his hospitality.

II

When Dalton came Becky met him on the front steps of the house.

"Dinner is late," she said, "let's go down into the garden."

The garden at Huntersfield was square with box hedges and peaked up with yew, and there were stained marble statues of Diana and Flora and Ceres, and a little pool with lily pads.

"You are like the pretty little girls in the picture books," said George, as they walked along. "Isn't that a new frock?"

"Yes," said Becky, "it is. Do you like it?"

"You are a rose among the roses," he said. He wondered a bit at its apparent expensiveness. Perhaps, however, Becky was skillful with her needle. Some women were. He did not care greatly for such skill, but he was charmed by the effect.

"You are a rose among the roses," he said again, and broke off a big pink bud from a bush near by.

"Bend your head a little. I want to put it in your hair."

His fingers caught in the bronze mesh. "It is wound around my ring." He fumbled in his pockets with his free hand and got his knife. "It may pull a bit."

He showed her presently the lock which he had cut. "It seems alive," he kissed it and put it in his pocket.

Her protest was genuine. "Oh, please," she said, "I wish you wouldn't."

"Wouldn't what?"

"Keep it."

"Shall I throw it away?"

"You shouldn't have cut it off."

"Other men have been tempted—in a garden—"

It might have startled George could he have known that old Mandy, eyeing him from the kitchen, placed him in Eden's bower not as the hero of the world's initial tragedy, but as its Satanic villain.

"He sutt'n'y have bewitched Miss Becky," she told Calvin; "she ain' got her min' on nothin' but him."

"Yo' put yo' min' on yo' roas' lamb, honey," Calvin suggested. "How-cum you got late?"

"That chile kep' me fixin' that pink dress. She ain' never cyard what she wo'. And now she stan' in front o' dat lookin'-glass an' fuss an' fiddle. And w'en she ain' fussin' an' fiddlin', she jus' moons around, waitin' fo' him to come ridin' up in that red car like a devil on greased light'in'. An' I say right heah, Miss Claudia ain' gwine like it."

"Why ain' she?"

"Miss Claudia know black f'um w'ite. An' dat man done got a black heart—"

"Whut you know 'bout hit, Mandy?"

"Lissen. You wait. He'll suck a o'ange an' th'ow it away. He'll pull a rose, and scattah the leaves." Mandy, stirring gravy, was none the less dramatic. "You lissen, an' wait—"

"W'en Miss Claudia comin'?"

"In one week, thank the Lord," Mandy pushed the gravy to the back of the stove and pulled forward an iron pot. "The soup's ready," she said; "you go up and tell the Jedge, Calvin."

All through dinner, Becky was conscious of that lock of hair in George's pocket. The strand from which the lock had been cut fell down on her cheek. She had to tuck it back. She saw George smile as she did it. She forgave him.

It was after dinner that George spoke of Becky's gown.

"It is perfect," he said, "all except the pearls—?"

She gave him a startled glance. "The pearls?"

"I want to see you without them."

She unwound them and they dripped from her hand in milky whiteness.

He made his survey. "That's better," he said, "if they were real it would be different—I don't like to have you cheapened by anything less than—perfect—"

"Cheapened?" She smiled inscrutably, then dropped the pearls into a small box on the table beside her. "Yes," she said, "if they were real it would be different—"

There was something in her manner which made him say hurriedly, "You must not think that I am criticizing your taste. If I had my way you should have everything that money can buy—"

Her candid eyes came up to his. "There are a great many things that money cannot buy."

"You've got to show me," George told her; "I've never seen anything yet that I couldn't get with money."

"Could you buy—dreams—"

"I'd rather buy—diamonds."

"And money can't buy happiness."

"It can buy a pretty good imitation."

"But imitation happiness is like imitation pearls."

He laughed and sat down beside her. "You mustn't be too clever."

"I am not clever at all."

"I believe you are. And you don't have to be. There are plenty of clever women but only one Becky Bannister."

It was just an hour later that Georgie-Porgie kissed her. She was at the piano in the music-room, and there was no light except the glimmer of tall white candles, and the silver moonlight which fell across the shining floor.

Her grandfather was nodding in the room beyond, and through the open window came the dry, sweet scent of summer, as if nature had opened her pot-pourri to give the world a whiff of treasured fragrance.

Becky had been singing, and she had stopped and looked up at him.

"Oh, you lovely—lovely, little thing," he said, and bent his head.

To Becky, that moment was supreme, sacred. She trembled with happiness. To her that kiss meant betrothal—ultimate marriage.

To George it meant, of course, nothing of the kind. It was only one of many moments. It was a romance which might have been borrowed from the Middle Ages. A rare tale such as one might read in a book. A pleasant dalliance—to be continued until he was tired of it. If he ever married, it must be a spectacular affair—handsome woman, big fortune, not an unsophisticated slip of a child from an impoverished Virginia farm.

III

In the days that followed, Becky's gay lover came and rode away, and came again. He sparkled and shone and worshipped, but not a word did he say about the future. He seemed content with this idyl of old gardens, scented twilights, starlight nights, with Beauty's eyes for him alone radiant eyes that matched the stars.

Yet as the days went on the radiance was dimmed. Becky was in a state of bewilderment which bordered on fear. George showed himself an incomparable lover, but always he was silent about the things which she felt cried for utterance.

So at last one day she spoke to the Judge.

"Granddad, did you kiss Grandmother before you asked her to marry you?"

"Asking always comes first, my dear. And you are too young to think of such things."

Grandfather was, thus obviously, no help. He sat in the Bird Room and dreamed of the days when the stuffed mocking-bird on the wax branch sang to a young bride, and his ideal of love had to do with the courtly etiquette of a time when men knelt and sued and were rewarded with the touch of finger tips.

As for George, he found himself liking this affair rather more than usual. There was no denying that the child was tremendously attractive—with her youth and beauty and the reserve which like a stone wall seemed now and then to shut her in. He had always a feeling that he would like to climb over the wall. It had pricked his interest to find in this little creature a strength and delicacy which he had found in no other woman.

He had had one or two letters from Madge, and had answered them with a line. She gave rather generously of her correspondence and her letters were never dull. In the last one she had asked him to join her on the North Shore.

"I am sorry," she said, "for the new little girl. I have a feeling that she won't know how to play the game and that you'll hurt her. You will probably think that I am jealous, but I can't help that. Men always think that women are jealous when it comes to other women. They never seem to understand that we are trying to keep the world straight.

"Oscar writes that Flora isn't well, that all her other guests are gone except you—and that she wants me. But why should I come? I wish he wouldn't ask me. Something always tugs at my heart when I think of Flora. She has so much and yet so little. She and Oscar would be much happier in a flat on the West Side with Flora cooking in a kitchenette, and Oscar bringing things home from the delicatessen. He would buy bologna and potato salad on Sunday nights, and perhaps they would slice up a raw onion. It sounds dreadful, doesn't it? But there are thousands of people doing just that thing, Georgie, and being very happy over it. And it wouldn't be dreadful for Flora and Oscar because they would be right where they belong, and the potato salad and the bologna and the little room where Oscar could sit with his coat off would be much more to their liking than their present pomp and elegance. You and I are different. You could never play any part pleasantly but that of Prince Charming, and I should hate the kitchenette. I want wide spaces, and old houses, and deep fireplaces—my people far back were like that—I sometimes wonder why I stick to Flora—perhaps it is because she clung to me in those days when Oscar was drafted and had to go, and she cried so hard in the Red Cross rooms that I took her under my wing—Take it all together, Flora is rather worth while and so is Oscar if he didn't try so hard to be what he is not.

"But then we are all trying rather hard to be what we are not. I am really and truly middle-class. In my mind, I mean. Yet no one would believe it to look at me, for I wear my clothes like a Frenchwoman, and I am as unconventional as English royalty. And two generations of us have inherited money. But back of that there were nice middle-class New Englanders who did their own work. And the women wore white aprons, and the men wore overalls, and they ate doughnuts for breakfast, and baked beans on Sunday, and they milked their own cows, and skimmed their own cream, and they read Hamlet and the King James version of the Bible, and a lot of them wrote things that will be remembered throughout the ages, and they had big families and went to church, and came home to overflowing hospitality and chicken pies—and they were the salt of the earth. And as I think I remarked to you once before, I want to be like my great-grandmother in my next incarnation, and live in a wide, low farmhouse, and have horses and hogs and chickens and pop-corn on snowy nights, and go to church on Sunday.

"I don't know why I am writing like this, except that I went to Trinity to vespers, when I stopped over in Boston. It was dim and quiet and the boys' voices were heavenly, and over it all brooded the spirit of the great man who once preached there—and who still preaches—

"And now it is Sunday again, and I am back at the Crossing, and I played golf all the morning, and bridge this afternoon, and all the women smoked and all the men, and I was in a blue haze, and I wanted to be back in the quiet church where the boys sang, and the lights were like stars—

"I wish you and I could go there some day and that you could feel as I do about it. But you wouldn't. You are always so sure and smug—and you have a feeling that money will buy anything—even Paradise. I wonder what you will be like on the next plane. You won't fit into my farmhouse. I fancy that you'll be something rather—devilish—like Don Juan—or perhaps you'll be just an 'ostler in a courtyard, shining boots and—kissing maids—

"Of course I don't quite mean that. But I do feel that you'd be rather worth while if you'd stop philandering and discover your soul.

"I am a bit homesick, and I haven't any home. If Dad hadn't married a second time, I believe he would still love me a bit. But his wife doesn't. And so here I am—and as restless as ever—seeking something—always seeking.

"And now, once more, don't break the heart of the new little girl. I don't need to warn you not to break your own. You are the greatest example of the truth of 'he who loves and runs away will live to love another day.' Oh, Georgie-Porgie, will you ever love any woman enough to rise with her to the heights?

"Perhaps there aren't any heights for you or me. But I should like to think there were. Different hilltops, of course, so that we could wave across. We shall never climb together, Georgie. Perhaps we are too much alike to help each other up the hills. We need stronger props.

"Tell me about Flora. Is she really ill? If she is, I'll come. But I'd rather not.

"I hope you won't read this aloud to Oscar. You might, you know, and it wouldn't do. He would hate to believe that he'd be happier buying things at a delicatessen, and he wouldn't believe it. But it's true, just as it is true that you would be happy shining boots and making love to the maids like a character in Dickens.

"Come on up, and we'll motor to Boston on Sunday afternoon and we'll go to Trinity; I want somebody to be good with me, Georgie, and there are so many of the other kind.

"Ever wistfully,

"Madge."

George knew that he ought to go, but he was not ready yet to run away. He was having the time of his life, and as for Becky, he would teach her how to play the game.

IV

Aunt Claudia was away for three weeks.

"I wish she would come home," young Paine said one morning to his mother.

"Why?" Caroline Paine was at her desk with her mind on the dinner. "Why, Randy?"

"Oh, Dalton's going there a lot."

Mrs. Paine headed her list with gumbo soup. "Do you think he goes to see Becky?"

"Does a duck swim? Of course he goes there to see her, and he's turning her head."

"He is enough to turn any woman's head. He has nice eyes." Mrs. Paine left the topic as negligible, and turned to more important things.

"Randy, would you mind picking a few pods of okra for the soup? Susie is so busy and Bob and Jefferson are both in the field."

"Certainly, Mother," his cool answer gave no hint of the emotions which were seething within him. Becky's fate was hanging in the balance, and his mother talked of okra! He had decided some weeks ago that boarders were disintegrating—and that a mother was not a mother who had three big meals a day on her mind.

He went into the garden. An old-fashioned garden, so common at one time in the South—with a picket fence, a little gate, orderly paths—a blaze of flowers to the right, and to the left a riot of vegetables—fat tomatoes weighing the vines to the ground, cucumbers hiding under their sheltering leaves, cabbages burgeoning in blue-green, and giving the promise of unlimited boiled dinners, onions enough to flavor a thousand delectable dishes, sweet corn running in countless rows up the hill, carrots waving their plumes, Falstaffian watermelons. It was evident with the garden as an index that the boarders at King's Crest were fed on more than milk and honey.

Randy picked the okra and carried it to the kitchen, and

returning to the Schoolhouse found the Major opening his morning mail.

Randy sat down on the step. "Once upon a time," he said, "we had niggers to work in our gardens. And now we are all niggers."

The Major's keen eyes studied him. "What's the matter?"

"I've been picking okra—for soup, and I'm a Paine of King's Crest."

"Well, you peeled potatoes in France."

"That's different."

"Why should it be different? If a thing is for the moment your job you are never too big for it."

"I wish I had stayed in the Army. I wish I had never come back."

The Major whistled for a moment, thoughtfully. Then he said, "Look here, Paine, hadn't you better talk about it?"

"Talk about what?"

"That's for you to tell me. There's something worrying you. You are more tragic than—Hamlet—"

"Well—it's—Becky—"

"And Dalton, of course. Why don't you cut him out, Paine—"

"Me? Oh, look here, Major, what have I to offer her?"

"Youth and energy and a fighting spirit," the Major rapped out the words.

"What is a fighting spirit worth," Randy asked with a sort of weary scorn, "when a man is poor and the woman's rich?"

The Major had been whistling a silly little tune from a modern opera. It was an air which his men would have recognized. It came to an end abruptly.

"Rich? Who is rich?"

"Becky."

The Major got up and limped to the porch rail. "I thought she was as poor as—"

"The rest of us? Well, she isn't."

It appeared that Becky's fortune came from the Nantucket grandmother, and that there would be more when the Admiral died. It was really a very large fortune, well invested, and yielding an amazing income. One of the clauses of the grandmother's will had to do with the bringing up of Becky. Until she was of age she was to be kept as much as possible away from the distractions and temptations of modern luxury. The Judge and the Admiral had agreed that nothing could be better. The result, Randy said, was that nobody ever thought of Becky Bannister as rich.

"Yet those pearls that she wears are worth more than I ever

expect to earn."

"It is rather like a fairy tale. The beggar-maid becomes a queen."

"You can see now why I can't offer her just youth and a fighting spirit."

"I wonder if Dalton knows."

"I don't believe he does," Randy said slowly. "I give him credit for that."

"He might have heard—"

"I doubt it. He hasn't mingled much, you know."

"It will be rather a joke on him—"

"To find that he has married—Mademoiselle Midas?"

"To find that she is Mademoiselle Midas, whether he marries her or not."

V

Of course Georgie-Porgie ran away. It was the inevitable climax. Flora's illness hastened things a bit.

"She wants to see her New York doctors," Waterman had said. "I think we shall close the house, and join Madge later at the Crossing."

George felt an unexpected sense of shock. The game must end, yet he wanted it to go on. The cards were in his hands, and he was not quite ready to turn the trick.

"When do we go?" he asked Oscar.

"In a couple of days if we can manage it. Flora is getting worried about herself. She thinks it is her heart."

George rode all of that afternoon with Becky. But not a word did he say about his departure. He never spoiled a thing like this with "Good-bye." Back at Waterman's, Kemp was packing trunks. In forty-eight hours there would be the folding of tents, and Hamilton Hill would be deserted. It added a pensiveness to his manner that made him more than ever charming. It rained on the way home, and it seemed to him significant that his first ride and his last with Becky should have been in the rain.

He stayed to dinner, and afterwards he and Becky walked together in the fragrance of the wet garden. A new moon hung low for a while and was then lost behind the hills.

"My little girl," George said when the moment came that he must go, "My dear little girl." He gathered her up in his arms—but did not kiss her. For once in his life, Georgie-Porgie was too deeply moved for kisses.

After he had gone, Becky went into the Bird Room, and stood

on the hearth and looked up at the Trumpeter Swan. There was no one to whom she could speak of the ecstasy which surged through her. As a child she had brought her joys here, and her sorrows—her Christmas presents in the early morning—the first flowers of the spring. She had sat here often in her little black frock and had felt the silent sympathy of the wise old bird.

He gazed down at her now with an almost uncanny intelligence. She laughed a little and standing on tiptoe laid her cheek against the cool glass. "When I am married," was her wordless question, "will you sound your trumpet high up near the moon?"

CHAPTER VII

MADEMOISELLE MIDAS

I

There came to Huntersfield the next morning at about the same moment, Kemp in his little car with a small parcel for Becky, and Calvin with a big box from the express office.

Becky was in her room at breakfast when Calvin brought the boxes up to her. It was a sunshiny morning, and the Judge had gone a-fishing with Mr. Flippin. Becky, in a lace cap and a robe that was delicately blue, sat in a big chair with a low table in front of her.

There were white roses on the table in a silver bowl. The Judge had sent them to her. The Judge had for the women of his family a feeling that was almost youthfully romantic, and which was, unquestionably, old-fashioned. He liked to think that they had roses for their little noses, ribbons and laces for their pretty faces. He wanted no harsh winds to blow on them. And in return for the softness and ease with which he would surround them, he wanted their deference to his masculine point of view.

With the box which George sent was a note. It was the first that Becky had ever received from her lover. George's code did not include much correspondence. Flaming sentiment on paper was apt to look silly when the affair ended.

To Becky, her name on the outside of the envelope seemed written in gold. She was all blushing expectation.

"There ain't no answer," Calvin said, and she waited for him to go before she opened it.

She read it and sat there drained of all feeling. She was as white as the roses on her table. She read the note again and her hands shook.

"Flora is very ill. We are taking her up to New York. After that we shall go to the North Shore. There isn't time for me to come and say, 'Good-bye.' Perhaps it is better not to come. It has been a wonderful summer, and it is you who have made it wonderful for me. The memory will linger with me always—like a sweet dream or a rare old tale. I am sending you a little token—for remembrance. Think of me sometimes, Becky."

That was all, except a scrawled "G. D." at the end. No word of coming back. No word of writing to her again. No word of any future in which she would have a part.

She opened the box. Within on a slender chain was a pendant—a square sapphire set in platinum, and surrounded by diamonds. George had ordered it in anticipation of this crisis. He had, hitherto, found such things rather effective in the cure of broken hearts.

Now, had George but known it, Becky had jewels in leather cases in the vaults of her bank which put his sapphire trinket to shame. There were the diamonds in which a Meredith great-grandmother had been presented at the Court of St. James, and there were the pearls of which her own string was a small part. There were emeralds and rubies, old corals and jade—not for nothing had the Admiral sailed the seas, bringing back from China and India lovely things for the woman he loved. And now the jewels were Becky's, and she had not cared for them in the least. If George had loved her she would have cherished his sapphire more than all the rest.

But he did not love her. She knew it in that moment. All of her doubts were confirmed.

The thing that had happened to her seemed incredible.

She put the sapphire back in its box, wrapped it, tied the string carefully and called Mandy.

"Tell Calvin to take this to Mr. Dalton."

Mandy knew at once that something was wrong. But this was not a moment for words. The Bannisters did not talk about things that troubled them. They held their heads high. And Becky's was high at this moment, and her eyes were blazing.

As she sat there, tense, Becky wondered what Dalton could have thought of her. If she had not had a jewel in the world, she would not have kept his sapphire. Didn't he know that?

But how could he know? To him it had been "a sweet dream—a rare old tale," and she had thought him a Romeo ready to die for her sake, an Aucassin—willing to brave Hell rather than give her up, a Lohengrin sent from Heaven!

She shuddered and hid her face in her hands. At last she crept into bed. Mandy, coming in to straighten the room, was told to lower the curtains.

"My—my head aches, Mandy."

Mandy, wise old Mandy, knew of course that it was her heart. "You res' an' sleep, honey," she said, and moved about quietly setting things in order.

But Becky did not sleep. She lay wide awake, and tried to get the thing straight in her mind. How had it happened? Where had she failed? Oh, why hadn't Sister Loretto told her that there were men like this? Why hadn't Aunt Claudia returned in time?

In the big box which Mandy had brought up were clothes—exquisite things which Becky had ordered from New York. She had thought it a miracle that George should have fallen in love with her believing her poor. It showed, she felt, his splendidness, his kingly indifference to—poverty. Yet she had planned a moment when he should know. When their love was proclaimed to the world he should see her in a splendor which matched his own. He had loved her in spite of her faded cottons, in spite of her shabby shoes. She had made up her list carefully, thinking of his sparkling eyes when he beheld her.

She got out of bed and opened the box. The lovely garments were wrapped in rosy tissue paper, and tied with ribbons to match. It seemed to Becky as if those rosy wrappings held the last faint glow of her dreams.

She untied the ribbons of the top parcel, and disclosed a frock of fine white lace—there was cloth of silver for a petticoat, and silver slippers. She would have worn her pearls, and George and she would have danced together at the Harvest Ball at the Merriweathers. It was an annual and very exclusive affair in the county. It was not likely that the Watermans and their guests would be invited, but there would have been a welcome for Dalton as her friend—her more than friend.

There was a white lace wrap with puffs of pink taffeta and knots of silver ribbon which went with the gown. Becky with a sudden impulse put it on. She stripped the cap from her head, and wound her bronze locks in a high knot. She surveyed herself.

Well, she was Becky Bannister of Huntersfield—and the mirror showed her beauty. And Dalton had not known or cared. He thought her poor, and had thrown her aside like an old glove!

Down-stairs the telephone rang. Old Mandy, coming up to say that Mr. Randy was on the wire, stood in amazement at the sight of Becky in the rosy wrap with her hair peaked up to a top-knot.

"Ain' you in baid?" she asked, superfluously.

"No. Who wants me, Mandy?"

"I tole you—Mr. Randy."

Becky deliberated. "I'll go down. When I come up we'll unpack all this, Mandy."

Randy at the other end of the wire was asking Becky to go to a barbecue the next day.

"The boarders are giving it—it is Mother's birthday and they want to celebrate. It is to be on Pavilion Hill. They want you and the Judge—"

"To-morrow? Oh, I don't know, Randy."

"Why not? Have you another engagement?"

"No."

"Then what's the matter? Can't you tear yourself away from your shining knight?"

Silence.

"Becky—oh, I didn't mean that. I'm sorry—*Becky*—"

Her answer came faintly, "I'll come."

"What's the matter with the wire? I can't hear you."

There was nothing the matter with the wire. The thing that was the matter was Becky's voice. She found it suddenly unmanageable. "We'll come," she told him finally, and hung up the receiver.

She ascended the stairs as if she carried a burden on her back. Mandy was on her knees before the hamper, untying the rosy packages.

"Is you goin' to try 'em on, honey?" she asked.

Becky stood in the doorway, the lace wrap hanging from her shoulders and showing the delicate blue of the negligee beneath—her face was like chalk but her eyes shone. "Yes," she said, "there's a pink gingham I want to wear to the barbecue to-morrow. There ought to be a hat to match. Did the hats come, Mandy?"

"Calvin he say there's another box, but he ain' brought it up from the deepot. He was ridin' dat Jo-mule, and this yer basket was all he could ca'y."

In the pink frock Becky looked like a lovely child.

"Huc-cum you-all gettin' eve'y thing pink, Miss Becky?" Mandy asked.

"For a change," said Becky.

And how could she tell old Mandy that she had felt that in a rose-colored world everything should be rose-color?

She tried on each frock deliberately. She tried on every pair of slippers. She tried on the wraps, and the hats which came up finally with Calvin staggering beneath the bulkiness of the box. She was lovely in everything. And she was no longer the little Becky Bannister whom Dalton had wooed. She was Mademoiselle Midas, appraising her beauty in her lovely clothes, and wondering what Dalton would think if he could see her.

II

Becky did not, after all, wear the pink gingham. The Judge elected to go on horseback, so Becky rode forth by his side correctly and smartly attired in a gray habit, with a straight black sailor and a high stock and boots that made her look like a charming boy.

They came to Pavilion Hill to find the boarders like the chorus in light opera very picturesque in summer dresses and summer flannels, and with Mrs. Paine in a broad hat playing the part of leading lady. Mr. Flippin, who was high-priest at all of the county barbecues, was superintending the roasting of a whole pig, and Mrs. Flippin had her mind on hot biscuits. The young mulatto, Daisy, and Mandy's John, with the negroes from the Paine household, were setting the long tables under the trees. There was the good smell of coffee, much laughter, and a generally festive atmosphere.

The Judge, enthroned presently in the Pavilion, was the pivotal center of the crowd. Everybody wanted to hear his stories, and with this fresh audience to stimulate him, he dominated the scene. He wore a sack suit and a Panama hat and his thin, fine face, the puff of curled white hair at the back of his neck, the gayety of his glance gave an almost theatric touch to his appearance, so that one felt he might at any moment come down stage and sing a topical song in the best Gilbertian manner.

It was an old scene with a new setting. It was not the first time that Pavilion Hill had been the backgrounds of a barbecue. But it was the first time that a Paine of King's Crest had accepted hospitality on its own land. It was the first time that it had echoed to the voices of an alien group. It was the first time that it had seen a fighting black man home from France. The old order had changed indeed. No more would there be feudal lords of Albemarle acres.

Yet old loyalties die hard. It was the Judge and Mrs. Paine and Becky and Randy who stood first in the hearts of the dusky folk who served at the long tables. The boarders were not in any sense "quality." Whatever they might be, North, East and West, their names were not known on Virginia records. And what was any family tree worth if it was not rooted in Virginia soil?

"Effen the Jedge was a king and wo' a crown," said Mandy's John to Daisy, "he couldn't look mo' bawn to a th'one."

Daisy nodded. "Settin' at the head o' that table minds me o' whut my old Mammy used to say, 'han'some is as han'some does.' The Bannisters *done* han'some and they *is* han'some."

"They sure is," John agreed; "that-all's whut makes you so good-lookin', Daisy."

He came close to her and she drew away. "You put yo' min' on passin' them plates," she said with severity, "or you'll be spillin' po'k gravy on they haids." Her smile took away the sting of her admonition. John moved on, murmuring, "Well, yo' does han'some and yo' is han'some, Daisy, and that's why I loves you."

There were speeches after dinner. One from Randy, in which he thanked them in the name of his mother, and found himself quite suddenly and unexpectedly being fond of the boarders. Major Prime was not there. He had been summoned back to Washington, but would return, he hoped, for the week-end.

It was after lunch that Randy and Becky walked in the woods. Nellie Custis followed them. They sat down at last at the foot of a hickory tree. Becky took off her hat and the wind blew her shining hair about her face. She was pale and wore an air of deep preoccupation.

"Randy," she asked suddenly out of a long silence, "did you ever kiss a girl?"

Her question did not surprise him. He and Becky had argued many matters. And they usually plunged in without preliminaries. He fancied that Becky was discussing kisses in the abstract. It never occurred to him that the problem was personal.

"Yes," he said, "I have. What about it?"

"Did you—ask her to marry you?"

"No."

"Why not?"

He pulled Nellie Custis' ears. "One of them wasn't a nice sort of girl—not the kind that I should have cared to introduce to—you."

"Yet you cared to—kiss her?"

Randy flushed faintly. "I know how it looks to you. I hated it afterwards, but I couldn't marry a girl—like that—"

"Who was the other girl?"

For a moment he did not reply, then he said with something of an effort, "It was you, Becky."

"Me? When?" She turned on him her startled gaze.

"Do you remember at Christmas—oh, ten years ago—and your grandfather had a party for you. There was mistletoe in the hall, and we danced and stopped under the mistletoe—"

"I remember, Randy—how long ago it seems."

"Yet ten years isn't really such a long time, is it, Becky? I was only a little boy, but I told myself then that I would never kiss any other girl. I thought then that—that some day I might ask you to marry me. I—I had a wild dream that I might try to make you love me. I didn't know then that poverty is a millstone about a man's neck." He gave a bitter laugh.

Becky's breath came quickly. "Oh, Randy," she said, "poverty wouldn't have had anything to do with it—not if we had—cared—"

"I care," said Randy, "and I think the first time I knew how much I cared was when I kissed that other girl. Somehow you came to me that night, a little white thing, so fine and different, and I loathed her."

He was standing now—tall and lean and black-haired, but with the look of race on his thin face, a rather princely chap in spite of his shabby clothes. "Of course you don't care," he said; "I think if I had money I should try to make you. But I haven't the right. I had thought that, perhaps, if no other man came that some time I might—"

Becky picked up her riding crop, and as she talked she tapped her boot in a sort of staccato accompaniment.

"That other man has come," *tap-tap*, "he kissed me," *tap-tap*, "and made me love him," *tap-tap*, "and he has gone away—and he hasn't asked me to marry him."

One saw the Indian in Randy now, in the lifted head, the square-set jaw, the almost cruel keenness of the eyes.

"Of course it is George Dalton," he said.

"Yes."

"I could kill him, Becky."

She laughed, ruefully. "For what? Perhaps he thinks I'm not a nice sort of girl—like the one you kissed—"

"For God's sake, Becky."

He sat down on a flat rock. He was white, and shaking a little. He wanted more than anything else in the wide world to kill George Dalton. Of course in these days such things were preposterous. But he had murder in his heart.

"I blame myself," Becky said, *tap-tap*, "I should have known that a man doesn't respect," *tap-tap*, "a woman he can kiss."

He took the riding crop forcibly out of her hands. "Look at me, look at me, Becky, do you love him?"

She whispered, "Yes."

"Then he's got to marry you."

But her pride was up. "Do you think I want him if he doesn't want—me?"

"He shall want you," said Randy Paine; "the day shall come when he shall beg on his knees."

Randy had studied law. But there are laws back of the laws of the white man. The Indian knows no rest until his enemy is in his hands. Randy lay awake late that night thinking it out. But he was not thinking only of Georgie. He was thinking of Becky and her self-respect. "She will never get it back," he said, "until that dog asks her to marry him."

He had faith enough in her to believe that she would not marry Dalton now if he asked her. But she must be given the chance.

CHAPTER VIII

ANCESTORS

I

The Judge and Mr. Flippin were fishing, with grasshoppers for bait. The fish that they caught they called "shiners." As an edible product "shiners" were of little account. But the Judge and Mr. Flippin did not fish for food, they fished for sport. It was mild sport compared to the fishing of other days when the Judge had waded into mountain streams with the water coming up close to the pocket of his flannel shirt where he kept his cigars, or had been poled by Bob Flippin from "riffle" to pool. Those had been the days of speckled trout and small-mouthed bass, and Bob had been a boy and the Judge at middle age. Now Bob Flippin had reached the middle years, and the Judge was old, but they still fished together. They were comrades in a very close and special sense. What Bob Flippin lacked in education and culture he made up in wisdom and adoration of the Judge. When he talked he had something to say, but as a rule he let the Judge talk and was always an absorbed listener.

There was in their relations, however, a complete adjustment to the class distinctions which separated them. The Judge accepted as his right the personal service with which Bob Flippin delighted to honor him. It was always Bob who pulled the boat and carried the basket. It was Bob who caught the grasshoppers and cooked the lunch.

There was one dish dedicated to a day's fishing—fried ham and eggs. Bob had a long-handled frying-pan, and the food was seasoned with the salt and savor of the out-of-doors.

There were always several dogs to bear their masters company. The Judge's three were beagles—tireless hunters of rabbits, and somewhat in disgrace as a species since Germany had gone to war with the world. Individually, however, they were beloved by the Judge because they were the children and grandchildren of a certain old Dinah who had slept in a basket by his bed until she died.

Bob Flippin had a couple of setters, and the five canines formed a wistful semicircle around the lunch basket.

The lunch basket was really a fishing-basket, lined with tin. In one end was a receptacle for ice. After the lunch was eaten, the fish were put next to the ice, and the basket thus served two purposes. Among the other edibles there were always corn-cakes for the dogs. They knew it, and had the patience of assured expectation.

"Truxton comes on Saturday," said the Judge as he watched Bob turn the eggs expertly in the long-handled pan, "and Claudia. I told Becky to ride over this morning and ask your wife if she could help Mandy. Mandy's all right when there's nobody but the family, but when there's company in prospect she moans and groans."

"Mollie's up at the Watermans'; Mrs. Waterman is worse. They expected to take her to New York, but she is too ill, and they are going to have the doctors bring another nurse."

"I had a note from Mr. Dalton," said the Judge, "saying they were going. It was rather sudden, and he was sorry. Nice fellow. He liked to come over and look at my birds."

Bob Flippin's eyes twinkled. "I reckon he liked to look at a pretty girl—"

The Judge stared at him. "At Becky?"

Flippin nodded. "Didn't you know it?"

"Bless my soul." The Judge was unquestionably startled. "But I don't know anything about him. I can't have him running after Becky."

"Seems to me he's been a-runnin'."

"But what would Claudia say? I don't know anything about his family. Maybe he hasn't any family. How do I know he isn't a fortune-hunter?"

"Well, he isn't a bird hunter, I can tell you that. I saw him kick one of your dogs. A man that will kick a dog isn't fit to hold a gun."

"No, he isn't," said the Judge, soberly. "I'm upset by what you've said, Flippin. Dalton's all right as far as I can see as a friend of mine. But when anybody comes courting at Huntersfield he's got to show credentials."

He ate his lunch without much appetite. He was guiltily aware of what Claudia would say if she knew what had happened.

But perhaps nothing had happened and perhaps she need not know. He cheered up and threw a bit of ham to the waiting dogs. Perhaps Becky wasn't interested. Perhaps, after all, Dalton had been genuine in his interest in the stuffed birds.

"Becky's too young for things like that," he began hopefully.

But Bob Flippin shook his head. "Girls are queer, Judge, and you never can tell what they're goin' to do next. Now, there's my Mary—running off and getting married, and coming home and not talking much about it. She—didn't even bring her marriage certificate. Said that he had kept it. But she's never lied to me, and I know when she says she's married, she's—married—but it's queer. He ain't written now for weeks, but she ain't worried. She says she knows the reason, but she can't tell me. And when I try to ask questions, she just looks me straight in the eye and says, 'I never lied to you, Father, did I? And it's all right.'"

"He has a good name," said the Judge. "Branch—it's one of our names—my wife's family."

"But I reckon there ain't never been any Truelove Branches in your family tree. I laugh at Mary when she calls him that. '"True-love" ain't any name for a man, Mary,' I tell her. But she says there couldn't be a better one. And she insisted on naming the child 'Fidelity.' But if anybody had told me that my little Mary—would take things into her own hands like that—why, Judge, before she went away to teach school, she leaned on me and her mother—and now she's as stiff as a poker when we try to ask about her affairs—"

"Does he support her?" the Judge asked.

"Sends her plenty of money. She always seems to have enough, even when he doesn't write. He'll be coming one of these days—and then we'll get the thing straight, but in the meantime there ain't any use in asking Mary."

He brought out the bag of corn-cakes and fed the dogs. They were a well-bred crew and took their share in turn, sitting in a row and going through the ceremony with an air of enjoying not only the food but the attention they attracted from the two men.

"Of course," said Mr. Flippin as he gathered up the lunch things, "I'm saying to you what I wouldn't say to another soul. Mary's my girl, and she's all right. But I naturally have the feelings of a father."

The Judge stretched himself on the grass, and pulled his hat over his eyes. "Girls are queer, and if that Dalton thinks he can court my Becky—" He stopped, and spoke again from under his hat, "Oh, what's the use of worrying, Bob, on a day like this?"

The Judge always napped after lunch, and Bob Flippin, stretched beside him, lay awake and watched the stream slip by in a sheet of silver, he watched a squirrel flattened on the limb above him, he watched the birds that fluttered down to the pools to bathe, he watched the buzzards sailing high above the hills.

And presently he found himself watching his own daughter Mary, as she came along the opposite bank of the stream.

She was drawing Fiddle-dee-dee in a small red cart and was walking slowly.

She walked well. Country-born and country-bred, there was nothing about her of plodding peasant. All her life she had danced with the Bannisters and the Beauforts. Yet she had never been invited to the big balls. When the Merriweathers gave their Harvest Dance, Mary and her mother would go over and help bake the cakes, and at night they would sit in the gallery of the great ballroom and watch the dancers, but Mary would not be asked out on the floor.

Seeing the Judge asleep, Mary stopped and beckoned from the other side.

Flippin rose and made his way across the stream, stepping from stone to stone.

"Mother wants you to come right up to the Watermans', Father. Mrs. Waterman is to have an operation, and you are to direct the servants in fitting up a room for the surgeons. The nurse will tell you what to do."

Mr. Flippin rubbed his face with his handkerchief. "I don't like to wake the Judge."

"I'll stay here and tell him," Mary said. "And you can send Calvin down to carry the basket."

She was standing beside him, and suddenly she laid her cheek against his arm. "I love you," she said, "you are a darling, Daddy."

He patted her cheek. "That sounds like my little Mary."

"Don't I always sound like your little Mary?"

"Not always."

"Well—I've had things on my mind." Her blue eyes met his, and she flushed a bit. "Not things that I am sorry for, but things that I am worried about. But now—well, I am very happy in my heart, Daddy."

He smiled down at her. "Have you heard from T. Branch?"

"Yes, by wireless—"

He looked his astonishment. "Wireless?"

"Heart-wireless, Daddy. Didn't you get messages that way when you were young—from Mother?"

"How do I know? It's been twenty-five years since then, and we haven't had to send messages. We've just held on to each other's hands, thank God." He bent and kissed her. "You stay and tell the Judge, Mary. He'll sleep for a half hour yet; he's as regular as the clock."

His own two dogs followed him, but the Judge's beagles lay with their noses on their paws at their master's feet. Now and then they snapped at flies but otherwise they were motionless.

Before the half hour was up Fiddle-dee-dee fell asleep, and the Judge waking, saw on the other side of a stream propped against the gray old oak, the young mother cool in her white dress, her child in her arms.

"Father had to go," she told him, and explained the need; "he'll send Calvin for the basket."

"I can carry my own basket, Mary; I'm not a thousand years old."

"It isn't that. But you've never carried baskets, Judge."

The Judge chuckled. "You say that is if it were an accusation."

"It isn't. Only some of us seem born to carry baskets and others are born to—let us carry them." Her smile redeemed her words from impertinence.

"Are you a Bolshevik, Mary?"

"No. I believe in the divine rights of kings and—Judges. I'd hate to see you carry a basket. It would rob you of something—just as I would hate to see a king without his crown or a queen without her scepter."

"Oh, Mary, Mary, your father has never said things like that to me."

"He doesn't feel them. Father believes in The God of Things as They are—"

"And don't you?"

"I believe in you," she rose and carrying her sleeping child, crossed the stream on the stones as easily as if she carried no burden; "you know I believe in you, don't you—and in all the Bannisters?"

It was said so lightly that he took it lightly. No one was so touchy as the Judge about his dignity if it were disregarded. But here was little Mary smiling up at him and telling him that he was a king with a crown and she liked it.

"Well, well. Let's sit down, Mary."

"Fish, if you want to, and I'll watch."

He baited his hook and cast his line into the stream. It had a bobbing red cork which fascinated Fiddle-dee-dee. She tried to wade out and get it, and had to be held by her very short skirts lest she drown in the attempt.

"So I'm a confounded autocrat," the Judge chuckled. "Nobody ever said that to me before, but maybe some of them have been thinking it."

"Maybe they have," said Mary gravely, "but they haven't really cared. Having the Bannisters at Huntersfield is like the English having a Victoria or an Edward or a George at Buckingham Palace or at Windsor; it adds flavor to their—democracy—"

"Mary—who's been saying all this to you?" he demanded.

"My husband."

"Truelove Branch?"

She nodded.

"I'd like to meet him, by Jove, I'd like to meet him. He has been teaching his wife to poke fun at her old friend—"

She faced him fearlessly. "I'm not poking fun. I—I'd hate to have the Bannisters lose one little bit of their beautiful traditions. I—I—Some day I'm going to teach little Fiddle those traditions, and tell her what it means when—when people have race back of them. You see, I haven't it, Judge, but I know what it's worth."

He was touched by her earnestness. "My dear Mary," he said, "I wish my own grandson looked at it that way. His letters of late have been very disturbing."

A little flush crept into her cheeks. "Disturbing?"

"He writes that we Americans have got to fit our practice to our theories. He says that we shout democracy and practice autocracy. That we don't believe that all men are free and equal, and that, well, in your words, Mary—we let other people carry our baskets."

Mary was smiling to herself. "You are glad he is coming home?"

"Truxton? Yes. On Saturday."

"Becky told me. She rode over to get Mother to help Mandy."

"I am going to have a lot of people to dine the day he arrives," said the Judge, "and next week there'll be the Merriweathers' ball. He will have a chance to see his old friends."

"Yes," said Mary, "he will."

They talked a great deal about Truxton after that.

"I wish he bore the Bannister name," said the Judge. "Becky is the only Bannister."

After the death of her husband Mrs. Beaufort had come to live with the Judge. Truxton's boyhood had been spent on the old estate. The Judge's income was small, and Truxton had known few luxuries. Like the rest of the boys of the Bannister family he was studying law at the University. He and Randy had been class-mates, but had gone into different branches of the service.

"When he comes back," the Judge told Mary, "he must show the stuff he is made of. I can't have him selling cars around the county like Randy Paine."

"Well, Randy has sold a lot of them," said Mary. "Father has given him an order—"

"You don't mean to say that Bob Flippin is going to buy a car—"

"He is."

"He didn't dare tell me," the Judge said; "what's he going to do with his horses?"

"Keep them," said Mary serenely; "the car is for Mother—she's going to drive it herself."

The Judge, with a vision of Mollie Flippin's middle-aged plumpness upon him, exclaimed: "You don't mean that your mother is going to—drive a car?"

"Yes," said Mary, "she is."

"I would as soon think of Claudia—"

"No," said Mary, "Mrs. Beaufort will never drive her own car. She has the coachman habit, and if she ever gets a car, there'll be a man at the wheel."

She brought the conversation back to Truxton. "Do you remember how we had a picnic here years ago, Mother packed the lunch, and Truxton ate up all the raspberry tarts?"

"He loved tarts," said the Judge, "and chocolate cake. Well, well, I shall be glad to see him."

"Perhaps—perhaps when he gets here you'll be disappointed."

"Why," sharply, "why should I?"

Mary did not answer. She stood up with Fiddle in her arms. "Calvin's coming for the basket," she said, "and I shall have to go up on the other side—I left the cart."

She said "good-bye" and crossed by the stepping-stones. The Judge wound up his fishing tackle. The day's sport resulted in three small "shiners." But he had enjoyed the day—there had been the stillness and the sunlight, and the good company of Bob Flippin and his daughter Mary.

The dogs followed, and Mary from the other side of the stream watched the little procession, Calvin in the lead with the load, the Judge straight and slim with his fluff of white hair, the three little dogs paddling on their short legs.

"Judge Bannister of Huntersfield," said Mary Flippin. Then she raised Fiddle high in her arms. "Say *Granddad*, Fiddle," she whispered, "say *Granddad*."

II

The Flippin farmhouse was wide and rambling. It had none of the classic elegance of the old Colonial mansions, but it had a hall in the middle with the sitting-room on one side and on the other an old-fashioned parlor with a bedroom back of it. The dining-room was back of the sitting-room, and beyond that was the kitchen, and a succession of detached buildings which served as dairy, granary, tool-house and carriage house in the old fashion. There was much sunlight and cleanliness in the farmhouse, and beauty of a kind, for the Flippins had been content with simple things, and Mary's taste was evidenced in the restraint with which the new had been combined with the old. She and her mother did most of the work. It was not easy in these days to get negroes to help. Daisy, the mulatto, had come down for the summer, but they had no assurance that when the winter came they could keep her. Divested of her high heels and city affectations, Daisy was just a darkey, of a rather plain, comfortable, efficient type. When Mary went in, she was getting supper.

"Has Mother come, Daisy?"

"No, Miss, she ain', an' yo' Poppa ain' come. An' me makin' biscuits."

"Your biscuits are always delicious, Daisy."

"An' me and John wants to go to the movies, Miss Mary. An' efen the supper is late."

"You can leave the dishes until mornin', Daisy."

Mary smiled and sighed as she went on with Fiddle to her own room. The good old days of ordered service were over.

She went into the parlor bedroom. It was the one which she and Fiddle occupied. She bathed and dressed her baby, and changed her own frock. Then she entered the long, dim parlor. There was a family Bible on the table. It was a great volume with steel engravings. It had belonged to her father's father. In the middle of the book were pages for births and deaths. The records were written legibly but not elegantly. They went back for two generations. Beyond that the Flippins had no family tree.

Mary had seen the family tree at Huntersfield. It was rooted in aristocratic soil. There were Huguenot branches and Royalist branches—D'Aubignes and Moncures, Peytons and Carys, Randolphs and Lees. And to match every name there was more than one portrait on the walls of Huntersfield.

Mary remembered a day when she and Truxton Beaufort had stood in the wide hall.

"A great old bunch," Truxton had said.

"If they were my ancestors I should be afraid of them."

"Why, Mary?"

"Oh, they'd expect so much of me."

"Oh, that," Truxton said airily, "who cares what they expect?"

Mr. and Mrs. Flippin came home in time for supper. The nurse had arrived and the surgeons would follow in the morning. "It's dreadful, Mary," Mrs. Flippin said, "to see her poor husband; money isn't everything. And he loves her as much as if they were poor."

Daisy washed the dishes in a perfect whirl of energy, donned her high-heeled slippers and her Washington manner, and went off with John. It was late that night when Mrs. Flippin went out to find Mary busy.

"My dear," she said, "what are you doing?"

Mary was rolling out pastry, with ice in a ginger-ale bottle. "I am going to make some tarts. There was a can of raspberries left—and—and well—I'm just hungry for—raspberry tarts, Mother."

III

It was the Judge who told Becky that Dalton had not gone. "Mrs. Waterman is very ill, and they are all staying down."

Becky showed no sign of what the news meant to her, but that night pride and love fought in the last ditch. It seemed to Becky that with Dalton at King's Crest the agony of the situation was intensified.

"Oh, why should I care?" she kept asking herself as she sat late by her window. "He doesn't. And I have known him only three weeks. Why should he count so much?"

She knew that he counted to the measure of her own constancy. "I can't bear it," she said over and over again pitifully, as the hours passed. "I think I shall—die."

It seemed to her that she wanted more than anything in the whole wide world to see him for a moment—to hear the quick voice—to meet the sparkle of his glance.

Well, why not? If she called him—he would come. She was sure of that. He was staying away because he thought that she cared. And he didn't want her to care. But he was not really—cruel—and if she called him—

She wandered around the room, stopping at a window and going on, stopping at another to stare out into the starless night. There had been rain, and there was that haunting wet fragrance from the garden. "I must see him," she said, and put her hand to her throat.

She went down-stairs. Everybody was in bed. There was no one to hear. Her grandfather's room was over the library; Mandy and Calvin slept in servants' quarters outside. To-morrow the house would be full of ears—and it would be too late.

A faint light burned in the lower hall. The stairway swept down from a sort of upper gallery, and all around the gallery and on the stairs and along the lower hall were the portraits of Becky's dead and gone ancestors.

They were really very worth-while ancestors, not as solid and substantial perhaps as those whose portraits hung in the Meredith house on Main Street in Nantucket, but none the less aristocratic, with a bit of dare-devil about the men, and a hint of frivolity about the women—with a pink coat here and a black patch there, with the sheen of satin and the sparkle of jewels—a Cavalier crowd, with the greatest ancestor of all in his curly wig and his sweeping plumes.

They stared at Becky as she went down-stairs, a little white figure in her thin blue dressing-gown, her bronze hair twisted into a curly topknot, her feet in small blue slippers.

The telephone was on a small table under the portrait of the greatest grandfather. He had a high nose, and a fine clear complexion, and he looked really very much alive as he gazed down at Becky.

She found the King's Crest number. It was a dreadful thing that she was about to do. Yet she was going to do it.

She reached for the receiver. Then suddenly her hand was stayed, for it seemed to her that into the silence her greatest grandfather shouted accusingly:

"Where is your pride?"

She found herself trying to explain. "But, Grandfather—"

The clamour of other voices assailed her:

"Where is your pride?"

They were flinging the question at her from all sides, those gentlemen in ruffles, those ladies in shining gowns.

Becky stood before them like a prisoner at the bar—a slight child, yet with the look about her of those lovely ladies, and with eyes as clear as those of the old Governor who had accused her.

"But I love him—"

It was no defense and she knew it. Not one of those lovely ladies would have tried to call a lover back, not one of them but would have died rather than show her hurt. Not one of those slender and sparkling gentlemen but would have found swords or pistols the only settlement for Dalton's withdrawal at such a moment.

And she was one of them—one of that prideful group. There came to her a sense of strength in that association. What had been done could be done again. Other women had hidden broken hearts. Other women had held their heads high in the face of disappointment and defeat. There were traditions of the steadfastness of those smiling men and women. Some day, perhaps, she would have her portrait painted, and she would be—smiling.

She had no fear now of their glances, as she passed them on

the stairs, as she met them in the upper hall. What she had to bear she must bear in silence, and bear it like a Bannister.

CHAPTER IX

"T. BRANCH"

I

Dalton felt that Fate had played a shabby trick. He had planned a graceful exit and the curtain had stuck; he had wanted to run away, and he could not. Flora was very ill, and it was, of course, out of the question to desert Oscar.

Madge had been sent for. She was to arrive on the noon train. He had promised Oscar that he would drive down for her. The house was in a hubbub. There were two trained nurses, and a half dozen doctors. The verdict was unanimous, Flora could not be moved, and an operation was imperative.

And in the meantime there was the thought of Becky beating at his heart. With miles between them, the thing would have been easy. Other interests would have crowded her out. But here she was definitely within reach—and he wanted her. He wanted her more than he had ever wanted Madge, more than he had ever wanted any other woman. There had been a sweetness about her, a dearness.

He thought it over as he lay in bed waiting for his breakfast. Since waking, he had led Kemp a life of it.

"Of all the fools," he said, when at last the tray came.

"Anything the matter, sir?"

George lifted a silver cover. "That's not what I ordered."

"You said a kidney omelette, sir."

"I wanted the kidney broiled—not in a messy sauce. Take it away."

"I'll get you another."

"I don't want another. Take it away." He flung his napkin on the tray and turned his face to the wall. "I've got a headache. Tell Waterman that if he asks for me, that I've told you to go down and meet Miss MacVeigh."

Kemp stood and looked at the figure humped up under the light silk cover. He had long patience. He might have been a stick or stone under his master's abuse. But he was not a stick or a stone. It seemed too that suddenly his soul expanded. No man had ever called him a fool, and he had worn a decoration in France. He knew what he was going to do. And for the first time in many months he felt himself a free man.

George's decision to have Kemp meet Madge had been founded on the realization that it would be unbearably awkward if he should pass Becky on the road. She had sent back his pendant without a word, and there was no telling how she was taking it. If the thing were ever renewed—and his mind dwelt daringly on that possibility, explanations would be easy—but he couldn't make explanation if she saw him first in a car with another woman.

It was thus that Madge, arriving on the noon train, found Kemp waiting for her. Kemp was very fond of Miss MacVeigh. She was not a snob and there were so many snobs among Dalton's friends. She talked to him as if he were a man and not a mechanical toy. Dalton, on the other hand, treated his valet as if he were a marionette to be pulled by strings, an organ controlled by stops, or a typewriter operated by keys.

Major Prime had come down on the same train. Randy, driving Little Sister, was there to meet him.

"It is good to get back," the Major said. "I've been homesick."

"We missed you a lot. Yesterday we had a barbecue, and you should have been here—"

"I wanted to be, Randy. I hope you are not going to turn me out with the rest of the boarders when you roll in affluence."

"Affluence, nothing—but I sold two cars yesterday—"

"Not bad for a poet."

"It is a funny sort of game," said Randy soberly; "all day I run around in this funny little car, and at night I think big thoughts and try to put them on paper."

He could not tell the Major that the night before his thoughts had not been the kind to put on paper. He had been in a white fury. He knew that if he met Dalton nothing could keep him from knocking him down. He felt that a stake and burning fagots would be the proper thing, but, failing that, fists would do. Yet, there was Becky's name to be considered. Revenge, if he took it, must be a subtle thing—his mind had worked on it in the darkness of the night.

Kemp was helping Madge into the Waterman car. "Who is she?" the Major asked. "She came down on my train."

"Miss MacVeigh. Mrs. Waterman is very ill. There is to be an operation at once."

"I watched her on the train," the Major confessed as he and Randy drove off. "She read all the way down, and smiled over her book. I saw the title, and it was 'Pickwick Papers.' Fancy that in these days. Most young people don't read Dickens."

"Well, she isn't young, is she?"

"Not callow, if that's what you mean, you ungallant cub. But she is young in contrast to a Methuselah like myself."

Kemp had to look after Miss MacVeigh's trunks, so Randy's little car went on ahead. Thus again Fate pulled wires, or Providence. If the big car had had the lead Madge would have gone straight as an arrow to Hamilton Hill. But as it happened, Little Sister barred the way to the open road.

II

The two cars had to pass the Flippins. Mrs. Flippin and Mary were baking cakes for the feast at Huntersfield. Mrs. Flippin was to go over in the afternoon and help Mandy, and to-morrow Truxton and his mother would arrive.

"The Judge is like a boy," said Mrs. Flippin; "he's so glad to have Truxton home."

"Perhaps he won't be so glad when he gets here—"

"Why not?" Mrs. Flippin turned and stared at her daughter.

Mary was seeding raisins, wetting her fingers now and then in a glass of water which stood on a table by her side. "Well, Truxton may be changed—most of the men are, aren't they?"

"Is Randy Paine changed?"

"Yes, Mother."

"How?"

"He's a grown-up."

"Well, he needed to grow, and it wouldn't hurt Truxton either."

"But if Truxton has grown up and wants his own way—the Judge won't like it. The Judge has always ruled at Huntersfield."

"Well, he supports Truxton; why shouldn't he?"

A bright flush stained Mary's skin. "Truxton has his officer's pay now."

"He won't have it when he gets out of the Army."

Mary rose and went to the stove. She came back with a kettle and poured boiling water over a dish of almonds to blanch them.

"We ought to have made this fruit cake a week ago to have it really good," she said, and shelved the subject of Truxton Beaufort.

"It will be good enough as it is," said Mrs. Flippin; "there isn't anybody in the county that can beat me when it comes to baking cakes."

"Where's Fiddle," Mary said, suddenly; "can you see her from the window, Mother?"

Mrs. Flippin could not.

"Well, she's probably sailing her celluloid fish in the chickens' water pan," said Mary; "I'll go out and look her up in a minute."

But Fiddle was not sailing celluloid fish. Columbuslike she

had decided that there were wider seas than the water pan. Once upon a time her grandmother had taken her to the bottom of the hill, and at the bottom of the hill there had been a lot of water, and Fiddle had walked in it with her bare feet, and had splashed. She had liked it much better than the chickens' pan.

So she had picked up her three celluloid fish and had trotted down the path. She wore her pink rompers, and as she bobbed along she was like a mammoth rose-petal blown by the wind.

At the foot of the hill she came upon a little brown stream. It was just a thread of a stream, very shallow with a lot of big flat stones. Fiddle walked straight into it, and the clear water swept over her toes. She put in her little fish, and quite unexpectedly, they swam away. She followed and came to where the stream was spanned by a rail-fence which separated the Flippin farm from the road. The lowest rail was about as high above the stream as her own fast-beating heart. She ducked under it and discovered one of her fish whirling in a small eddy. It was a red fish and she was very fond of it. She made a sudden grab, caught it, lost her balance and sat down in the water. After the first shock, she found that she liked it. The other fish had continued on their journey towards the river. Perhaps some day they would come to the sea. Fiddle forgot them. She held the little red fish fast and splashed the water with her heels.

Now on each side of the water was a road, which went up a hill each way, so that cars coming down, put on speed to go up, and forded the stream which was a mere thread of water except after high rains.

Randy was talking to the Major as he came down the hill. He did not see Fiddle until he was almost upon her. He was driving at high speed, and there was only a second in which to jam things down and pull things up and stop the car.

Kemp was behind him. He was not prepared for Randy's sudden stop. He swerved sharply to the left, slammed into a tele-graph pole—and came back to life to find somebody bending over him. "Who is looking after the lady, sir?" he managed to murmur.

"Young Paine and Mr. Flippin are carrying her to the house. You are cut a bit. Let me tie up your head." The Major gave efficient first aid and after that Kemp got to his feet painfully. "Is Miss MacVeigh badly hurt?"

"She is conscious, and not in great pain. I'm not much of a prop to lean on, but I think we can make that hill together."

They climbed slowly, the man of crutches and the man with the bound-up head.

"It's like a little bit of over there, Kemp, isn't it?"

"Yes it is, sir—many's the time I've seen them helping each other—master and man."

When they got to the house, they found Madge on the sofa, and Mrs. Flippin bending over her. "My husband has gone for the doctor," she told the Major. "I think the blood comes from her hand; she must have put it up to save her face."

"I bent my head," murmured Madge, "and my hat was broad. Think what might have happened if I had worn a little hat."

She had started the sentence lightly but she stopped with a gasp of pain. "Oh—my foot—" she said, "the pain—is—dreadful—"

The Major drew up a chair, and handed his crutches to Randy. "If you'll let us take off your shoe, it might help till the doctor comes."

She fainted dead away while they did it, and came back to life to find her foot bandaged, and her uncut hand held in the firm clasp of the man with the crutches. He was regarding her with grave gray eyes, but his face lighted as she looked up at him.

"Drink this," he told her. "The doctor is on the way, and I think it will help the pain until he comes."

She liked his voice—it had a deep and musical quality. She was glad he was there. Something in his strength seemed to reach out to her and give her courage.

When the pain began again, he gave her another drink from the glass, and when she drifted off, she came back to the echo of a softly-whistled tune.

"I beg your pardon," the Major said as she opened her eyes; "it is a bad habit that I permit myself when I have things on my mind. My men said they always knew by the tune I whistled the mood I was in. And that there was only one tune they were afraid of."

"What was that?"

"'Good-night, Ladies—'" He threw back his head and laughed. "When I began on that they knew it was all up with them—"

She tried to laugh with him, but it was a twisted grin. "Oh," she said and began to tremble. She saw his eyes melt to tenderness. "Oh, you poor little thing."

She was conscious after that of the firm hand which held hers. The deep voice which soothed. Through all that blinding agony she was conscious of his call to courage—she wondered if he had called his men like that—over there—

When the doctor came, he shook his head. "We'd better keep

her here. She is in no condition to be moved to Hamilton Hill, not over these roads. Can you make room for her, Mrs. Flippin?"

"She can have my room," said Mary; "Fiddle and I can go up-stairs—"

They moved Madge, and Mrs. Flippin and Mary got her to bed. The Major sat in the sitting-room and talked to Randy, and as he talked he held Madge's hat in his hand. It had a brim of straw and a crown of mauve silk. The Major, turning it round and round on a meditative finger, thought of the woman who had worn it. She was a pretty woman, a very oddly pretty woman.

"Is she related to Mrs. Waterman, Kemp?" he asked.

"No, sir. But she's been there all summer. And then she went away, and they sent for her because Mrs. Waterman is ill."

Randy rather indiscreetly flung out, "It seems as if the trail of that Waterman crowd is over our world. I suppose we shall have to get the news of this up to them somehow."

"I can telephone Mr. Dalton, sir."

"Is Dalton still there?"

"Yes, sir. And he had a headache this morning, and stayed in bed, or he would have been in the car, sir—"

Randy wished bloodthirstily that Dalton had been in the car. Why couldn't Dalton have been smashed instead of Madge?

"I might call up Mr. Waterman instead of Mr. Dalton," Kemp suggested. "If Mr. Dalton's in bed, he'll hate to be disturbed."

"Are you afraid of him, Kemp?"

Kemp's honest eyes met Randy's burning glance. "No, I am not afraid. I am leaving his service, sir."

They stared at him. "Leaving his service, why?" Randy demanded.

"He called me a fool this morning. And I am not a fool, sir."

"What made him say that?" Randy asked, with interest.

"He ordered a kidney omelette for breakfast, and I brought it, and he wouldn't eat it, and blamed me. I am willing to serve any man, but not without self-respect, sir."

"What are you going to do now, Kemp?" the Major asked.

"Find a better man to work for."

"It won't be hard," Randy interpolated.

"Work for me," said the Major.

Kemp was eager—! "For you, sir?"

"Yes. I need somebody to be legs for me—I'm only half a man. The place is open for you if you want it."

"I shall want it in a week," said Kemp; "I shall have to give him notice."

"There will be three musketeers in the old Schoolhouse, Paine. We have all seen service."

"It will be the best thing that ever happened to me, sir," said Kemp ecstatically, "to know that I can wait on a fighting man." He swung down the hall to the telephone as if he marched to the swirl of pipes.

"Isn't Dalton a brute?" said Randy.

"He that calleth his brother a fool—" mused the Major. He was still turning the mauve hat in his hands. "It is queer," he said unexpectedly, "how some women make you think of some flowers. Did you notice everything Miss MacVeigh wore was lilac—and there's the perfume of it about her things—"

"Becky's a rose," said Randy, "from her own garden. She's as fresh and sweet," his voice caught. "Oh, hang Dalton," he said, "I hate the whole tribe of them—"

Kemp came back to say that Oscar Waterman would be down at once. He insisted that Miss MacVeigh should be brought up to Hamilton Hill.

"He must talk with the doctor."

"He is bringing a doctor of his own. One who came down for Mrs. Waterman."

Randy picked up his hat. "I'm going home. The same house won't hold us—"

Kemp was discreet. "Can I help you with your car, sir?"

"I'll come over later and look at it." Randy, escaping by the back way, walked over the hills.

The Major stayed, and was in the sitting-room with the county doctor when the others arrived.

Dr. Dabney, the county doctor, was not old. He rode to hounds and he enjoyed life. But he was none the less a good doctor and a wise one. Waterman's physician confirmed the diagnosis. It would be very unwise to move Miss MacVeigh.

"But she can't stay here," said Dalton.

"Why not?"

"She can't be made comfortable." Dalton surveyed the Flippin sitting-room critically. He was aware that Mr. Flippin was in the doorway, and that Mrs. Flippin and Mary could not fail to catch his words. But he did not care who heard what he said. All was wrong with his world. It was bad enough to have Flora ill, but to have Madge out of commission would be to forge another chain to hold him to Hamilton Hill.

"She can be made very comfortable here," said Dr. Dabney. "Mrs. Flippin is a famous housekeeper. And anyone who has ever slept in that east room in summer knows that there is nothing better."

Dalton ignored him. "What do you think?" He turned to the Washington doctor. "What do you think?"

"I think it best not to move her. We can send a nurse, and with Dr. Dabney on the case, she will be in good hands."

"The only trouble is," said Dr. Dabney, unexpectedly, "that we may impose too much on Mrs. Flippin's hospitality."

"We will pay—" said Dalton with a touch of insolence.

From the doorway, Mr. Flippin answered him. "We don't want pay—Neighbors don't ask for money when they—help out—"

There was a fine dignity about him. He was a rough farmer in overalls, but Dalton would never match the simple grace of his fine gesture of hospitality.

The Major, who had been silent, now spoke up. "You are having more than your share of trouble, Mr. Waterman. First your wife, and now your guest."

"Oh, I am, I am," said Oscar, brokenly. "I don't see what I've done to deserve it."

He was a pathetic figure. Whatever else he lacked, he loved his wife. If she died—he felt that he could not bear it. For the first time in his life Oscar faced a situation in which money did not count. He could not buy off Death—all the money in the world would not hold back for one moment the shadow of the Dark Angel from his wife's door.

III

The window of the east room looked out on the old orchard. There was a screened door which opened upon a porch and a stretch of lawn beyond which was the dairy.

Within the room there was a wide white bed, and a mahogany dresser with a scarf with crocheted trimming, above the dresser was an old steel engraving of Samson destroying the temple. The floor was spotless, a soft breeze shook the curtains. Madge, relieved from pain and propped on her pillows, watched a mother cat who with her kittens sat just outside the door.

She was a gray cat with white paws and breast, not fat at the moment but with a comfortable well-fed look. She alternately washed herself and washed her offspring. There were four of them, a rollicking lot not easy to keep in order.

"Aren't they—ripping?" Madge said to Mary.

"They always come up on the step about this time in the afternoon; they are waiting for the men to bring the milk to the dairy."

A little later Madge saw the men coming—two of them, with the foaming pails. The mother cat rose and went to meet them. Her tail was straight up, and the kittens danced after her.

"They will get a big dish of it, and then they will go around to the kitchen door to wait for supper and the table scraps. And after that Bessie will coax the kittens out to the barn and go hunting for the night."

"Is that her name—Bessie?"

"Yes, there has always been a Bessie-cat here. And we cling to old customs."

"I like old customs," said Madge, "and old houses."

After a little she asked, "Who makes the butter?"

"I do. It's great fun."

"Oh, when I am well, may I help?"

"You—?" Mary came over and stood looking down at her; "of course you may help. But perhaps you wouldn't like it."

"I am sure I should. And I don't think I am going to get well very soon—"

Mary was solicitous. "Why not?"

"I don't want to get well. I want to stay here. I think this place is—heavenly."

Mary laughed. "It is just a plain farmhouse. If you want the show places you should go to Huntersfield and King's Crest—"

"I want just this. Do you know I am almost afraid to go to sleep for fear I shall wake up and find it a—dream—"

A little later, she asked, "Are those apples in the orchard ripe?"

"Yes."

"May I have one?"

"The doctor may not want you to have it," said her anxious nurse.

"Just to hold in my hand," begged Madge.

So Mary picked a golden apple, and when the doctor came after dark, he found the room in all the dimness of shaded lamp-light, and the golden girl asleep with that golden globe in her hand.

Up-stairs the mulatto girl, Daisy, was putting Fiddle-dee-dee to sleep.

"You be good, and Daisy gwine tell you a story."

Fiddle liked songs better. "Sing 'Jack-Sam bye.'"

Daisy, without her corsets and in disreputable slippers, settled herself to an hour of ease. She had the negro's love of the white child, and a sensuous appreciation of the pleasant twilight, the bedtime song, the rhythm of the rocking-chair.

"Well, you lissen," she said, and rocked in time to the tune.

> *Bye, oh, bye, little Jack-Sam, bye.*
> *Bye, oh, bye, my baby,*
> *When you wake, you shall have a cake—*
> *And all the pretty little horses—*

Her voice was low and pleasant, with queer, quavering minor cadences. But Fiddle-dee-dee was not sleepy.

"'Tory," she begged, when the song was ended.

So Daisy told the story of the three bears. Fiddle was too young to fully comprehend, but she liked the sound of Daisy's voice at the climaxes, "Who's been sittin' in *my* chair?" and "Who's been sleepin' in *my* bed?" and "Who's been eatin' *my* soup?" Daisy was dramatic or nothing, and she entered into the spirit of her tale. It was such an exciting performance altogether that Fiddle was wider awake than ever when the story was finished.

"Ain' you evah gwine shut yo' eyes?"

"Daisy, sing," said Fiddle.

"I'se sung twel my th'oat's dry," said Daisy. And just then Mary came in. "Isn't she asleep, Daisy?—I'll take her. Bannister's John is down-stairs and wants to see you."

"Well, I ain' wantin' to see him," Daisy tossed her head; "you jus' take Miss Fiddle whilst I goes down and settles *him*. I ain' dressed and I ain' ready, Miss Mary. You jes' look at them feet." She stuck them out for inspection. Her shoes were out at the toes and down at the heels. "This ain' my comp'ny night." As she went down-stairs, her voice died away in a querulous murmur.

Mary, with her child in her arms, sat by the window and looked out upon the quiet scene. There was faint rose in the sky, and a silver star. But while she watched the rose faded.

Fiddle, warm and heavy in her arms, slept finally. Then Mary took off her dress and donned a thin white kimono. She let down her hair and braided it—

There was no light in the room, and her mother, coming up, asked softly, "Are you there?"

"Yes."

"Fiddle asleep?"

"Yes, Mother."

Mrs. Flippin found her way to the window and sat down. "The nurse is here, and a lot of clothes and things just came over for Miss MacVeigh from Hamilton Hill. Mary, I wish you could see them."

"I shall in the morning, Mother."

"The nurse got her into a satin nightgown before I came up, with nothing but straps for sleeves—but she looked like a Princess—"

"Aren't you tired to death, dear?"

Mrs. Flippin laughed. "Me? I like it. I am sorry to have Miss MacVeigh hurt, but having her in the house with all those pretty things and people coming and going is better than a circus."

Mary laughed a little. "You are such a darling—making the best of things—"

"Well, making the best is the easiest way," said Mrs. Flippin. "I ain't taking any credit, Mary."

"You've had a hard day. You'd better go to bed."

"I'll have a harder one to-morrow. Nothing would do but I must go back to Huntersfield. Mandy's off her head, and the Judge wants the whole house turned upside down for Truxton."

"And Truxton comes—on the noon train."

"Yes."

There was a long silence. Then Mary said in a queer voice, "Mother, I've got to tell you something—to-night—"

"You ain't got anything to tell me, honey."

"But I have—something—I should have told you—months ago."

"There isn't anything you can tell me that I don't know."

"Mother—"

"Girls can't fool their mothers, Mary. Do you think that when Fiddle grows up, she is going to fool you?"

IV

The next morning Mr. Flippin was at the foot of the stairs when his daughter came down.

"So you lied to me, Mary."

She shook her head, "No."

"You said his name was Truelove Branch."

"He is my true love, Father. And his name is T. Branch—Truxton Branch Beaufort."

"What do you think the Judge is going to say about this?"

"He is going to hate it. He is going to think that your daughter isn't good enough for his grandson."

"You are good enough for anybody, Mary. But this wasn't the right way."

"It was the only way. Didn't Mother tell you that he begged me to let him write to you and go to the Judge, and I wouldn't?"

"Why not?"

"I wanted to have him here, so that we might face it together."

"Your mother says she guessed it long ago. But she didn't say anything. Talking might make it worse."

"Talking would have made it worse, Dad. We had done it—and I'd do it again," there was a lift of her head, a light in her eyes, "but it hasn't been easy—to know that you wondered—that other people wondered. But it wouldn't have been any better if I had told. Truxton had to be here to make it right if he could."

"Why didn't he come a-runnin' to you as soon as he got on this side?"

"He couldn't. His orders kept him in New York, and he wanted me to come. But I wouldn't. I made him ask his mother. I could spare him for three weeks,—he will be mine for the rest of his life—and he is to tell her before they get here."

"I wouldn't have had it happen for a thousand dollars," said troubled Bob Flippin. "I've always done everything on the square with the Judge."

"I know," said Mary, with the sudden realization of how her act had affected others, "I know. That's the only thing I am sorry about. But—I don't believe the Judge would be so silly as to let anything I did make any difference about you—"

"Where are you going to live?"

For the first time Mary's air of assurance left her. "He is hoping his grandfather will want us at Huntersfield—"

"He can keep on a-hoping," said Bob Flippin. "I know the Judge."

Mary flared. "We can find a little house of our own—"

Her father laid his hand on her shoulder. "Look at me, daughter," he said, and turned her face up to him. "Our house is yours, Mary," he said. "I don't like the way you did it, and I hate to think what will happen when the Judge finds out. But our home is yours, and it's your husband's. As long as you like to stay—"

And now Mary sobbed—a little slip of a thing in her father's arms. All the long months she had kept her secret, holding it safe in her heart, dreading yet longing for the moment when she could tell the world that she was the wife of Truxton Beaufort, whom she had adored from babyhood.

"I would have married him, Dad, if—if I had had to tramp the road."

Truxton came on the noon train. He drove at once to Huntersfield with his mother, was embraced by the Judge, kissed Becky, and suddenly disappeared.

"Where's he gone?" the Judge asked, irritably. "Where has he gone, Claudia?"

"He will be back in time for lunch," said Mrs. Beaufort. "May I speak to you in the library, Father?"

Becky, from the moment of her aunt's arrival, had known that something was wrong. She had expected to see Mrs. Beaufort glowing with renewed youth, radiant. Instead, she looked as if a blight had come upon her, shrivelled—old. When she smiled it was without joy; she was dull and flat.

It was a half hour before Aunt Claudia came out from the library. "My dear," she said, finding Becky still on the porch, "I have something to tell you. Will you go up-stairs with me?—I—think I should like to—lie down—"

Becky put a strong young arm about her and they went up together.

"It's—it's about Truxton," Aunt Claudia said, prone on the couch in her room. "Becky—he's married—"

"Married?"

"Married, my dear. He did not tell me until—last night. He wanted me to be happy—as long as I could. He's a dear boy, Becky—but—he's married—" She went on presently with an effort. "He has been married over two years—and, Becky—he has married—Mary Flippin."

"Aunt Claudia—"

"He married her in Petersburg—before he went to France with the first ambulance corps. They decided not to tell anyone. Mary took Truxton's middle name. When the baby came, Truxton was wild to write us, but Mary—wouldn't. She felt if he was here when it was told that we would forgive him—If anything—happened to him—she didn't want him to die feeling that we had—blamed him—I must say that Mary—was wise—but—to think that my son has married—Mary Flippin."

"Mary's a dear," said Becky stoutly.

"Yes," Aunt Claudia agreed, "but not a wife for my son. I had such hopes for him, Becky. He could have married anybody."

Becky knew the kind of woman that Aunt Claudia had wanted Truxton to marry—one whose ancestors were like those whose portraits hung in the hall at Huntersfield—a woman with a high-held head—a woman whose family traditions paralleled those of the Bannisters and Beauforts.

"Then Fiddle is Truxton's child."

"And I am a grandmother, Becky. Mrs. Flippin and I are grandmothers—" She said it with a sort of bitter mirth.

"What did Grandfather say?"

"I left him—raging. It was—very hard on me. I had hoped—he would make it easy. He declares that Mary Flippin shan't step inside of his front door. That he is going to recall all the invitations that he had sent out for to-night. I tried to show him that now that the thing is done—we might as well—accept it. But he wouldn't listen. If he keeps it up like this, I don't want Truxton to come back—to lunch. I had hoped that he might bring Mary with him—She's his wife, Becky—and I've got to love her—"

"Aunt Claudia," Becky came over and put her arms about the pitiful black figure, "you are the best sport—ever—"

"No, I'm not," but Aunt Claudia kissed her, and for a moment they clung together; "you mustn't make me cry, Becky."

But she did cry a little, wiping her eyes with her black-bordered handkerchief, and saying all the time, "He's my son, Becky. I—I can't put him away from me—"

"He loved her," said Becky, with a catch of her breath. "I—I think that counts a great deal, Aunt Claudia."

"Yes, it does. And they did no wrong. They were only foolish children."

"If anyone was to blame," she went on steadily, "it was Truxton. He had been brought up a—gentleman. He knew what was expected of a man of his birth and breeding. Secrecy is never honorable and I told him—last night—that I was sorry to be less proud of my son than of the men who had gone before him."

"Did you tell him that?"

"Yes. If pride of family means anything, Becky, it means holding on to the finest of your traditions. If you break the rules—you are a little less fine—a little less worthy—"

What a stern little thing she was. Yet one felt the stimulus of her strength. "Aunt Claudia," said Becky, tremulously, "if I could only be as sure of things as you are—"

"What things?"

"Of right and wrong and all the rest of it."

"I don't know what you mean by all the rest. But right is right, and wrong is wrong, my dear. There is no half way, in spite of all the sophistries with which people try to salve their consciences."

She stopped, and plunged again into the discussion of her problem. "I must telephone to Truxton—he mustn't come—not until his grandfather asks him, Becky."

"He is coming now," said Becky, who sat by the window. "Look, Aunt Claudia."

Tramping up the hill towards the second gate was a tall figure in khaki. Resting like a rose-petal on one shoulder was a mite of a child in pink rompers.

"He is bringing Fiddle with him," Becky gasped. "Oh, Aunt Claudia, he is bringing Fiddle."

Aunt Claudia rose and looked out—"Well," she said, "let her come. She's his child. If Father turns them out, I'll go with them."

Truxton saw them at the window and waved. "Shall we go down?" Becky said.

"No—wait a minute. Father's in the hall." Aunt Claudia stood tensely in the middle of the room. "Becky, listen over the stair rail to what they are saying."

"But—"

"Go on," Aunt Claudia insisted; "there are times when—one breaks the rules, Becky. I've got to know what they are saying—"

The voices floated up. Truxton's a lilting tenor—

"Are you going to forgive us, Grandfather?"

"I am not the grandfather of Mary Flippin's child," the Judge spoke evidently without heat.

"You are the grandfather of Fidelity Branch Beaufort," said Truxton coolly; "you can't get away from that—"

"The neighborhood calls her Fiddle Flippin," the Judge reminded him.

"What's in a name?" said Truxton, and swung his baby high in the air. "Do you love your daddy, Fiddle-dee-dee?"

"'Ess," said Fiddle, having accepted him at once on the strength of sweet chocolate, and an adorable doll.

"What are they saying?" whispered Aunt Claudia, still tense in the middle of the room.

"Hush," Becky waved a warning hand.

"There is," said the Judge, in a declamatory manner, "every-thing in a name. The Bannisters of Huntersfield, the Paines of King's Crest, the Randolphs of Cloverdale, do you think these things don't count, Truxton?"

"I think there's a lot of rot in it," said young Beaufort, "when we were fighting for democracy over there—"

The shot told. "Democracy has nothing to do with it—"

"Democracy," said Truxton, "has a great deal to do with it. The days of kings and queens are dead, they have married each other for generations and have produced offspring like—William of Germany. Class assumptions of superiority are withered branches on the tree of civilization. Mary is as good as I am any day."

"You wrote things like this," said the Judge, interested in spite of himself, and loving argument.

"I wrote them because I believed them. I am ready to apologize for not telling you of my marriage before this. I have no apologies to make for my wife—

"I have no apologies to make for my wife," Truxton repeated. "I fought for democratic ideals. I am practising them. Mary is a lady. You must admit that, Grandfather."

"I do admit it," said the Judge slowly, "in the sense that you mean it. But in the county sense? Do you think the Merriweathers will ask her to their ball? Do you think Bob Flippin will dine with my friends to-night?"

"I don't think he will expect to dine with you, Grandfather. I think if you ask him, he will refuse. But if you take your friendship from him it will break his heart—"

"Who said I would take my friendship away from Bob Flippin?"

"He is afraid—you may—"

"Because you married Mary?"

"Yes."

The Judge was breathing hard. "Whom does he think I'd go fishing with?"

"Do you think he'll want to go fishing with you if you cast off Mary?"

The Judge had a vision of life without Bob Flippin. On sunshiny days there would be no one to cut bait for him, no one to laugh with him at the dogs as they sat waiting for their corn-cakes, no one to listen with flattering attention to his old, old tales.

It had not occurred to him that Bob Flippin, too, might have his pride.

He sat down heavily in a porch chair.

"Go and get Mary," he exploded; "bring her here. The thing is done. The milk is spilled. And there's no use crying over it. And if you think you two young people can separate me and Bob Flippin—"

Mrs. Beaufort and Becky came down presently, to find the old man gazing, frowning, into space.

"I have told him to bring Mary, Claudia, but I must say that I am bitterly disappointed."

"Mary is a good little thing, Father." Aunt Claudia's voice shook.

The old man looked up at her. "It is hardest for you, my dear. And I have helped to make it hard."

He reached out his hand to her. She took it. "He is my

son—and I love him—"

"And I love you, Claudia."

"May I get the blue room ready?"

The blue room was the bridal chamber at Huntersfield; kept rather sacredly at other times for formal purposes.

"Do as you please. The house is yours, my dear."

And so that night the lights of the blue room shone on Fiddle Flippin and her new grandmother.

"Do you think she would let me put her to bed?" Mrs. Beaufort had asked Mary.

"If you will sing, 'Jack-Sam Bye.'"

Mary pulled the last little garment from the pink plump body, and Fiddle, like a rosy Cupid, counted her toes gleefully in the middle of the wide bed.

"I told Truxton," Mary said suddenly, "that he might not want to call her 'Fiddle.' The whole neighborhood says 'Fiddle Flippin.'"

"It is a dear little name," Aunt Claudia was bending adoringly over the baby, "but Fidelity is better—Fidelity Branch Beaufort—"

"I want her to be as proud of her name as I am," Mary's voice had a thrilling note. "It is a great thing to know that my child has in her the blood of all those wonderful people whose portraits hang in the hall. I want her to be worthy of her name."

She could have said nothing better. Aunt Claudia's face was lighted by the warmth in her heart. "Such a lot of ancestors for one little fat Fidelity," she said; "put on her nightgown, Mary, and I'll rock her to sleep."

CHAPTER X

A GENTLEMAN'S LIE

I

Becky was not well. Aunt Claudia, perceiving her listlessness, decided that she needed a change. Letters were written to the Nantucket grandfather, and plans made for Becky's departure. She was to spend a month on the island, come back to Boston to the Admiral's big old house on the water-side of Beacon Street, and return to Huntersfield for Christmas.

Becky felt that it was good of everybody to take so much trouble. She really didn't care in the least. She occupied herself steadily with each day's routine. She bent her head over the fine embroidery of a robe she was making for Mary. She cut the flowers for the vases and bowls, she recited nursery rhymes to Fiddle, entrancing that captious young person with "Oranges and Lemons" and "Lavender's Blue." She read aloud to the Judge, planned menus for Aunt Claudia, and was in fact such an angel in the house that Truxton, after three days of it, protested.

"Oh, what's the matter with Becky, Mums?"

"Why?"

"She hasn't any pep."

"I know."

"Isn't she well?"

"I have tried to have her see a doctor. But she won't. She insists that she is all right—"

"She is not. She is no more like the old Becky than champagne is like—milk—Becky was the kind that—went to your head—Mums. You know that—sparkling."

"I have wondered," Mrs. Beaufort said, slowly, "if anything happened while I was away."

"What could happen—"

His mother sighed. "Nothing, I suppose—" She let it go at that. Her intuitions carried her towards the truth. She had learned from Mandy and the Judge that Dalton had spent much time at Huntersfield in her absence. Becky never mentioned him. Her silence spoke eloquently, Mrs. Beaufort felt, of something concealed. Becky was apt to talk of things that interested her. And there had been no doubt of her interest in Dalton before her aunt had gone away.

Randy, coming often now to Huntersfield, had his heart torn for his beloved. No one except himself knew what had happened, and the knowledge stirred him profoundly. He held that burning torches and a stake were none too good for Dalton. He sighed for the old days in Virginia when gentlemen settled such matters in the woods at dawn, with pistols, seconds, a shot or two. Farther back it would have been an affair of knives and toma- hawks—Indian chiefs in a death struggle.

But neither duels nor death struggles were in the modern mode, nor would any punishment which he might inflict on Dalton help Becky in this moment of deep humiliation. He knew her pride and the hurt that had come to her, he knew her love, and the deadly inertia which had followed the loss of illusion.

Randy's love was not a selfish love. In that tense moment of Becky's confession on the day of the barbecue, his own hopes had died. The boy in him had died, too, and he had reached the full stature of a man. He wanted to protect and shield—he was all ten- derness. He felt that he would dare anything, do anything, if he could bring back to Becky the dreams of which Dalton robbed her.

Night after night he sat in his room up-stairs in the old Schoolhouse, and wrote on "The Trumpeter Swan." It was an outlet for his pent-up emotions, and something of the romance which was denied him, something of the indignation which stirred him, something of the passions of love and revenge which fought within him, drove his pen onward, so that his little tale took on color and life. Crude, perhaps, in form, it was yet a song of youth and patriotism. It was Randy's call to his comrades. There was to be no compromise. They must make men look up and listen—to catch the sound of their clear note. The ideals which had made them fight brutality and greed were living ideals. They were not to be doffed with their khaki and overseas caps. Their country called, the whole world called, for men with faith and courage. There was no place for pessimism, no place for materi- alism, no place for sordidness.

His hero was, specifically, a man who had come back from the fighting, flaming with the thought of his high future. He had found the world smiling and unconcerned. It was this world which needed to listen to the call of trumpets—high up—

The chapters in which he wrote of love—for there was a woman in the story—were more beautiful than Randy realized. It was of a boy's love that he told—delicately. It was his own story of love denied, yet enriching a life.

Yet—because man cannot live up always to the measure of his own vision, there came often between Randy and the written page the image of George Dalton, smiling and insolent. And he would lay down his pen, and lean his head on his hand, and gaze into space, and sometimes he would speak out in the silence. "I will make him suffer."

It was in one of these moments that he saw how it might be done. "He would let fruit drop to the ground and rot if no other man wanted it," he analyzed keenly, "but if another man tried to pick it up, he would fight for it."

Dalton was still at King's Crest. Mrs. Waterman had not responded satisfactorily to the operation. The doctors had grave doubts as to her recovery. Madge was convalescing at the Flippins'.

Randy had been content, hitherto, to receive bulletins indirectly from both of the invalids. But on the morning following the birth of his great idea he rode on horseback to King's Crest. He looked well on horseback, and in his corduroys, with a soft shirt and flowing tie, a soft felt hat, he was at his best.

He found George and Oscar on the west terrace, shaded by blue and white-striped awnings, with a macaw, red and blue on a perch—a peacock glimmering at the foot of the steps—and the garden blazing beyond.

There were iced drinks in tall glasses—a litter of cigarettes on smoking-stands, magazines and newspapers on the stone floors, packs of cards on a small table. Oscar, hunched up in a high-backed Chinese chair, was white and miserable. George looked bored to extinction.

Randy, coming in, gave a clear-cut impression of strength and youth.

"Mother sent some wine jelly for Mrs. Waterman," he said to Oscar. "It was made from an old recipe, and she thought it might be different. And there were some hundred-leaved roses from our bush. I gave them to your man."

Oscar brightened. He was grateful for the kindness of these queer neighbors of his who would have nothing to do with him and his wife when they were well, and who had seemed to care not at all for his money. But who, now that sickness had come and sorrow, offered themselves and their possessions unstintedly.

"I'll go and see that Flora gets them," he said. "She hasn't any appetite. She's—it's rather discouraging—"

Randy, left alone with Dalton, was debonair and delightful. George, looking at him with speculative eyes, decided that there was more to this boy than he would have believed. He had exceedingly good manners and an ease that was undeniable. There was of course good blood back of him. And in a way it counted. George knew that he could never have been at ease in old clothes in the midst of elegance.

It was Randy who spoke first of Becky. Dalton's heart jumped when he heard her name. Night after night he had ridden towards Huntersfield, only to turn back before he reached the lower gate. Once he had ventured on foot as far as the garden, and in the hush had called softly, "Becky." But no one had answered. He wondered what he would have done if Becky had responded to his call. "I am not going to be fool enough to marry her," he told himself, angrily, yet knew that if he played the game with Becky there could be no other end to it.

Randy said, quite naturally, that Becky was going away. To Nantucket. He asked if George had been there.

"Once, on Waterman's yacht. It's quaint—but a bit spoiled by summer people—"

"Becky doesn't know the summer people. Her great-grandparents were among the first settlers, and the Merediths have never sold the old home."

"She is a pretty little thing," George said. "And she's buried down here."

"I shouldn't call it exactly—buried."

George, with his eyes on the peacock, smiled and shrugged his shoulders.

Randy smiled and his eyes, too, were on the peacock. He was thinking that there were certain points of resemblance between the gorgeous bird and Dalton. They glimmered in the sunlight and strutted a bit—

He came back to say easily, "Has Becky told you of our happiness—"

George gave him a startled glance. "Happiness?"

"We are to be married when she comes back—at Christmas."

"Married—"

"Yes," coolly, "it was rather to be expected, you know. We played together as children—our fathers played together—our grandfathers—our great-grandfathers."

A cold wave seemed to sweep over George. So this young cub would have her beauty!

"Aren't you rather young—?" he demanded, "and what have you to give her?"

"Love," said Randy calmly, "a man's respect for her goodness and worth—for her innocence. She's a little saint in a shrine."

"Is she?" Georgie-Porgie asked, and smiled to himself; "few

women are that."

After Randy had gone George Dalton walked the floor. He knew innocence when he saw it, and he knew that Randy had told the truth. Becky Bannister was as white as the doves that were fluttering down to the garden pool to drink. He had never cared particularly for innocence. But he cared for Becky. He knew now that he cared tremendously. Randy had made him know it. It had not seemed so bad to think of Becky as breaking her heart and waiting for a word from him. It seemed very bad, indeed, when he thought of her as married to Randy.

He felt that, of course, she did not love Randy; that he, Georgie-Porgie, had all that she had to give—But womanlike, she had taken this way to get back at him. He wondered if she had sent Randy.

Up and down the terrace he raged like a lion. He wanted to show that cub—oh, if he might show him—!

Randy had known that he would rage, and as he rode home he had the serene feeling that he had stuck a splinter in George's flesh.

Oscar Waterman joined George on the terrace, but noticed nothing. His mind was full of Flora. "I am sorry young Paine went so soon. I wanted to thank him. Flora can't eat the jelly, but it was good of them to send it. She can't eat anything. She's worse, George. I don't know how I am going to stand it."

George was in no mood for condolence. Yet he was not quite heartless. "Look here," he said, "you mustn't give up."

"George, if she dies," Oscar said, wildly, "what do you think will happen to me? I never planned for this. I planned for a good time. I thought maybe that when we were old—one of us might go. But it wouldn't be fair to take her now—and leave me."

"I have given her—everything—" he went on. "I—I think I've been a good husband. I have always loved her a lot, George, you know that."

He was a plain little man, but at this moment he gained something of dignity. And there was this to say for him, that what he felt for Flora was a deeper emotion than George had ever known.

"The doctor says the crisis comes to-night. I am not going to bed. I couldn't sleep. George—I've been wondering if I oughtn't to call in—some kind of clergyman—to see her."

"People don't, nowadays, do they?" George asked rather uncomfortably.

"Well, I don't see why they shouldn't. There ought to be somebody to pray for Flora."

There was, it developed upon inquiry, a little old rector who lived not far away. George went for him in his big car.

The little man, praying beside Flora's gorgeous bed, felt that this was the hundredth sheep who had wandered and was found. The other ninety and nine were safely in the fold. He had looked after the spiritual condition of the county for fifty years. There had been much to discourage him, but in the main if they strayed they came back.

He prayed with fervor, the fine old prayers of his church.

"Look down from heaven, we humbly beseech thee, with the eyes of mercy upon this child now lying upon the bed of sickness: Visit her, O Lord, with thy salvation; deliver her in thy good appointed time from bodily pain, and save her soul for thy mercies' sake; that, if it shall be thy pleasure to prolong her days here on earth, she may live for thee, and be an instrument of thy glory, by serving thee faithfully, and doing good in her generation; or else receive her into those heavenly habitations, where the souls of those who sleep in the Lord Jesus enjoy perpetual rest and felicity."

Flora, lying inert and bloodless, opened her eyes. "Say it again," she whispered. "Say it again."

II

Randy rode straight from Hamilton Hill to Huntersfield. He found Becky in the Bird Room. She had her head tied up in a white cloth, and a big white apron enveloped her. She was as white as the whiteness in which she was clad, and there were purple shadows under her eyes. The windows were open and a faint breeze stirred the curtains. The shade of the great trees softened the light to a dim green. After the glare of Oscar's terrace it was like coming from a blazing desert to the bottom of the sea.

There was a wide seat under a window which looked out towards the hills. Becky sat down on it. "Everybody is out," she said, "except Aunt Claudia. She is taking a nap up-stairs."

"I didn't come to see everybody, Becky. I came to see you."

"I am glad you came. I can rest a bit."

"You work as hard as if you had to do it."

She leaned back against the green linen cushions of the window seat and looked up at him. "I do have to do it. There is nobody else. Mandy is busy, and, anyhow, Grandfather doesn't like to have the servants in here. And neither do I—It is almost as if the birds were alive—and loved me."

Randy hugged his knee and meditated. "But there are lots of rich women who wouldn't dust a room."

She made a gesture of disdain. "Oh, *that* kind of rich people."

"What kind?"

"The kind that aren't used to their money. Who think ladies—are idle. Sister Loretto says that is the worst kind—the awful kind. She talked to me every day about it. She said that money was a curse when people used it only for their ease. Sister Loretto hates laziness. She had money herself before she took her vows, but now she works every hour of the day and she says it brings her happiness."

Randy shook his head. "Most of us need to play around a bit, Becky."

"Do we? I—I think most women would be better off if they were like Sister Loretto."

"They would not. Stop talking rot, Becky, and take that thing off your head. It makes you look like a nun."

"I know. I saw myself in the glass. I don't mind looking like a nun, Randy."

"Well, I mind. Turn your head and I'll take out that pin."

"Don't be silly, Randy."

He persisted. "Keep still while I take it out—"

He found the pin and unwound the white cloth. "There," he said, drawing a long breath, "you look like yourself again. You were so—austere, you scared me, Becky."

He was again hugging his knees. "When are you going away?"

"On the twenty-ninth. I shall stay over until next week for the Merriweathers' ball."

"I didn't know whether you would feel equal to it."

"I shall go on Mary's account. It will be her introduction to Truxton's friends, and if I am there it will be easier for her. She has a lovely frock, jade green tulle with a girdle of gold brocade. It came down for me with a lot of other clothes, and it needed only a few changes for her to wear it."

"You will be glad to get away?"

"It will be cooler—and I need the change. But it is always more formal up there—they remember that I have money. Here it is forgotten."

"I wish I could forget it."

"Why should you ever think of it?" she demanded with some heat. "I am the same Becky with or without it."

"Not quite the same," he was turning his hat in his hand. Then, raising his eyes and looking at her squarely, he said what he had come to say, "I have—I have just been to see Dalton, Becky."

A wave of red washed over her neck, touched her chin, her

cheeks. "I don't see what that has to do with me."

"It has a great deal to do with you. I told him you were going to marry me."

The wave receded. She was chalk-white.

"Randy, how dared you do such a thing?"

"I dared," said Randy, with tense fierceness, "because a man like Dalton wants what other men want. He will think about you a lot, and I want him to think. He won't sleep to-night, and I want him to stay awake. He will wonder whether you love me, and he will be afraid that you do—and I want him to be afraid."

"But it was a lie, Randy. I am not going to marry you."

"Do you think that I meant that—? That I am expecting anything for myself?"

"No," unsteadily, her slender body trembling as if from cold, "but what did you mean?"

"I told you. Dalton's got to come back to you and beg—on his knees—and he will come when he thinks you are mine—"

"I don't want him to come. And when you talk like that it makes me feel—smirched—"

Dead silence. Then, "It was a gentleman's lie—"

"Gentlemen do not lie. Go to him this minute, Randy, and tell him that it isn't true."

"Give me three days, Becky. If in that time he doesn't try to see you or call you up, I'll go—But give me three days."

She wavered. "What good will it do?"

He caught up her cold little hands in his. "You will have a chance to get back at him. And when you stick in the knife, you can turn it—until it hurts."

III

It was while the family at Huntersfield were at dinner that the telephone rang. Calvin answered, and came in to say that Miss Becky was wanted. She went listlessly. But the first words over the wire stiffened her.

It was George's voice, quick imploring. Saying that he had something to tell her. That he must see her—

"Let me come, Becky."

"Of course."

"You mean that I—may—?"

"Why not?"

He seemed to hesitate. "But I thought—"

Her laugh was light and clear. "I must get back to my dinner. I have only had my soup. And I am simply—*starving*—"

It was not what he had expected. Not in the least. As he hung up the receiver he was conscious too of a baffled feeling that Becky had, in a sense, held the reins of the situation.

In spite of her famished condition, Becky did not at once go to the dining-room. She called up King's Crest, and asked for Randy.

She wanted to know, she said, whether he had anything on for the evening. No? Then could he come over and bring the boarders? Oh, as many of them as would come. And they would dance. She was bored to *death*. Her laugh was still clear and light, and Randy wondered.

Then she went back to the dinner table and ate the slice of lamb which the Judge had carved for her. She ate mint sauce and mashed potatoes, she ate green corn pudding, and a salad, and watermelon. Her cheeks were red, and Aunt Claudia felt that Becky was looking much better. For how could Aunt Claudia know that everything that Becky ate was like sawdust to her palate. She found herself talking and laughing a great deal, and Truxton teased her.

After dinner she went up-stairs with Mary and showed her a new way to do her hair, and found an entrancing wisp of a frock for Mary to wear.

"It will be great fun having the boarders from King's Crest. There are a lot of young people of all kinds—and not many of them our kind, Mary."

Mary smiled at her. "I am not quite your kind, am I?"

"Why not? And oh, Mary, you are happy, happy. And you are lovely with your hair like that, close to your head and satin-smooth."

Mary, surveying herself in the glass, gave an excited laugh. "Do you know when I married Truxton I never thought of this?"

"Of what?" Becky asked.

"Of pretty clothes—and dances—and dinners. I just knew that he—loved me, and that he had to leave me. But I don't suppose I could make the world believe it."

"Truxton believes it, doesn't he, Mary?"

"Yes."

"And I believe it. And what do you care for the others? It is what we know of ourselves, Mary," she drew a quick breath. "It is what we know of ourselves—"

Becky was wearing the simple frock of pale blue in which George had seen her on that first night when he came to Huntersfield.

"Aren't you going to change?" Mary asked.

"No. It is too much trouble." Becky was in front of the mirror.

Her pearls caught the light of the candles. Her bronze hair was a shining wave across her forehead. "It is too much trouble," she said, again, and turned from the mirror.

She had a dozen frocks that had come in the rosy hamper—frocks that would have made the boarders open their eyes. Frocks that would have made Dalton open his. But Becky had the feeling that this was not the moment for lovely clothes. She felt that she would be cheapened if she decked herself for George.

When the two girls went down-stairs Truxton was waiting for his wife. "I thought you would never come," he said. He drew her within the circle of his arm, and they went out into the garden. The Judge and Mrs. Beaufort were on the porch. Becky sat on the step and leaned her head against Aunt Claudia's knee.

"What in the world made you ask all those people over, Becky?" the Judge demanded.

"Oh, they're great fun, Grandfather, and I felt like it."

"Have you planned anything for them to eat, Claudia?"

"Watermelons. Calvin has put a lot of them in the spring."

The stars were thick overhead. Becky looked up at them and relaxed a little. Since Dalton had spoken to her over the wire she had gone through the motions of doing normal things. She had eaten and talked, and now she was sitting quite still on the step while Aunt Claudia smoothed her hair, and the Judge talked of things to eat.

But shut up within her was a clock which ticked and never stopped. *"He will come—when he thinks—you are mine—He will come—when he thinks—you are mine—"*

Randy and his mother arrived in Little Sister, with two of the boarders for good measure in the back seat. They had dropped Major Prime at Flippins', where he was to make a call on Madge MacVeigh. He had promised to come later, however, if Randy would drive over and get him.

The rest of the boarders were packed variously into their cars and the surrey, and as soon as they arrived they proceeded to occupy the lawn and the porch, and to overflow the garden. They made a great deal of pleasant noise about it, and the white gowns of the women, and the white flannels of the men gave an impressionistic effect of faint blue against the deeper blue of the night.

Within the house, the rugs were up in the drawing-room, the library, the dining-room, and the wide hall; there sounded, presently, the tinkling music of the phonograph, and there was the unceasing movement of white-clad figures which seemed to float in a golden haze.

Becky danced a great deal, with Randy, with the younger boarders, and with the genial gentleman. She laughed with an air of unaffected gayety. And she felt that her heart stopped beating, when at last she looked up and saw Dalton standing in the door.

She at once went towards him, and gave him her hand. "I wonder if you know everybody?"

Her clear eyes met his without self-consciousness. He attempted a swagger. "I don't want to know everybody. How do they happen to be here?"

"I asked them. And they are really very nice."

He did not see the niceness. He had thought to find her in the setting which belonged to her beauty. The silent night, the fragrance of the garden, the pale statues among the trees, and himself playing the game with a greater sense of its seriousness than ever before.

Throughout the evening George watched for a chance to see Becky alone. Without conspicuously avoiding him, she had no time for him. He complained constantly. "I want to talk to you. Run away with me, Becky—and let these people go."

"It isn't proper for a hostess to leave her guests."

"Are you trying to—punish me?"

"For what?"

So—she too was playing—! She had let him come that he might see her—indifferent.

Becky had danced with George once, and with Randy three times. George had protested, and Becky had said, "But I promised him before you came—"

"You knew I was coming?"

"Yes."

"You might have kept a few—"

She seemed to consider that. "Yes, I might. But not from Randy—"

At last he said to her, "I have been out in the garden. There is a star shining in the little pool where the fishes are. I want you to see the star."

It was thus he had won her. He had always seen stars shining in little pools, or a young moon rising from a rosy bed. But it had never meant anything. She shook her head. "I should like to see your little star. But I haven't time."

"Are you afraid to come?"

"Why should I be?"

"Well, there's Love—in the garden," he was daring—his sparkling eyes tried to hold hers and failed.

She was looking straight beyond him to where Randy stood by a window, tall and thin with his Indian profile, and his high-held head.

"We are going to have watermelons in a minute," was her romantic response to Dalton's fire. "You'd better stay and eat some."

"I don't want to eat. And if you aren't afraid you'll come."

Calvin and Mandy and their son, John, with Flippins' Daisy, had assembled the watermelons on a long table out-of-doors. Above the table on the branch of a tree was hung an old ship's lantern brought by Admiral Meredith to his friend, the Judge. It gave a faint but steady light, and showed the pink and green and white of the fruit, the dusky faces of the servants as they cut and sliced, and handed plates to the eager and waiting guests.

Becky, standing back in the shadows with Randy by her side, watched the men surge towards the table, and retire with their loads of lusciousness. Grinning boys were up to their ears in juice, girls, bare-armed and bare-necked, reached for plates held teasingly aloft. It was all rather innocently bacchanal—a picture which for Becky had an absolutely impersonal quality. She had entertained her guests as she had eaten her dinner, outwardly doing the normal and conventional thing, while her mind was chaotic. This jumble of people on the lawn seemed unreal and detached. The only real people in the world were herself and Dalton.

"How did you happen to ask us?" Randy was saying.

"Because I wanted you—"

"That doesn't explain it. It has something to do with Dalton—"

"He said he was coming—and I wanted a crowd."

"Were you afraid to see him alone?"

"He says that I am."

"When did he say it?"

"Just now. He's in the garden, Randy."

"Waiting for you?"

"He says that he is waiting."

Randy gave a quick exclamation. "Surely you won't go."

"Why not? I've got to turn—the knife—"

He groaned. "So this is what I've let you in for—"

"Well, I shall see it through, Randy."

"Becky, don't go to him in the garden."

"Why not?"

"The whole thing is wrong," the boy said, slowly. "I lied to give you your opportunity, and now, I'd rather die than think of you out there—"

"Then you don't trust me, Randy?"

"My dear, I do. But I don't trust—him."

IV

George had known that she would come. Yet when he saw the white blur of her gown against the blackness of the bushes, his heart leaped. All through the ages men have waited for women in gardens—"*She is coming, my own, my sweet*—" and farther back, "*Make haste, my beloved,*" and in the beginning, as Mandy could have told, a serpent waited.

Dalton was not, of course, a serpent. He was merely a very selfish man, who had always had what he wanted, and now he wanted Becky. He was still, perhaps, playing the game, but he was playing it in dead earnest with Randy as his opponent and Becky the prize.

She recognized a new note in his voice and was faintly disturbed by it.

"So you are not afraid?"

"No."

She sat down on the bench. Behind them was the pale statue of Diana, the pool was at their feet with its little star.

"Why should I be afraid?" she asked.

"You are trying to shut me out of your heart, Becky—and you are afraid I may try to—open the door."

"Silly," she said, clearly and lightly, but with a sense of panic. Oh, why had she come? The darkness seemed to shut her in; his voice was beating against her heart—

He was saying that he loved her, *loved* her. Did she understand? That he had been *miserable*? His defense was masterly. He played on her imagination delicately, as if she were a harp, and his fingers touched the strings. He realized what a cad he must have seemed. But she was a saint in a shrine—it will be seen that he did not hesitate to borrow from Randy. She was a saint in a shrine, and well, he knelt at her feet—a sinner. "You needn't think that I don't know what I have done, Becky. I swept you along with me without a thought of anything serious in it for either of us. It was just a game, sweetheart, and lots of people play it, but it isn't a game now, it is the most serious thing in life."

There is no eloquence so potent as that which is backed by genuine passion. Becky coming down through the garden had been so sure of herself. She had felt that pride would be the rock to which she would anchor her resistance to his enchantments. Yet here in the garden—

"Oh, *please*," she said, and stood up.

He rose, too, and towered above her. "Becky," he said, hoarsely, "it's the real thing—for me—"

His spell was upon her. She was held by it—drawn by it against her will. Her cry was that of a frightened and fascinated bird.

He bent down. His face was a white circle in the dark, but she could see the sparkle of his eyes. "Kiss me, Becky."

"I shall never kiss you again."

"I love you."

"Love," she said, with a sort of tense quiet, "does not kiss and run away."

"My heart never ran away. I swear it. Marry me, Becky."

He had never expected to ask her. But now that he had done it, he was glad.

She was swayed by his earnestness, by the thought of all he had meant to her in her dreams of yesterday. But to-day was not yesterday, and George was not the man of those dreams. Yet, why not? There was the quick laughter, with its new ring of sincerity, the sparkling eyes, the Apollo head.

"Marry me, Becky."

Beyond the pool which reflected the little star was the dark outline of the box hedge, and beyond the hedge, the rise of the hill showed dark against the dull silver of the sky—a shadow seemed to rise suddenly in that dim brightness, the tall thin shadow of a man with a clear-cut profile, and a high-held head!

Becky drew a sharp breath—then faced Dalton squarely. "I am going to marry Randy."

His laugh was triumphant—

"Do you think I am going to let you? You are mine, Becky, and you know it. *You are mine—*"

V

Randy, having made a record run with Little Sister to the Flippins', had brought back Major Prime. When he returned Becky had disappeared. He looked for her, knowing all the time that she had gone down into the garden to meet Dalton. And he had brought Dalton back to her, he had given him this opportunity to plead his cause, had given him the incentive of a man of his kind to still pursue; he had, as he had said, let Becky in for it, and now he was raging at the thought.

Nellie Custis, padding at his heels, had known that something disturbed him. He walked restlessly from room to room, from porch to porch, across the lawn, skirted the garden, stopped now and then to listen, called once when he saw a white figure alone by the big gate, "Becky!"

Nellie knew who it was that he wanted. And at last she instituted a search on her own account. She went through the garden, passed the pool, found Becky's feet in blue slippers, and rushed back to her master with an air of discovery.

But Randy would not follow her. He must, he knew, set a curb on his impatience. He walked beyond the gate, following the ridge of the hill to the box hedge. He was not in the least aware that his shadow showed up against the silver of the sky. Perhaps Fate guided him to the ridge, who knows? At any rate, it seemed so afterwards to Becky, who felt that the shadow of Randy against the silver sky was the thing that saved her.

She gave the old Indian cry, and he answered it.

His shadow wavered on the ridge. He was lost for a moment against the blackness of the hedge, and emerged on the other side of the pool.

"Randy," she was a bit breathless, "here we are. Mr. Dalton and I. I saw you on the ridge. You have no idea how tall your shadow seemed—"

She was talking in that clear light voice which was not her own. Dalton said sullenly, "Hello, Paine." And Randy's heart was singing, "She called me."

The three of them walked to the house together. Becky had insisted that she must go back to her guests. George left them at the step. He was for the moment beaten. As he drove his car madly back to King's Crest, he tried to tell himself that it was all for the best. That he must let Becky alone. He would be a fool to throw himself away on a shabby slender slip of a thing because she had clear eyes and bronze hair.

But it was not because of her slenderness and clear eyes and bronze hair that Becky held him, it was because of the force within her which baffled him.

The guests were leaving. They had had the time of their lives. They packed themselves into their various cars, and the surrey, and shouted "good-bye." The Major stayed and sat on the lawn to talk to the Judge and Mrs. Beaufort. Mary and Truxton ascended the stairs to the Blue Room, where little Fiddle slept in the Bannister crib that had been brought down from the attic.

Becky and Randy went into the Bird Room and sat under the swinging lamp. "I have something to tell you, Randy," Becky had said, and as in the days of their childhood the Bird Room seemed the place for confidences.

Becky curled herself up in the Judge's big chair like a tired child. Randy on the other side of the empty fireplace said, "You ought to be in bed, Becky."

"I shan't—sleep," nervously. There were deep shadows under her troubled eyes. "I shan't sleep when I go."

Randy came over and knelt by her side. "My dear, my dear," he said, "I am afraid I have let you in for a lot of trouble."

"But the things you said were true—he came—because he thought I—belonged to—you."

She hesitated. Then she reached out her hand to him. "Randy," she said, "I told him I was going to marry—you."

His hand had gone over hers, and now he held it in his strong clasp. "Of course it isn't true, Becky."

"I am going to make it true."

Dead silence. Then, "No, my dear."

"Why not?"

"You don't love me."

"But I like you," feverishly, "I like you, tremendously, and don't you want to marry me, Randy?"

"God knows that I do," said poor Randy, "but I must not. It—it would be Heaven for me, you know that. But it wouldn't be quite—cricket—to let you do it, Becky."

"I am not doing it for your sake. I am doing it for my own. I want to feel—safe. Do I seem awfully selfish when I say that?"

A great wave of emotion swept over him. She had turned to him for protection, for tenderness. In that moment Randy grew to the full stature of a man. He lifted her hand and kissed it. "You are making me very happy, Becky, dear."

It was a strange betrothal. Behind them the old eagle brooded with outstretched wings, the owl, round-eyed, looked down upon them and withheld his wisdom, the Trumpeter, white as snow, in his glass case, was as silent as the Sphinx.

"You are making me very happy, Becky, dear," said poor Randy, knowing as he said it that such happiness was not for him.

CHAPTER XI

WANTED—A PEDESTAL

I

The Major's call on Miss MacVeigh had been a great success. She was sitting up, and had much to say to him. Throughout the days of her illness and convalescence, the Major had kept in touch with her. He had sent her quaint nosegays from the King's Crest garden, man-tied and man-picked. He had sent her nice soldierly notes, asking her to call upon him if there was anything he could do for her. He had sent her books, and magazines, and now on this first visit, he brought back the "Pickwick" which he had picked up in the road after the accident.

"I have wondered," Madge said, "what became of it."

They were in the Flippin sitting-room. Madge was in a winged chair with a freshly-washed gray linen cover. The chair had belonged to Mrs. Flippin's father, and for fifty years had held the place by the east window in summer and by the fireplace in winter. Oscar had wanted to bring things from Hamilton Hill to make Madge comfortable. But she had refused to spoil the simplicity of the quiet old house. "Everything that is here belongs here, Oscar," she had told him, "and I like it."

She wore a mauve negligee that was sheer and soft and flowing, and her burnt-gold hair was braided and wound around her head in a picturesque and becoming coiffure.

As she turned the pages of the little book the Major noticed her hands. They were white and slender, and she wore only one ring—a long amethyst set in silver.

"Do you play?" he asked abruptly.

"Yes. Why?"

"Your hands show it."

She smiled at him. "I am afraid that my hands don't quite tell the truth." She held them up so that the light of the lamp shone through them. "They are really a musician's hands, aren't they? And I am only a dabbler in that as in everything else."

"You can't expect me to believe that."

"But I am. I have intelligence. But I'm a 'dunce with wits.' I know what I ought to do but I don't do it. I think that I have brains enough to write, I am sure I have imagination enough to paint, I have strength enough when I am well to"—she laughed,—"scrub floors. But I don't write or play or paint—or scrub floors—I don't believe that there is one thing in the world that I can do as well as

Mary Flippin makes biscuits."

Her eyes seemed to challenge him to deny her assertion. He settled himself lazily in his chair, and asked about the book.

"Tell me why you like Dickens, when nobody reads him in these days except ourselves."

"I like him because in my next incarnation I want to live in the kind of world he writes about."

He was much interested. "You do?"

She nodded. "Yes. I never have. My world has always been—cut and dried, conventional, you know the kind." The slender hand with the amethyst ring made a little gesture of disdain. "There were three of us, my mother and my father and myself. Everything in our lives was very perfectly ordered. We were not very rich—not in the modern sense, and we were not very poor, and we knew a lot of nice people. I went to school with girls of my own kind, an exclusive school. I went away summers to our own cottage in an exclusive North Shore colony. We took our servants with us. After my mother died I went to boarding-school, and to Europe in summer, and when my school days were ended, and I acquired a stepmother, I set up an apartment of my own. It has Florentine things in it, and Byzantine things, and things from China and Japan, and the colors shine like jewels under my lamps—you know the effect. And my kitchen is all in white enamel, and the cook does things by electricity, and when I go away in summer my friends have Italian villas—like the Watermans, on the North Shore, although all of my friends are not like the Watermans." She threw this last out casually, not as a criticism, but that he might, it seemed, withhold judgment of her present choice of associates. "And I have never known the world of good cheer that Dickens writes about—wide kitchens, and tea-kettles singing and crickets chirping and everybody busy with things that interest them. Do you know that there are really no bored people in Dickens except a few aristocrats? None of the poor people are bored. They may be unhappy, but there's always some recompense in a steaming drink or savory stew, or some gay little festivity;—even the vagabonds seem to get something out of life. I realize perfectly that I've never had the thrills from a bridge game that came to the Marchioness when she played cards with Dick Swiveller—by stealth."

She talked rapidly, charmingly. He could not be sure how much in earnest she might be—but she made out her case and continued her argument.

"When I was a child I walked on gray velvet carpets, and there were etchings on the wall, and chilly mirrors between the long windows in the drawing-room. And the kitchen was in the basement and I never went down. There wasn't a cozy spot anywhere. None of us were cozy, my mother wasn't. She was very lovely and sparkling and went out a great deal and my father sparkled too. He still does. But there was really nothing to draw us together—like the Cratchits or even the Kenwigs. And we were never comfortable and merry like all of these lovely people in Pickwick."

She went on wistfully, "When I was nine, I found these little books in our library and after that I enjoyed vicariously the life I had never lived. That's why I like it here—Mrs. Flippin's kettle sings—and the crickets chirp—and Mr. and Mrs. Flippin are comfortable—and cozy—and content."

It was a long speech. "So now you see," she said, as she ended, "why I like Dickens."

"Yes. I see. And so—in your next incarnation you are going to be like—"

"Little Dorrit."

He laughed and leaned forward. "I can't imagine—you."

"She really had a heavenly time. Dickens tried to make you feel sorry for her. But she had the best of it all through. Somebody always wanted her."

"But she was imposed upon. And her unselfishness brought her heavy burdens."

"She got a lot out of it in the end, didn't she? And what do selfish people get? I'm one of them. I live absolutely for myself. There isn't a person except Flora who gets anything of service or self-sacrifice out of me. I came down here because she wanted me, but I hated to come. The modern theory is that unselfishness weakens. And the modern psychologist would tell you that little Dorrit was all wrong. She gave herself for others—and it didn't pay. But does the other thing pay?"

"Selfishness?"

"Yes. I'm selfish, and Oscar is, and Flora, and George Dalton, and most of the people we know. And we are all bored to death. If being unselfish is interesting, why not let us be unselfish?" Her lively glance seemed to challenge him, and they laughed together.

"I know what you mean."

"Of course you do. Everybody does who *thinks*."

"And so you are going to wait for the next plane to do the things that you want to do?"

"Yes."

"But why—wait?"

"How can I break away? I am tied into knots with the people whom I have always known; and I shall keep on doing the things I have always done, just as I shall keep on wearing pale purples and letting my skin get burned so that I may seem distinctive."

It came to him with something of a shock that she did these things with intention. That the charms which seemed to belong to her were carefully planned.

Yet how could he tell if what she said was true, when her eyes laughed?

"I shall get all I can out of being here. Mary Flippin is going to let me help her make butter, and Mrs. Flippin will teach me to make corn-bread, and some day I am going fishing with the Judge and Mr. Flippin and learn to fry eggs out-of-doors—"

"So those are the things you like?"

She nodded. "I think I do. George Dalton says it is only because I crave a change. But it isn't that. And I haven't told him the way I feel about it—the Dickens way—as I have told you."

He was glad that she had not talked to Dalton as she had talked to him.

"I wonder," he said slowly, "why you couldn't shake yourself free from the life which binds you?"

"I'm not strong enough. I'm like the drug-fiend, who doesn't want his drug, but can't give it up."

"Perhaps you need—help. There are doctors of everything, you know, in these days."

"None that can cure me of the habit of frivolity—of the claims of custom—"

"If a man takes a drug, he is cured by substituting something else for a while until he learns to do without it."

"What would you substitute for—my drug?"

"I'll have to think about it. May I come again and tell you?"

"Of course. I am dying to know."

Mrs. Flippin entered just then with a tall pitcher of lemonade and a plate of delicate cakes. "I think Miss MacVeigh is looking mighty fine," she said; "don't you, Major?"

He would not have dared to tell how fine she looked to him.

He limped across the room with the plate of cakes, and poured lemonade into a glass for Madge. Her eyes followed his strong soldierly figure. What a man he must have been before the war crippled him. What a man he was still, and his strength was not merely that of body. She felt the strength too of mind and soul.

"I think," said Mrs. Flippin that night, "that Major Prime is one of the nicest men."

Madge was in bed. The nurse had made her ready for the night, and was out on the porch with Mr. Flippin. Mrs. Flippin had fallen into the habit of having a little nightly talk with Madge. She missed her daughter, and Madge was pleasant and friendly.

"I think that Major Prime is one of the nicest men," repeated Mrs. Flippin as she sat down beside the bed, "but what a dreadful thing that he is lame."

"I am not sure," Madge said, "that it is dreadful."

She hastened to redeem herself from any possible charge of bloodthirstiness.

"I don't mean," she said, "that it isn't awful for a man to lose his leg. But men who go through a thing like that and come out—conquerors—are rather wonderful, Mrs. Flippin."

Madge had hold of Mrs. Flippin's hand. She often held it in this quiet hour, and the idea rather amused her. She was not demonstrative, and it seemed inconceivable that she should care to hold Mrs. Flippin's hand. But there was a motherliness about Mrs. Flippin, a quality with which Madge had never before come closely in contact. "It is like the way I used to feel when I was a little girl and said my prayers at night," she told herself.

Madge did not say her prayers now. Nobody did, apparently. She thought it rather a pity. It was a comfortable thing to do. And it meant a great deal if you only believed in it.

"Do you say your prayers, Mrs. Flippin?" she asked suddenly.

Mrs. Flippin was getting used to Madge's queer questions. She treated them as a missionary might treat the questions of a beautiful and appealing savage, who having gone with him to some strange country was constantly interrogatory.

"She don't seem to know anything about the things we do," Mrs. Flippin told her husband. "She got the nurse to wheel her out into the kitchen this afternoon, and watched me frost a cake and cut out biscuits. And she says that she has never seen anything so sociable as the teakettle, the way it rocks and sings."

So now when Madge asked Mrs. Flippin if she said her prayers, Mrs. Flippin said, "Do you mean at night?"

"Yes."

"Bob and I say them together," said Mrs. Flippin. "We started on our wedding night, and we ain't ever stopped."

It was a simple statement of a sublime fact. For thirty years this plain man and this plain woman had kept alive the spiritual flame on the household altar. No wonder that peace was under this roof and serenity.

Madge, as she lay there holding Mrs. Flippin's hand, looked

very young, almost like a little girl. Her hair was parted and the burnished braids lay heavy on her lovely neck. Her thin fine gown left her arms bare. "Mrs. Flippin," she said, "I wish I could live here always, and have you come every night and sit and hold my hand."

Her eyes were smiling and Mrs. Flippin smiled back. "You'd get tired."

"No," said Madge, "I don't believe anybody ever gets tired of goodness. Not real goodness. The kind that isn't hypocritical or priggish. And in these days it is so rare, that one just loves it. I am bored to death with near-bad people, Mrs. Flippin, and near-good ones. I'd much rather have them real saints and real sinners."

The nurse came in just then, and Mrs. Flippin went away. And after a time the house was very still. Madge's bed was close to the window. Outside innumerable fireflies studded the night with gold. Now and then a screech-owl sounded his mournful note. It was a ghostly call, and there was the patter of little feet on the porch as the old cat played with her kittens in the warm dark. But Madge was not afraid. She had a sense of great content as she lay there and thought of the things she had said to Major Prime. It was not often that she revealed herself, and when she did it was still rarer to meet understanding. But he had understood. She was sure of that, and she would see him soon. He had promised. And she would not have to go back to Oscar and Flora until she was ready. Flora was better, but still very weak. It would be much wiser, the doctor had said, if she saw no one but her nurses for several days.

II

Truxton Beaufort rode over to King's Crest the next morning, and sat on the steps of the Schoolhouse. Randy and Major Prime were having breakfast out-of-doors. It was ten o'clock, but they were apparently taking their ease.

"I thought you had to work," Truxton said to Randy.

"I sold a car yesterday—"

"And to-day you are playing around like a plutocrat. I wish I could sell cars. I wish I could do *anything*. Look here, you two. I wonder if you feel as I do."

"About what?"

"Coming back. I came home expecting a pedestal—and I give you my word nobody seems to think much of me except my family. And they aren't worshipful—exactly. They can't be. How can they rave over my one decoration when that young nigger John has two, and deserved them, and when the butcher and baker and candlestick-maker are my ranking officers? War used to be a gentleman's game. But it isn't any more."

"We've got to carve our own pedestals," said the Major. "We are gods of yesterday. The world won't stop to praise us. We did our duty, and we would do it again. But our laurel wreaths are doffed. Our swords are beaten into plowshares. Peace is upon us. If we want pedestals, we've got to carve them."

Truxton argued that it wasn't quite fair. The Major agreed that it might not seem so, but the thing had been so vast, and there were so many men involved, so many heroes.

"Every little family has a hero of its own," Truxton supplemented. "Mary thinks none of the others did *anything*—I won the *whole* war. That's where I have it over you two," he grinned.

"It is a thing," said the Major, cheerfully, "which can be remedied."

"It can," Truxton told him; "which reminds me that our young John is going to marry Flippins' Daisy, and our household is in mourning. Mandy doesn't approve of Daisy, and neither does Calvin. Mandy took to her bed when she heard the news, and young John cooked breakfast to the tune of his Daddy's lamentations. But it was a good breakfast."

"Marriage," said the Major, "seems rather epidemic in these days."

Randy rose restlessly and sat on the porch rail. "Why in the world does John want to marry Daisy—"

"Why not?" easily. "There's some style about Daisy—"

"But there are lots of nice, comfortable, hard-working girls in this neighborhood."

"Lead me to 'em," Truxton mimicked young John, "lead me to 'em. Mary says that Daisy is the best of the lot. She has plenty of good sense back of her foolishness, and she is one of the best cooks in the county. She and John are planning to go up to Washington and open an old-fashioned oyster house. She says that people are complaining that they can't get oysters as they did in the old days, and she is going to show them. I wouldn't be surprised if they made a success of it. And I tell you this—I envy John. He will have a paying business, and here I am without a thing ahead of me, and I have married a wife and the ravens won't feed us."

Randy stuck his hands in his pockets with an air of sudden resolution.

"Look here," he said, "why can't we go halves in this car business? It will pay our expenses, and we can finish our law course at the University."

"Law? Oh, look here, Randy, I thought you had given that up."

"I haven't, and why should you? We will finish, and some day we will open an office together."

The Major, whistling softly, listened and said nothing.

"I have been thinking a lot about it," Randy went on, "and I can't see much of a future ahead of me. Not the kind of future that our families are expecting of us. You and I have got to stand for something, Truxton, or some day the world will be saying that all the great men died with Thomas Jefferson."

The Major went on with his lilting tune. What a pair they were, these lads! Randy, afire with his dreams, and rather tragic in his dreaming. Truxton, light as a feather—laughing.

"Why can't we give to the world as much as the men who have gone before us?" Randy was demanding. "Are we going to take everything from our ancestors, and give nothing to our descendants?"

Truxton chuckled. "By Jove," he said, "now that I come to think of it, I am the head of a family—there's Fiddle-dee-dee, and I shall have to reckon with Fiddle-dee-dee's children and grandchildren and great-grandchildren—who will expect that my portrait will hang on the wall at Huntersfield."

"It is all very well to laugh," said Randy hotly, "but that is the way it looks to me; that we have got to show to the world that our ambitions are—big. It is all very well to talk about the day's work. I am going to do it, and pay my way, but there's got to be something beyond that to think about—something bigger than I have ever known."

He gained dignity through the sincerity of his purpose. The Major, still whistling softly, wondered what had come over the boy. He recognized a difference since he had last talked to him. Randy was not only roused; he was ready to look life in the face, to wrest from it the best. "If that is what love of the little girl is doing for him," said the Major to himself, "then let him love her."

Truxton continued to treat the situation lightly. "Look here," he said, "do you think you are going to be the only great man in our generation?"

Randy laughed; but the fire was still in his eyes. "The county will hold the two of us."

And now the Major spoke. "No man can be great by simply saying it. But I think most of our great men have expected things of themselves. They have dreamed dreams of greatness. I fancy that Lincoln did in his log cabin, and Roosevelt on the plains. And it wasn't egotism—it was a boy's wish to give himself to the world. And the wish was the urge. And the trouble with many of our men in these days is that they are content to dream of what they can get instead of what they can do. Paine has the right idea. There must be a day's work no matter how hard, and it must be done well, but beyond that must be a dream of bigger things for the future—"

Truxton stood up. "I asked for bread and you have given me—caviar. Sufficient unto the day is the greatness thereof. And in the meantime, Randy, I will make the grand gesture—and help you sell cars." He was grinning as he left them. "Good-bye, Major. Good-bye, T. Jefferson, Jr. Let me know when you want me in your Cabinet."

It was late that afternoon that Mary, looking for her husband, found him in the Judge's library.

"What are you doing?" she asked, with lively curiosity.

Truxton was sitting on the floor with a pile of calf-bound books beside him.

"What are you doing, lover?"

"Come here and I'll tell you." He made a seat for her of four of the big books. His arm went around her and he laid his head against her shoulder.

"Mary," he said, "I am carving a pedestal."

"You are what?"

He explained. He laughed a great deal as he gave her an account of his conversation with the Major and Randy that morning.

"You see before you," with a final flourish, "a potential great man. A Thomas Jefferson, up-to-date; a John Randolph of the present day; the Lincoln of my own time; the ancestor of Fiddle's great-grandchildren."

She rumpled his hair. "I like you as you are."

He caught her hand and held it. "But you'd like me on—a pedestal?"

"If you'll let me help you carve it."

He kissed the hand that he held. "If I am ever anything more than I am," he said, and now he was not laughing, "it will be because of you—my dearest darling."

CHAPTER XII

INDIAN—INDIAN

I

The Merriweather fortunes had not been affected by the fall of the Confederacy. There had been money invested in European ventures, and when peace had come in sixty-five, the old grey stone house had again flung wide its doors to the distinguished guests who had always honored it, and had resumed its ancient custom of an annual harvest ball.

The ballroom, built at the back of the main house, was connected with it by wide curving corridors, which contained the family portraits, and which had long windows which opened out on little balconies. On the night of the ball these balconies were lighted by round yellow lanterns, so that the effect from the outside was that of a succession of full moons.

The ballroom was octagonal, and canopied with a blue ceiling studded with silver stars. There were cupids with garlands on the side walls, and faded blue brocade hangings. Across one end of the ballroom was the long gallery reserved for those whom the Merriweathers still called "the tenantry," and it was here that Mary and Mrs. Flippin always sat after baking cakes.

Mrs. Flippin had not baked the cakes to-day, nor was she in the gallery, for her daughter, Mary, was among the guests on the ballroom floor, and her mother's own good sense had kept her at home.

"I shall look after Miss MacVeigh," she had said. "I want Truxton to bring you over and show you in your pretty new dress."

When they came, Madge, who was sitting up, insisted that she, too, must see Mary. "My dear, my dear," she said, "what a wonderful frock."

"Yes," Mary said, "it is. It is one of Becky's, and she gave it to me. And the turquoises are Mrs. Beaufort's."

Madge, who knew the whole alphabet of smart costumers, was aware of the sophisticated perfection of that fluff of jade green tulle. The touch of gold at the girdle, the flash of gold for the petticoat. She guessed the price, a stiff one, and wondered that Mary should speak of it casually as "one of Becky's."

"The turquoises are the perfect touch."

"That was Becky's idea. It seemed queer to me at first, blue with the green. But she said if I just wore this band around my hair, and the ring. And it does seem right, doesn't it?"

"It is perfect. What is Miss Bannister wearing?"

"Silver and white—lace, you know. The new kind, like a cobweb—with silver underneath—and a rose-colored fan—and pearls. You should see her pearls, Miss MacVeigh. Tell her about them, Truxton."

"Well, once upon a time they belonged to a queen. Becky's great-grandfather on the Meredith side was a diplomat in Paris, and he bought them, or so the story runs. Becky only wears a part of them. The rest are in the family vaults."

Madge listened, and showed no surprise. But that account of lace and silver, and priceless pearls did not sound in the least like the new little girl about whom George had, in the few times that she had seen him of late, been so silent.

"If only Flora would get well, and let me leave this beastly hole," had been the burden of his complaint.

"I thought you liked it."

"It is well enough for a time."

"What about the new little girl?"

He was plainly embarrassed, but bluffed it out. "I wish you wouldn't ask questions."

"I wish you wouldn't be—rude—Georgie-Porgie."

"I hate that name, Madge. Any man has a right to be rude when a woman calls him 'Georgie-Porgie.'"

"So that's it? Well, now run along. And please don't come again until you are nice—and smiling."

"Oh, look here, Madge."

"Run along—"

"But there isn't any place to run."

Laughter lurked in her eyes. "Oh, Georgie-Porgie—for once in your life can't you run away?"

"Do you think you are funny?"

"Perhaps not. Smile a little, Georgie."

"How can anybody smile, with everybody sick?"

"Oh, no, we're not. We are better. I am so glad that Flora is improving."

"Oscar thinks it is because that little old man prayed for her. Fancy Oscar—"

Madge meditated. "Yet it might be, you know, George. There are things in that old man's petition that transcend all our philosophy."

"Oh, you're as bad as Oscar," said George. He rose and stood frowning on the threshold. "Well, good-bye, Madge."

"Good-bye, Georgie, and smile when you come again."

She had guessed then that something had gone wrong in the game with the new little girl. She had a consuming curiosity to know the details. But she could never force things with Georgie. Some day, perhaps, he would tell her.

And now here was news indeed! She waited until young Beaufort and his wife had driven away, and until Mrs. Flippin had time for that quiet hour by her bedside.

"Mary looked lovely," said Madge.

"Didn't she?" Mrs. Flippin rocked and talked. "You would never have known that dress was made for anybody but for Mary. Becky gave Mary another dress out of a lot she had down from New York. It is yellow organdie, made by hand and with little embroidered scallops."

Madge knew the house which made a specialty of those organdie gowns with embroidered scallops, and she knew the price.

"But how does—Becky manage to have such lovely things?"

"Oh, she's rich," Mrs. Flippin was rocking comfortably. "You would never know it, and nobody thinks of it much. But she's got money. From her grandmother. And there was something in the will about having her live out of the world as long as she could. That's why they sent her to a convent and kept her down here as much as possible. She ain't ever seemed to care for clothes. She could always have had anything she wanted, but she ain't cared. She told Mary that she had a sudden notion to have some pretty things, and she sent for them, and it was lucky for Mary that she did. She couldn't have gone to this ball, for there wasn't any time to get anything made. Mr. Flippin and I are going to buy her some nice things when she goes to Richmond. But they won't be like the things that Becky gets, of course."

Madge, listening to further details of the Meredith fortunes, wondered how much of this Georgie knew. "Becky's mother died when she was five, and her father two years later," Mrs. Flippin was saying. "She might have been spoiled to death if she had been brought up as some children are. But she has spent her winters at the convent with Sister Loretto, and she's never worn much of anything but the uniform of the school. You wouldn't think that she had any money to see her, would you, Miss MacVeigh?"

"No, you wouldn't," said Madge, truthfully.

It was after nine o'clock—a warm night—with no sound but the ticking of the clock and the insistent hum of locusts.

"Mrs. Flippin," said Madge, "I wish you'd call up Hamilton Hill and ask for Mr. Dalton, and tell him that Miss MacVeigh would like to have him come and see her if he has nothing else on hand."

Mrs. Flippin looked her astonishment. "To-night?"

"Oh, I am not going to receive him this way," Madge reassured her. "If he can come, I'll get nurse to dress me and make me comfy in the sitting-room."

Having ascertained that Dalton would be over at once, the nurse was called, and Madge was made ready. It was a rather high-handed proceeding, and both Mrs. Flippin and the nurse stood aghast.

The nurse protested. "You really ought not, Miss MacVeigh."

"I love to do things that I ought not to do."

"But you'll tire yourself."

"If you were my Mary," said Mrs. Flippin severely, "I wouldn't let you have your way—"

"I love to have my own way, Mrs. Flippin. And—I am not your Mary"—then fearing that she had hurt the kind heart, she caught Mrs. Flippin's hand in her own and kissed it,—"but I wish I were. You're such a lovely mother."

Mrs. Flippin smiled at her. "I'm as near like your mother as a hen is mother to a bluebird."

Madge, robed in the mauve gown, refused to have her hair touched. "I like it in braids," and so when George came there she sat in the sitting-room, all gold and mauve—a charming picture for his sulky eyes.

"Oh," she said, as he came in, in a gray sack suit, with a gray cap in his hand, "why, you aren't even dressed for dinner!"

"Why should I be?" he demanded. "Kemp has left me."

She had expected something different. "Kemp?"

"Yes."

"Why?"

"He didn't give any reason. Just said he was going—and went. He said he had intended to go before, and had only stayed until Mrs. Waterman was better. Offered to stay on a little longer if it would embarrass me any to have him leave. I told him that if he wanted to go, he could get out now. And he is packing his bags."

"But what will you do without him?"

"I have wired to New York for a Jap."

"Where will Kemp go?"

"To King's Crest. To work for that lame officer—Prime."

"Oh—Major Prime? How did it happen?"

"Heaven only knows. I call it a mean trick."

"Well, of course, Kemp had a right to go if he wanted to. And perhaps you will like a Jap better. You always said Kemp was too independent."

"He is," shortly, "but I hate to be upset. It seems as if everything goes wrong these days. What did you want with me, Madge?"

Her eyelashes flickered as she surveyed him. "I wanted to see you—smile, Georgie."

"You didn't bring me down here to tell me that—" But in spite of himself the corners of his lips curled. "Oh, what's the answer, Madge?" he said, and laughed in spite of himself.

"I wanted to talk a little about—your Becky."

His laughter died at once. "Well, I'm not going to talk about her."

"Please—I am dying of curiosity—I hear that she is very—rich, Georgie."

"Rich?"

"Yes. She has oodles of money—"

"I don't believe it."

"But it is true, Georgie."

"Who told you?"

"Mrs. Flippin."

"It is all—rot—"

"It isn't rot, Georgie. Mrs. Flippin knows about it. Becky inherits from her Meredith grandmother. And her grandfather is Admiral Meredith of Nantucket, with a big house on Beacon Street in Boston. And they all belong to the inner circle."

He stared at her. "But Becky doesn't look it. She doesn't wear rings and things."

"'Rings on her fingers and bells on her toes'? Oh, George, did you think it had to be like that when people had money? Why, her pearls belonged to a queen." She told him their history.

It came back to him with a shock that he had said to Becky that the pearls cheapened her. "If they were *real*," he had said.

"It was rather strange the way I found it out," Madge was saying. "Mary Flippin had on the most perfect gown—with all the marks on it of exclusive Fifth Avenue. She was going to the Merriweather ball, and Becky is to be there."

She saw him gather himself together. "It is rather a Cinderella story, isn't it?" he asked, with assumed lightness.

"Yes," she said, "but I thought you'd like to know."

"What if I knew already?"

She laughed and let it go at that. "I'm lonesome, Georgie, talk to me," she said. But he was not in a mood to talk. And at last she sent him away. And when he had gone she sat there a long time and thought about him. There had been a look in his eyes which made her almost sorry. It seemed incredible as she came to think of it that anybody should ever be sorry for Georgie.

II

Since that night with Becky in the garden at Huntersfield George had been torn by conflicting emotions. He knew himself at last in love. He knew himself beaten at the game by a little shabby girl, and a lanky youth who had been her champion.

He would not acknowledge that the thing was ended, and in the end he had written her a letter. He cried to Heaven that a marriage between her and young Paine would be a crime. "How can you love him, Becky—you are mine."

The letter had been returned unopened. His burning phrases might have been dead ashes for all the good they had done. She had not read them.

And now Madge had told him the unbelievable thing—that Becky Bannister, the shabby Becky of the simple cottons and the stubbed shoes, was rich, not as Waterman was rich, flamboyantly, vulgarly, with an eye to letting all the world know. But rich in a thoroughbred fashion, scorning display—he knew the kind, secure in a knowledge of the unassailable assets of birth and breeding and solid financial standing.

No wonder young Paine wanted to marry her. George, driving through the night, set his teeth. He was seeing Randy, poor as Job's turkey, with Becky's money for a background.

Well, he should not have it. He should not have Becky.

George headed his car for the Merriweathers'. Becky was there, and he was going to see Becky. How he was to see her he left to the inspiration of the moment.

He parked his car by the road, and walked through the great stone gates. The palatial residence was illumined from top to bottom, its windows great squares of gold against the night. The door stood open, but except for a servant or two there was no one in the wide hall. The guests were dancing in the ballroom at the back, and George caught the lilt of the music as he skirted the house, then the sound of voices, the light laughter of the women, the deeper voices of the men.

The little balconies, lighted by the yellow lanterns, were empty. As soon as the music stopped they would be filled with dancers seeking the coolness of the outer air. He stood looking up, and suddenly, as if the stage had been set, Becky stepped out on the balcony straight in front of him, and stood under the yellow lantern. The light was dim, but it gave to her white skin, to her lace frock, to the pink fan, a faint golden glow. She might have been transmuted from flesh into some fine metal. George had not heard the Major's name for her, "Mademoiselle Midas," but he had a feeling that the little golden figure was symbolic—here was the real Golden Girl for him—not Madge or any other woman.

Randy was with her, back in the shadow, but unmistakable, his lean height, the lift of his head.

George moved forward until, hidden by a bush, he was almost under the balcony. He could catch the murmur of their voices. But not a word that they said was intelligible.

They were talking of Mary. Her introduction to her husband's friends had been an ordeal for Bob Flippin's daughter. But she had gone through it simply, quietly, unaffectedly, with the Judge by her side standing sponsor for his son's wife in chivalrous and stately fashion, with Mrs. Beaufort at her elbow helping her over the initial small talk of her presentation. With Truxton beaming, and with Becky drawing her into that charmed circle of the younger set which might so easily have shut her out. More than one of those younger folk had had it in mind that at last year's ball Mary Flippin had sat in the gallery. But not even the most snobbish of them would have dared to brave Becky Bannister's displeasure. Back of her clear-eyed serenity was a spirit which flamed and a strength which accomplished. Becky was an amiable young person who could flash fire at unfairness or injustice or undue assumption of superiority.

The music had stopped and the balconies were filled. George, in the darkness, was aware of the beauty of the scene—the lantern making yellow moons—the golden groups beneath them. Mary and Truxton with a friend or two were in the balcony adjoining the one where Becky sat with young Paine.

"Isn't she a dear and a darling, Randy?" Becky was saying; "and how well she carries it off. Truxton is so proud of her, and she is so pretty."

"She can't hold a candle to you, Becky."

"It is nice of you to say it." She leaned on the stone balustrade and swung her fan idly.

"I am not saying it to be nice."

"Aren't you—oh—!" She gave a quick exclamation.

"What's the matter?"

"I dropped my fan."

"I'll go and get it," he said, and just then the music started.

"No," said Becky, "never mind now. This is your dance with

Mary—and she mustn't be kept waiting."

"Aren't you dancing this?"

"It is Truxton's, and I begged off. Run along, dear boy."

When he was gone she leaned over the rail. Below was a tangle of bushes, and the white gleam of a stone bench. Beyond the bushes was a path, and farther on a fountain. It was a rather imposing fountain, with a Neptune in bronze riding a seahorse, with nymphs on dolphins in attendance. Neptune poured water from a shell which he held in his hand, and the dolphins spouted great streams. The splash of the water was a grateful sound in the stillness of the hot night, and the mist which the slight breeze blew towards a bed of tuberoses seemed to bring out their heavy fragrance. Always afterwards when Becky thought of that night, there would come to her again that heavy scent and the splash of streaming water.

"Becky," a voice came up from below, "I have your fan."

She peered down into the darkness, but did not speak.

"Becky, I am punished enough, and I am—starved for you—"

"Give me my fan—"

"I want to talk to you—I must—talk to you—"

"Give me my fan—"

"I can't reach—"

"You can stand on that bench."

He stood on it, and she could see his figure faintly defined.

"I am afraid I am still too far away. Lean over a bit, Becky—and I'll hand it to you."

She stretched her white arm down into the darkness. Her hand was caught in a strong clasp. "Becky, give me just five minutes by the fountain."

"Let me go."

"Not until you promise that you'll come."

"I shall never promise."

"Then I shall keep your fan—"

"Keep it—I have others."

"But you will think about this one, because I have it." There was a note of triumph in his soft laugh.

He kissed her finger-tips and reluctantly released her hand. "The fan is mine, then, until you ask for it."

"I shall never ask."

"Who knows? Some day you may—who knows?" and he was gone.

He could not have chosen a better way in which to fire her imagination. His voice in the dark, his laughing triumph, the daring theft of her fan. Her heart followed him, seeing him a Conqueror even in this, seeing him a robber with his rose-colored booty, a Robin Hood of the Garden, a Dick Turpin among the tuberoses.

The spirit of Romance went with him. The things that Pride had done for her looked gray and dull. She had promised to marry Randy, and felt that she faced a somewhat sober future. Set against it was all that George had given her, the sparkle and dash and color of his ardent pursuit.

He was not worth a thought, yet she thought of him. She was still thinking of him when Randy came back.

"Did you get your fan?" he asked.

"No. Never mind, Randy. I will have one of the servants look for it."

"But I do mind."

She hesitated. "Well, don't look for it now. Let's go in and join the others. Are they going down to supper?"

Supper was served in the great Hunt Room, which was below the ballroom. It was a historic and picturesque place, and had been the scene for over a century of merry-making before and after the fox-hunts for which the county was famous. There were two great fireplaces, almost hidden to-night by the heaped-up fruits of the harvest, orange and red and green, with cornstalks and goldenrod from the fields for decorations.

Becky found Mary alone at a small table in a corner. Truxton had left her to forage for refreshments and Randy followed him.

"Are you having a good time, Mary?"

Mary did not answer at once. Then she said, bravely, "I don't quite fit in, Becky. I am still an—outsider."

"Oh, Mary!"

"I am not—unhappy, and Truxton is such a dear. But I shall be glad to get home, Becky."

"But you look so lovely, Mary, and everybody seems so kind."

"They are, but underneath I am just plain—Mary Flippin. They know that, and so do I, and it will take them some time to forget it."

There was an anxious look in Becky's eyes. "It seems to me that you are feeling it more than the others."

"Perhaps. And I shouldn't have said anything. Don't let Truxton know."

"Has anyone said anything to hurt you, Mary?"

"No, but when I dance with the men, I can't speak their language. I haven't been to the places—I don't know the people. I am on the outside."

Becky had a sudden forlorn sense that things were wrong with the whole world. But she didn't want Mary to be unhappy.

"Truxton loves you," she said, "and you love him. Don't let anything make you miserable when you have—that. Nothing else counts, Mary."

There was a note of passion in her voice which brought a pulsing response from Mary.

"It *is* the only thing that counts, Becky. How silly I am to worry."

Her young husband was coming towards her—flushed and eager, a prince among men, and he was hers!

As he sat down beside her, her hand sought his under the table.

He looked down at her. "Happy, little girl?"

"Very happy, lover."

III

Caroline Paine was having the time of her life. She wore a new dress of thin midnight blue which Randy had bought for her and which was very becoming; her hair was waved and dressed, and she had Major Prime as an attentive listener while she talked of the past and linked it with the present.

"Of course there was a time when the men drank themselves under the tables. Everybody calls them the 'good old times,' but I reckon they were bad old times in some ways, weren't they? There was hot blood, and there were duels. There's no denying it was picturesque, Major, but it was foolish for all that. Men don't settle things now by shooting each other, except in a big way like the war. The last duel was fought by the old fountain out there—one of the Merriweathers met one of the Paines. Merriweather was killed, and the girl died of a broken heart."

"Then it was Merriweather that she loved?"

"Yes. And young Paine went abroad, and joined the British army and was killed in India. So nobody was happy, and all because there was, probably, a flowing bowl at the harvest ball. I am glad they don't do it that way now. Just think of my Randy stripped to his shirt and with pistols for two. We are more civilized in these days and I'm glad of it."

"Are we?" said the Major; "I'm not sure. But I hope so."

Randy came by just then and spoke to them. "Are you getting everything you want, Mother?"

"Yes, indeed. The Major looked after me. I've had salad twice, and everything else—"

"That sounds greedy, but it isn't, not when you think of the groaning boards of other days. Has she been telling you about them, Major?"

"Yes, she has peopled the room with ghosts—"

"Now, Major!"

"Pleasant ghosts—in lace ruffles and velvet coats, smoking long pipes around a punch bowl; beautiful ghosts in patches and powder," he made an expressive gesture; "they have mingled with the rest of you—shadow-shapes of youth and loveliness."

"Well, if anybody can tell about it, Mother can," said Randy, "but I don't believe there were ever any prettier girls than are here to-night."

"Becky looks like an angel," Mrs. Paine stated, "but she's pale, Randy."

"She is tired, Mother. I think she ought to go home. I shall try to make her when I come back. She dropped her fan and I am going to get it."

He had not told Becky where he was going. He had slipped away—his mind intent on regaining her property. But when he reached the bushes and flashed his pocket-light on the ground beneath, there was no fan. It must have fallen here. He was sure he had made no mistake.

He decided finally that someone else had found it. It seemed unlikely, however, for the spot was remote, and the thickness of the bushes offered a barrier to anyone strolling casually through the grounds.

He went slowly back to the house. Ever since that night when Becky had said she would marry him he had lived in a dream. They were pledged to each other, yet she did not love him. How could he take her? And again, how could he give her up? She had offered herself freely, and he wanted her in his future. And there was a fighting chance. He had youth and courage and a love for her he challenged any man to match. Why not? Was it beyond the bounds of reason that some day he could make Becky love him?

They had agreed that no one was to be told. "Not until I come back from Nantucket," Becky had stipulated.

"By that time you won't want me, my dear."

"Well, I shan't if you talk like that," Becky had said with some spirit.

"Like what?"

"As if I were a queen and you were a slave. When you were a little boy you bossed me, Randy."

There had been a gleam in his eye. "I may again."

He wondered if, after all, that would be the way to win her. Yet he shrank from playing a game. When she came to him, if she ever came, it must be because she found something in him that was love-worthy. At least he could make himself worthy of love, whether she ever came to him or not.

He stopped by the fountain; just beyond it the long windows of the Hunt Room opened out upon the lawn. The light lay in golden squares upon the grass. Randy, still in the shadow, stood for a moment looking in. There were long tables and little ones, kaleidoscopic color, movement and light, and Becky back in her corner in the midst of a gay group.

He was aware, suddenly, that he was not the only one who watched. Half hidden by the shadows of one of the great pillars of the lower porch was a man in light flannels and a gray cap.

He was not skulking, and indeed he seemed to have a splendid indifference to discovery. He was staring at Becky and in his hand, a blaze of lovely color against his coat, was Becky's fan!

Randy took a step forward. George turned and saw him.

"I was looking for that," Randy said, and held out his hand for the fan.

But Dalton did not give it to him. "She knows I have it."

"How could she know?" Randy demanded; "she dropped it from the balcony."

"And I was under the balcony"—George's laugh was tantalizing,—"a patient Romeo."

"You picked it up."

"I picked it up. And she knew that I did. Didn't she tell you?"

She had not told him. He remembered now her unwillingness to have him search for it.

He had no answer for George. But again he held out his hand.

"She will be glad to get it. Will you give it to me?"

"She told me I might—keep it."

"Keep it—?"

"For remembrance."

There was a tense pause. "If that is true," said Randy, "there is, of course, nothing else for me to say."

He turned to go, but George stopped him. "Wait a minute. You are going to marry her?"

"Yes."

"And she is very—rich."

"Her money does not enter into the matter."

"Some people might think it did. There are those who might be unkind enough to call you a—fortune-hunter."

"I shall be called nothing of the kind by those who know me."

"But there are so many who don't know you."

"I wonder," said Randy, fiercely, "why I am staying here and letting you say such things to me. There is nothing you can say which can hurt me. Becky knows—God knows, that I wish she were as poor as poverty. Perhaps money doesn't mean as much to us as it does to you. I wish I had it, yes—so that I could give it to her. But love for us means a tent in the desert—a hut on a mountain—it can never mean what we could buy with money."

"Does love mean to her," George's tone was incisive, "a tent in the desert, a hut on a mountain?"

Randy's anger flamed. "I think," he said, "that I should beg Becky's pardon for bringing her name into this at all—And now, will you give me her fan?"

"When she asks for it—yes."

Randy was breathing heavily. "Will you give me her—fan—"

The mist from the fountain blew cool against his hot cheeks. The water which old Neptune poured from his shell flashed white under the stars.

"Let her ask for it—" George's laugh was light.

It was that laugh which made Randy see red. He caught George's wrists suddenly in his hands. "Drop it."

George stopped laughing. "Let her ask for it," he said again.

Randy twisted the wrists. It was a cruel trick. But his Indian blood was uppermost.

"Drop it," he said, with another twist, and the fan fell.

But Randy was not satisfied. "Do you think," he said, "that I am through with you? What you need is tar and feathers, but failing that—" he did not finish his sentence. He caught George around the body and began to push him back towards the fountain.

George fought doggedly—but Randy was strong with the muscular strength of youth and months of military training.

"I'll kill you for this," George kept saying.

"No," said Randy, conserving his breath, "they don't—do it—in—these—days—"

He had Dalton now at the rim and with a final effort of strength he lifted him—there was a splash, and into the deeps of the great basin went George, while the bronze Neptune, and the bronze dolphins, and the nymphs with flowing hair, splashed and spouted a welcoming chorus that drowned his cry!

Randy, head up, eyes shining, marched into the house and had a servant brush him off and powder a scratch on his chin;

then he went down-stairs to the Hunt Room and strode across the room until he came to where Becky sat in her corner.

"I found your fan," he told her, and laid it, a blaze of lovely color, on the table in front of her.

CHAPTER XIII

THE WHISTLING SALLY

I

Becky, as she journeyed towards the north, had carried with her a vision of a new and rather disturbing Randy—a Randy who, striding across the Hunt Room with high-held head, had delivered her fan, and had, later, asked for an explanation.

"How did he get it, Becky?"

She had told him.

"Why didn't you tell me when I came back and said I would go for it?"

"I was afraid he might still be there."

"Well?"

"And that something might happen."

Something had happened later by the fountain. But Randy did not speak of it. "I saw the fan in his hand and asked for it," grimly, "and he gave it to me—"

On the night before she went away, Randy had said, "I can't tell you all that you mean to me, Becky, and I am not going to try. But I am yours always—remember that—" He had kissed her hand and held it for a moment against his heart. Then he had left her, and Becky had wanted to call him back and say something that she felt had been left unsaid, but had found that she could not.

Admiral Meredith met his granddaughter in New York, and the rest of the trip was made with him.

Admiral Meredith was as different from Judge Bannister in his mental equipment as he was in physical appearance. He was a short little man, who walked with a sailor's swing, and who laughed like a fog-horn. He had ruddy cheeks, and the manners of a Chesterfield. If he lacked the air of aristocratic calm which gave distinction to Judge Bannister, he supplied in its place a sophistication due to his contact with a world which moved faster than the Judge's world in Virginia.

He adored Becky, and resented her long sojourn in the South. "I believe you love the Judge better than you do me," he told her, as he turned to her in the taxi which took them from the train to the boat.

"I don't love anybody better than I do you," she said, and tucked her hand in his.

"What have they been doing to you?" he demanded; "you are

as white as paper."

"Well, it has been hot."

"Of all the fool things to keep you down there in summer. I am going to take you straight to 'Sconset to the Whistling Sally and keep you there for a month."

"The Whistling Sally" was the Admiral's refuge when he was tired of the world. It was a gray little house set among other gray little houses across the island from Nantucket town. It stood on top of the bluff and overlooked a sea which stretched straight to Spain. It was called "The Whistling Sally" because a ship's figure-head graced its front yard, the buxom half of a young woman who blew out her cheeks in a perpetual piping, and whose faded colors spoke eloquently of the storms which had buffeted her.

The Admiral, as has been indicated, had an imposing mansion in Nantucket town. For two months in the summer he entertained his friends in all the glory of a Colonial background—white pillars, spiral stairway, polished floors, Chinese Chippendale, lacquered cabinets, old china and oil portraits. He gave dinners and played golf, he had a yacht and a motor boat, he danced when the spirit moved him, and was light on his feet in spite of his years. He was adored by the ladies, lionized by everybody, and liked it.

But when the summer was over and September came, he went to Siasconset and reverted to the type of his ancestors. He hobnobbed with the men and women who had been the friends and neighbors of his forbears. He doffed his sophistication as he doffed his formal clothes. He wore a slicker on wet days, and the rain dripped from his rubber hat. He sat knee to knee with certain cronies around the town pump. He made chowder after a famous recipe, and dug clams when the spirit moved him.

His housekeeper, Jane, adjourned from the town house to "The Whistling Sally" when Becky was there; at other times the Admiral did for himself, keeping the little cottage as neat as a pin, and cooking as if he were born to it.

It seemed to Becky that as the long low island rose from the sea, the burdens which she had carried for so long dropped from her. There were the houses on the cliff, the glint of a gilded dome, and then, gray and blue and green the old town showed against the skyline, resolving itself presently into roofs, and church towers, and patches of trees, with long piers stretching out through shallow waters, boat-houses, fishing smacks, and at last a thin line of people waiting on the wharf.

The air was like wine. The sky was blue with the deep sapphire which follows a wind-swept night. There was not a hint of mist or fog. Flocks of gulls rose and dipped and rose again, or rested unafraid on the wooden posts of the pier.

The 'Sconset bus was waiting and they took it. Until two years ago no automobiles had been allowed on the island, but there had been the triumph of utility over the picturesque and quaint, and now one motored across the moor on smooth asphalt, in one-half the time that the trip had been made in the old days.

The Admiral did not like it. He admitted that it was quicker. "But we used to see the pheasants fly up from the bushes, and the ducks from the pools, and now they are gone before we can get our eyes on them."

Becky was not in a captious mood. The moor was before her, rising and falling in low unwooded hills, amber with dwarf gold-enrod, red with the turning huckleberry, purple with drying grasses, green with a thousand lovely growing things still unpainted by the brush of autumn. The color was almost unbelievably gorgeous. Even the pools by the roadside were almost unbelievably blue, as if the water had been dyed with indigo, and above all was that incredible blue sky—!

Then out of the distance clear cut like cardboard the houses lifted themselves above the horizon, with the sea a wall to the right, and to the left, across the moor, the Sankaty lighthouse, white and red with the sun's rays striking across it.

They entered the village between rows of pleasant informal residences, many of them closed until another season; they passed the tennis courts, and came to the post-office, with its flag flying. The bus stopped, and they found Tristram waiting for them.

"Tristram" is an old name in Nantucket. There was a Tristram among the nine men who had purchased the island from Thomas Mayhew in 1659 for "30 pounds current pay and two beaver hats." The present Tristram wore the name appropriately. Fair-haired and tall, not young but towards the middle-years, strong with the strength of one who lives out-of-doors in all weathers, browned with the wind and sun, blue-eyed, he called no man master, and was the owner of his own small acres.

Like the Admiral, he gave himself up for two months of the year to the summer people. If his association with them was a business rather than a social affair, it was, none the less, interesting. The occupation of Nantucket by "off-islanders" was a matter of infinite speculation and amusement. Into the serenity of his life came restless men and women who golfed and swam and rode and danced, who chafed when it rained, and complained of the fog, who seemed endlessly trying to get something out of life and who were endlessly bored, who wondered how Tristram could stand the solitudes and who pitied him.

Tristram knew that he did not need their pity. He had a thousand things that they did not have. He was never bored, and he was too busy to manufacture amusements. There were always things happening on the island—each day brought something different.

To-day, it was the winter gulls. "They are coming down—lots of them from the north," he told the Admiral as they drove through the quaint settlement with its gray little houses, "the big ones—"

There was also the *gerardia*, pale pink and shading into mauve. He had brought a great bunch to "The Whistling Sally," and had put it in a bowl of gray pottery.

When Becky saw the flowers, she knew whom to thank. "Oh, Tristram," she said, "you found them on the moor."

Tristram, standing in the little front room of the Admiral's cottage, seemed to tower to the ceiling. "The Whistling Sally" from the outside had the look of a doll's house, too small for human habitation. Within it was unexpectedly commodious. It had the shipshape air of belonging to a seafaring man. The rooms were all on one floor. There was the big front room, which served as a sitting-room and dining-room. It had a table built out from the wall with high-backed benches on each side of it, and a rack for glasses overhead. There was a window above the table which looked out towards the sea. The walls were painted blue, and there was an old brick fireplace. A model of a vessel from which the figure-head in the front yard had been taken was over the mantel, flanked by an old print or two of Nantucket in the past. There were Windsor chairs and a winged chair; some pot-bellied silver twinkled in a corner cupboard.

The windows throughout were low and square and small-paned and white-curtained. The day was cool, and there was a fire on the hearth. The blaze and the pink flowers, and the white curtains gave to the little room an effect of brightness, although outside the early twilight was closing in.

Jane came in with her white apron and added another high light. She kissed Becky. "Did your grandfather tell you that Mr. Cope is coming over to have chowder?" she asked.

It would be impossible to describe Jane's way of saying "chowder." It had no "r," and she clipped it off at the end. But it is the only way in the world, and the people who so pronounce it are usually the only people in the world who can make it.

"Who is Mr. Cope?" Becky asked.

Mr. Cope, it seemed, had a cottage across the road from the Admiral's. He leased it, and it was his first season at 'Sconset. His sister had been with him only a week ago. She had gone "off-shore," but she was coming back.

"Is he young?" Becky asked.

"Well, he isn't old," said Jane, "and he's an artist."

Becky was not in the least interested in Mr. Cope, so she talked to Tristram until he had to go back to his farm and the cows that waited to be milked. Then Becky went into her room, and took off her hat and coat and ran a comb through the bronze waves of her hair. She did not change the straight serge frock in which she had travelled. She went back into the front room and found that Mr. Cope had come.

He was not old. That was at once apparent. And he was not young. He did not look in the least like an artist. He seemed, rather, like a prosperous business man. He wore a Norfolk suit, and his reddish hair was brushed straight back from his forehead. He had rather humorous gray eyes, and Becky thought there was a look of delicacy about his white skin. Later he spoke of having come for his health, and she learned that he had a weak heart.

He had a pleasant laughing voice. He belonged to Boston, but had lived abroad for years.

"With nothing to show for it," he told her with a shrug, "but one portrait. I painted my sister, and she kept that. But before we left Paris we burned the rest—"

"Oh, how dreadful," Becky cried.

"No, it wasn't dreadful. They were not worth keeping. You see, I played a lot and made sketches and things, and then there was the war—and I wasn't very well."

He had had two years of aviation, and after that a desk in the War Department.

"And now I am painting again."

"Gardens?" Becky asked, "or the sea?"

"Neither. I am trying to paint the moor. I'll show you in the morning."

The Admiral was in the kitchen, superintending the chowder. Jane knew how to make it, and he knew that she knew. But he always went into the kitchen at the psychological moment, tied on an apron, and put in the pilot crackers. Then he brought the chowder in, in a big porcelain tureen which was shaped like a goose. Becky loved him in his white apron, with his round red face, and the porcelain goose held high.

"If you could paint him like that," she suggested to Archibald Cope.

"Do you think he would let me?" eagerly.

After supper the two men smoked by the fire, and Becky sat between them and watched the blaze. She heard very little of the conversation. Her mind was in Albemarle. How far away it seemed! Just three nights ago she had danced at the Merriweathers' ball, and George had held her hand as she leaned over the balcony.

"If you can bring yourself back for a moment, Becky, to present company," her grandfather was saying, "you can tell Mr. Cope whether you will walk with us to-morrow to Tom Never's."

"I'd love it."

"Really?" Cope asked. "You are sure you won't be too tired?"

"Not in this air. I feel as if I could walk forever."

"How about a bit of a walk to-night—up to the bluff? Is it too late, Admiral?"

"Not for you two. I'll finish my pipe, and read my papers."

The young people followed the line of the bluff until they came to an open space which looked towards the east. To the left of them was the ridge with a young moon hanging low above it, and straight ahead, brighter than the moon, whitening the heavens, stretching out and out until it reached the sailors in their ships, was the Sankaty light.

"I always come out to look at it before I go to bed," said Cope; "it is such a *living* thing, isn't it?"

The wind was rising and they could hear the sound of the sea. Becky caught her breath. "On dark nights I like to think how it must look to the ships beyond the shoals—"

"The sea is cruel," said Cope; "that's why I don't paint it."

"Oh, it isn't always cruel."

"When isn't it? Last year, with the submarines, it was—a monster. I saw a picture once in a gallery, 'The Eternal Siren,' just the sea. And a woman asked, 'Where's the Siren?'"

Becky laughed. "If you had sailor blood in you, you wouldn't feel that way. Ask Grandfather."

"The Admiral is prejudiced. He loves—the siren—"

"He would tell you that the sea isn't a siren. It's a bold, blustering lass like the Whistling Sally out there in the front yard. Man has tamed her even if he hasn't quite mastered her."

"He will never master her. She will go on and on, after we are dead, through the ages, wooing men to—destruction—"

Becky shivered. "I hate to think of things—after we are dead."

"Do you? I don't. I like to think way beyond the ages to the time when there shall be no more sea—"

He pulled himself up abruptly. "I am talking rather dismally, I am afraid, about death and destruction. You won't want to walk with me again."

"Oh, yes, I shall. And I want to see your pictures."

"You may not care for them. Lots of people don't. But I have to work in my own way—"

As they walked back, he told her what he was trying to do. As she listened, Becky seemed to have two minds, one that caught his words, and answered them, and another which went back and back to the things which had happened since she had last walked this bluff with the wind in her face and the sound of the sea in her ears.

It seemed to her as if a lifetime had elapsed since last she had looked at the Sankaty light.

II

When Becky wrote to Randy, she had a great deal to say about Archibald Cope.

"He is trying to paint the moor. He wants to get its meaning, and then make other people see what it means. He doesn't look in the least like that, Randy—as if he were finding the spirit of things. He has red hair and wears correct clothes, and says the right things, and you feel as if he ought to be in Wall Street buying bonds. But here he is, refusing to believe that anything he has done is worth while until he does it to his own satisfaction.

"We walked to Tom Never's Head yesterday. It was one of those clear silver days, a little cloudy and without much color. The cranberries are ripe, and the moor was carpeted with them. When we got to Tom Never's we sat on the edge of the bluff, and Mr. Cope told me what he meant about the moor. It has its moods, he said. On a quiet, cloudy morning, it is a Quaker lady. With the fog in, it is a White Spirit. There are purple twilights when it is—Cleopatra, and windy nights with the sun going down blood-red, when it is—Medusa—He says that the trouble with the average picture is that it is just—paint. I am not sure that I understand it all, but it is terribly interesting. And when he had talked a lot about that, he talked of the history of the island. He said that he should never be satisfied until somebody put a bronze statue of an Indian right where we stood, with his back to the sea. And when I said, 'Why with his back to it?' he said, 'Wasn't the sea cruel to the red man? It brought a conquering race in ships.'

"I told him then about our Indians in Virginia, and that some of us had a bit of red blood in our veins, and I told him that you and I always used the old Indian war cry when we called to each other, and he asked, 'Who is Randy?' and I said that you were an old friend, and that we had spent much of our childhood together."

As a matter of fact, Cope had been much interested in her account of young Paine. "Do you mean to say that he is still living on all that land?"

"Yes."

"Master of his own domain. I can't see it. The way I like to live is with a paint box, and a bag, and nothing to keep me from moving on."

"We aren't like that in the South."

"Do you like to stay in one place?"

"I never have. I have always been handed around."

"Would you like a home of your own?"

"Of course—after I am married."

"North, south, east or west?"

She put the question to him seriously. "Do you think it would make any difference if you loved a man, where you lived?"

"Well, of course, there might be difficulties—on a desert island."

"Not if you loved him."

"My sister wouldn't agree with you."

"Why not?"

"She is very modern. She says that love has nothing to do with it. Not romantic love. She says that when she marries she shall choose a man who lives in New York, who likes to go to Europe, and who hates the tropics. He must fancy pale gray walls and willow-green draperies, and he must loathe Florentine furniture. He must like music and painting, and not care much for books. He must adore French cooking, and have a prejudice against heavy roasts. He must be a Republican and High Church. She is sure that with such a man she would be happy. The dove of peace would hover over the household, because she and her husband would have nothing to quarrel about."

"Of course she doesn't mean it."

"She thinks she does."

"She won't if she is ever really in love."

He glanced at her. "Then you believe in the desert island?"

"I think I do—"

She stood up. "Did you feel a drop of rain? And Grandfather is waving."

The Admiral on the porch of the closed Lodge was calling to them to come under shelter.

It was a gentle rain, and they decided to walk home in it. They went at a smart pace, which they moderated as Cope showed signs of fatigue. "It's a beastly nuisance," he said, "to give out. I wish you would go on ahead, and let me rest here—"

They rested with him. The two men talked, and Becky was rather silent. When they started on again, Cope said to her, "Are you tired? It is a long walk."

"No," she said, "I am not tired. And I have been thinking a lot about the things you said to me."

He was not a conceited man, and he was aware that it was the things which he had said to her which had set her mind to work, not any personal fascination. She was quaint and charming, and he was glad that she had come. He had been lonely since his sister left. And his loneliness had fear back of it.

It was because of this conversation with Cope that Becky ended her letter to Randy with the following paragraph:

"Mr. Cope has a sister, Louise. She thinks that people ought to marry because they like the same things. She thinks that if two people care for the same furniture and the same religion and the same things to eat, that life will be lovely. She couldn't love a man enough to live on a desert island with him, because she adores New York. Of course, there is something in that, and if it is so, you and I ought to be very happy, Randy. We like old houses and the Virginia hills, and lots of books, and fireplaces—and dogs and horses and hot biscuits and fried chicken. It sounds awfully funny to put it that way, doesn't it, and practical? But perhaps Louise Cope is right, and one isn't likely, of course, to have the desert island test. Do you *really* think that anybody could be happy on a desert island, Randy?"

Randy replied promptly.

"If you were in love with me, Becky, you wouldn't be asking questions. You would believe that we could be blissful on a desert island. I believe it. It may not be true, yet I feel that a hut on a mountain top would be heaven for me if you were in it, Becky. In a way Cope's sister is right. The chances for happiness are greatest with those who have similar tastes, but not fried chicken tastes or identical religious opinions. These do not mean so much, but it would mean a great deal that we think alike about honesty and uprightness and truth and courage—

"And now, Becky, I might as well say it straight from the

shoulder. I haven't the least right in the world to let you feel that you are engaged to me. I shall never marry you unless you love me—unless you love me so much that you would have the illusion of happiness with me on a desert island.

"I have no right to let you tie yourself to me. The whole thing is artificial and false. You are strong enough to stand alone. I want you to stand alone, Becky, for your own sake. I want you to tell yourself that Dalton isn't worth one single thought of yours. Tell yourself the truth, Becky, about him. It is the only way to own your soul.

"You may be interested to know that the Watermans left Hamilton Hill yesterday. Dalton went with them. I haven't seen him since the night of the Merriweathers' ball. I didn't tell you, did I, that after I took the fan away from him, I dropped him into the fountain? I had much rather have tied him to a stake, and have built a fire under him, but that isn't civilized, and of course, I couldn't. But I am glad I dropped him in the fountain—"

Becky read Randy's letter as she sat alone on the beach. It was cool and sunshiny and she was wrapped in a red cape. The winter gulls were beating strong wings above the breakers, and their sharp cries cut across the roar of the waters.

There had been a storm the night before—wind booming out of the northeast and the sea still sang the song of it.

Becky felt, suddenly, that she was very angry with Randy. It was as if he had broken a lovely thing that she had worshipped. She hated to think of that struggle in the dark—She hated to think of Randy as—the Conqueror. She hated to think of George as dank and dripping. She wanted to think of him as shining and splendid, and Randy had spoiled that.

But she wanted to be fair. Hadn't George, after all, spoiled his own splendidness? He had wooed her and had run away. And he had not run back until he thought another man wanted her.

"Of course," said somebody behind her, "you won't tell me what you are thinking about. But if you will just let me sit here and think, by your side, it will be a great privilege."

It was Mr. Cope, and she was not sure that she wanted him at this moment. Perhaps something of her thought showed in her eyes, for when she said, "Oh, yes," he stood looking down at her.

"Would you rather be alone with your letters? Don't hedge and be polite. Tell me."

"Well," she admitted, "my letters are a bit on my mind. But if you don't care if I am stupid, you can stay—"

He sat down. He had known her for ten days, and dreaded to

think that in ten days more she might be gone. "I won't talk if you don't wish it."

Becky's eyes were on the sea. "I think I should like to talk. I have been thinking—about that Indian that you want commemorated in bronze up there on the bluff. Do you think he was cruel?"

"Who knows? He was, perhaps, a savage. Yet he may have been tender-hearted. I hope so, if he is going to be fixed in bronze for the ages to stare at."

"Did you," Becky asked, deliberately, "ever want to tie a man to a stake and build a fire under him?"

He turned and stared at her. "My dear child, what ever put such an idea in your head?"

"Well, did you?"

He considered it. "There was a time in France when I wanted to do worse than that."

"But that was war."

"No, it was a brute in my own company. He broke the heart of a little girl that he met in Brittany. He—he—well he murdered her—dreams."

"Perhaps he didn't know what he was doing."

"He knew. Every man knows."

"And you wanted to make him—suffer—"

"Yes."

She shivered. "Are all men like that?"

"Like what?"

"Cruel."

"It can't be cruelty. It's a sense of justice."

"I hope it is." She kept thinking about George rising dank and dripping from the fountain. She hated to think about it.

So she changed the subject. "I thought you were painting."

"I was. But the moor is fickle. Yesterday she billowed towards the south, all gray and blue. And last night the storm spoiled it; she is gorgeous and gay to-day, and I don't like her."

"Oh, why not?"

"She is too obvious. Anybody can paint a Persian carpet, but one can't put soul into a—carpet—"

He was petulant. "I shall never paint the pictures I want to paint. Life is too short."

"Life isn't short. Look at Grandfather. You will have forty years yet in which to paint."

And now it was he who changed the subject, quickly, as if he were afraid of it.

"My sister is coming to-morrow. I rather think you will like her."

"Will she like me, that's more important."

"She will love you, as I do, as everybody does, Becky."

They had reached that point in ten days that he could say such things to her and win her smile. She did not believe in the least that he loved her. He always laughed when he said it.

She liked him very much. She felt that the Admiral and Tristram and Archibald Cope were all of them the best of comrades. Except for Jane, she had had practically no feminine society since she came. And Jane was not especially inspiring, not like Tristram, who seemed to carry one's imagination back to Viking days.

Cope was immensely enthusiastic about Tristram. "If I could paint figures as I want to," he said, "I'd do Tristram as 'The Islander.' One feels that he belongs here as inevitably as the moors or the sands or the sea. Perhaps it is he who ought to be in bronze on the bluff, instead of the Indian."

"But he'd have to face the sea," said Becky.

"Yes," Cope agreed, "he would. He loves it and his ancestors lived by it. I'll stick to my Indian and the moor."

Becky gathered up her letters. "It is time for lunch, and Jane doesn't like to be kept waiting. Won't you lunch with us? Grandfather will be delighted."

"I shall get to be a perpetual guest. I feel as if I were taking advantage of your hospitality."

"We shouldn't ask you if we didn't want you."

"Then I'll come."

They walked up the beach together. Becky was muffled in her red cape, Cope had a sweater under his coat. The air was sharp and clear as crystal.

"How anybody can go in bathing in this weather," Becky shivered, as a woman ran down the sands towards the sea. She cast off her bathing cloak and stood revealed, slim and rather startling, in yellow.

"She goes in every day," said Cope, "even when it storms."

"Who is she?"

"A dancer—from New York. Haven't you seen her before?"

"No. Where is she staying?"

"At the hotel."

"I thought the hotel was closed."

"Not for three weeks. There aren't many guests. This one came up a month ago. She dances on the moor—practising for some play which opens in October."

"What's her name?"

"I don't know. They call her 'The Yellow Daffodil' because of that bathing suit."

The girl was swimming now beyond the breakers.

Becky was envious. "I wish I could swim like that."

"You can do other things—that she can't do."

"What things?"

"Well, be a lady, for example. That's not exactly cricket, is it, to draw a deadly parallel? But I don't want people like that dancing on my moor."

CHAPTER XIV

THE DANCER ON THE MOOR

I

Randy's letter had set Becky adrift. She was not in love with him. She was sure of that. And he had said he would not marry her without love. He had said that if she owned her soul she would think of Dalton as a cad and as a coward.

It seemed queer that Randy should be demanding things of her. He had always been so glad to take anything she would give, and now she had offered him herself, and he wouldn't have her. Not till she owned her soul.

She knew what he meant. The thought of George was always with her. She kept seeing him as she had first seen him at the station; as he had been that wonderful day when they had had tea in the Pavilion; the night in the music room when he had kissed her; the old garden with its pale statues and box hedges; and always there was his sparkling glance, his quick voice.

She would never own her soul until she forgot George. Until she put him out of her life; until the thought of him would not make her burn hot with humiliation; until the thought of him would not thrill to her finger-tips.

She found Cope's easy and humorous companionship a balance for her hidden emotions. And when Louise Cope came, she proved to be a rather highly emphasized counterpart of her brother. Her red-gold hair was thick and she wore it bobbed. Her skin was white but lacked the look of delicacy which seemed to contradict constantly Cope's vivid personality. She seemed to laugh at the world as he did. She called Becky "quaint," but took to her at once.

"Archie has been writing to me of you," she told Becky; "he says you came up like a bird from the south."

"Birds don't fly north in the fall—"

"Well, you were the—miracle," Cope asserted.

Louise Cope's shrewd glance studied him. "He has fallen in love with you, Becky Bannister," was her blunt assurance, "but you needn't let it worry you. As yet it is only an æsthetic passion. But there is no telling what may come of it—"

"Does he fall in love—like that?" Becky demanded.

"He has never been in love," Louise declared, "not really. Except with me."

Becky felt that the Copes were a charming pair. When she

answered Randy's letter she spoke of them.

"Louise adores her brother, and she thinks he would be a great artist if he would take himself seriously. But neither of them seems to take anything seriously. They always seem to be laughing at the world in a quiet way. Louise is not pretty, but she gives an effect of beauty—She wears a big gray cape and a black velvet tam, and I am not sure that the color in her cheeks is real. She is different from other people, but it doesn't seem to be a pose. It is just because she has lived in so many places and has seen so many people and has thought for herself. I have always let other people think for me, haven't I, Randy?

"And now that I have done with the Copes, I am going to talk about the things that you said to me in your letter, and which are really the important things.

"I hated to think that you dropped Mr. Dalton in the fountain. I hated to think that you wanted to burn him at the stake—there was something—cruel—and—dreadful in it all. I have kept thinking of that struggle between you—in the dark—I have hated to think that a few years ago if you had felt as you do about him—that you might have—killed him. But perhaps men are like that. They care more for justice than for—mercy.

"I am trying to take your advice and tell myself the truth about Mr. Dalton. That he isn't worth a thought of mine. Yet I think of him a great deal. I am being very frank with you, Randy, because we have always talked things out. I think of him, and wonder which is the real man—the one I thought he was—and I thought him very fine and splendid. Or is he just trifling and commonplace? Perhaps he is just between, not as wonderful as I thought him, nor as contemptible as I seem forced to believe.

"Yet I gave him something that it is hard to take back. I gave a great deal. You see I had always been shut up in a glass case like the bob-whites and the sandpipers in the Bird Room, and I knew nothing of the world. And the first time I tried my wings, I thought I was flying towards the sun, and it was just a blaze that—burned me.

"Of course you are right when you say that you won't marry me unless I love you. I had a queer feeling at first about it—as if you were very far away and I couldn't reach you. But I know that you are right, and that you are thinking of the thing that is best for me. But I know I shall always have you as a friend. I don't think that I shall ever love anybody. And after this we won't talk about it. There are so many other things that we have to say to each other that don't hurt—"

Becky could not, of course, know the effect of her letter on Randy. The night after its receipt, he roamed the woods. She had thought him cruel—and dreadful. Well, let her think it. He was glad that he had dropped George in the fountain. He should always be glad. But women were not like that—they were tender—and hated—hardness. Perhaps that was because they were—mothers—

And men were—hard. He had been hard, perhaps, in the things he had said in his letter. Her words rang in his ears. "I had a queer feeling at first that you were very far away, and that I could not reach you." And she had said that, when his soul ached to have her near.

Yet he had tried to do the best that he could for Becky. He had felt that she must not be bound by a tie that was no longer needed to protect her from Dalton. She was safe at 'Sconset, with the Admiral and her new friends the Copes. He envied them, their hours with her. He was desperately lonely, with a loneliness which had no hope.

He worked intensively. The boarders had gone from King's Crest, and he and the Major had moved into the big house. Randy spent a good deal of time in the Judge's library at Huntersfield. He and Truxton had great plans for their future. They read law, sold cars, and talked of their partnership. The firm was to be "Bannister, Paine and Beaufort"; it was to have brains, conscience, and business acumen.

"In the order named," Truxton told the Major. "The Judge has brains, Randy has a conscience. There's nothing left for me but to put pep into the business end of it."

Randy worked, too, on his little story. He did not know in the least what he was going to do with it, but it was an outlet for the questions which he kept asking himself. The war was over and the men who had fought had ceased to be important. He and the Major and Truxton talked a great deal about it. The Major took the high stand of each man's satisfaction in the thing he had done. Truxton was light-heartedly indifferent. He had his Mary, and his future was before him. But Randy argued that the world ought not to forget. "It was a rather wonderful thing for America. I want her to keep on being wonderful."

The Major in his heart knew that the boy was right. America must keep on being wonderful. Her young men must go high-hearted to the tasks of peace. It was the high-heartedness of people which had won the war. It would be the high-heartedness of men and women which would bring sanity and serenity to a troubled world.

"The difficulty lies in the fact that we are always trying to make laws to right the world, when what we need is to form individual ideals. The boy who says in his heart, 'I want to be like Lincoln,' and who stands in front of a statue of Lincoln, and learns from that rugged countenance the lesson of simple courage and honesty, has a better chance of a future than the boy who is told, 'There is evil in the world, and the law punishes those who transgress.' Half of our Bolsheviks would be tamed if they had the knowledge and love of some simple hero in their hearts, and felt that there was a chance for them to be heroic. The war gave them a chance. We have now to show them that there is beauty and heroism in orderly living—"

He was talking to Madge. She was still with the Flippins. The injury to her foot had been more serious than it had seemed. She might have gone with Oscar and Flora when they left Hamilton Hill. But she preferred to stay. Flora was to go to a hospital; Madge would not be needed.

"I am going to stay here as long as you will let me," she said to Mrs. Flippin; "you will tell me if I am in the way—"

Mrs. Flippin adored Madge. "It is like having a Princess in the house," she said, "only she don't act like a Princess."

The Major came over every afternoon. Kemp drove him, as a rule, in the King's Crest surrey. If the little man missed Dalton's cars, he said no word. He made the Major very comfortable. He lived a life of ease if not of elegance, and he loved the wooded hills, the golden air, the fine old houses, the serene autumn glory of this southern world.

On the afternoon when the Major talked to Madge of the world at peace, they were together under the apple tree which Madge had first seen from the window of the east room. There were other apple trees in the old orchard, but it was this tree that Madge liked because of its golden globes. "The red ones are wonderful," she said, "but red isn't my color. With my gold skin, they make me look like a gypsy. If I am to be a golden girl, I must stay away from red—"

"Is that what you are—a golden girl?"

"That was always George Dalton's name for me."

"I am sorry."

"Why?"

"Because I should like it to be mine for you. I should like to link my golden West with the thought of you."

"And you won't now, because it was somebody else's name

for me?"

Kemp, before he went away, had made her comfortable with cushions in a chairlike crotch of the old tree. The Major was at her feet. He meditated a moment. "I shall make it my name for you. What do I care what other men have called you."

"Do you know what you called me—once?" she was smiling down at him.

"No."

"A little lame duck. It was when I first tried to use my foot. And you laughed, and said that it—linked us—together. And now you are trying to link me with your West—"

"You know why, of course."

"Yes, I do."

He drew a long breath. "Most women would have said, 'No, I don't know.' But you told the truth. I want to link you with my life in every way I can because I love you. And you know that I care—very much—that I want you for my wife—my golden girl in my golden West—?"

"You have never told me before that—you cared."

"There was no need to tell it. You knew."

"Yes. I was afraid it was true—"

He was startled. "Afraid? Why?"

"Oh, I oughtn't to let you care," she said. "You don't know what a slacker I've been. And I don't want you to find out—"

"The only thing that I want to find out is whether you care for me."

She flushed a little under his steady gaze, then quite unexpectedly she reached her hand down to him. He took it in his firm clasp. "I do care—an awful lot," she said, "but I've tried not to. And I shouldn't let you care for me."

"Why—shouldn't?"

"I'm not—half good enough. My life has always been lived at loose ends. Nothing bad, but a thousand things that you wouldn't—like to hear—I'm not a golden girl—I'm a gilded one—"

"Why should you tell me things like that? I don't believe it."

"Please believe it," she said earnestly, "don't whitewash things. Just let me begin again—loving you—"

Her voice broke. He drew himself up, and took her in his arms. "My dear girl," he said, "my dear girl—"

"I never met a man like you, I never believed there were—such men—" He felt her tears against his hand.

"Listen," he said quietly; "let me tell you something of my

life." He told her the things he had told Randy. Of the little wife he had not loved. "Perhaps if it had not been for her, I should not have had the courage to offer to you my—maimed—self. When I married her I was strong and young and had wealth to give her. Yet I did not give her love. And love is more than all the rest. I have that to give you—you know it."

"Yes."

"I have some money. I don't think it is going to count much with either of us. What will count is the way we plan our future. I have a big old ranch, and we'll live in it—with the dairy and the wide kitchen that you've talked about—and you won't have to wait for another world, dearest, to get your heart's desire—"

"I have my heart's desire," she whispered; "you are—my world."

II

Madge wrote to George Dalton that she was going to marry Major Prime.

"There is no reason why we should put it off, Georgie. The clergyman who prayed for Flora will perform the ceremony, and the wedding will be at the Flippins' farm.

"It seems, of course, too good to be true. Not many women have such luck. Not my kind of women anyway. We meet men as a rule who want us to be gilded girls, and not golden ones. But Mark wants me to be gold all through. And I shall try to be—We are to live on his ranch, a place that passes in California for a farm—a sort of glorified country place. Mrs. Flippin is teaching me to make butter, so that I can superintend my own dairy, and I have learned a great deal about chickens and eggs.

"I am going to be a housewife in what I call a reincarnated sense—loving my house and the things which belong to it, and living as a part of it, not above it, and looking down upon it. Perhaps all American women will come to that some day and I shall simply be blazing the way for them. I shall probably grow rosy and round, and if you ever ride up to my door-step, you will find me a buxom and blooming matron instead of a golden girl. And you won't like it in the least. But my husband will like it, because he thinks a bit as I do about it, and he doesn't care for the woman who lives for her looks.

"I shall come and see Flora before I go West. But I am going to be married first. We both have a feeling that it must be now—that something might happen if we put it off, and nothing must happen. I love him too much. Of course you won't believe that. I can hardly believe it myself. But I have someone to climb the heights with me, Georgie, and we shall ascend to the peak—together."

For a wedding present George sent Madge the pendant he had bought for Becky. To connect it up with Madge's favorite color scheme, he had an amethyst put in place of the sapphire. He was glad to give it away. Every time he had come upon it, it had reminded him of things that he wished to forget.

Yet he could not forget. Even as Becky had thought of him, he had thought of her; of her radiant youth on the morning that Randy had arrived; at the Horse Show in her shabby shoes and sailor hat; in the Bird Room in pale blue under the swinging lamp; in the music room between tall candles; in the garden, with a star shining into the still pool; that last night, on the balcony, leaning over, with a yellow lantern like a halo behind her.

There were other things that he thought of—of Randy, in khaki on the station platform; Randy, lean and tall among the boarders; Randy, left behind with Kemp in the rain; Randy, debonair and insolent, announcing his engagement on the terrace at Hamilton Hill; Randy, a shadow against a silver sky, answering Becky's call; Randy, in the dark by the fountain, with muscles like iron, forcing him inevitably back, lifting him above the basin, letting him drop—; Randy, the Conqueror, marching away with Becky's fan as his trophy—!

New York was, of course, at this season of the year, a pageant of sparkling crowds, and of brilliant window displays, of new productions at the theaters. People were coming back to town. Even the fashionable folk were running down to taste the elixir of the early days in the metropolis.

But George found everything flat and stale. He did the things he had always done, hunted up the friends he had always known. He spent week-ends at various country places, and came always back to town with an undiminished sense of his need of Becky, and his need of revenge on Randy.

He had heard before he left Virginia that Becky was at Nantucket. He had found some consolation in the fact that she was not at Huntersfield. To have thought of her with Randy in the old garden, on Pavilion Hill, in the Bird Room, would have been unbearable.

He had a feeling that, in a sense, Madge's marriage was a desertion. He did not in the least want to marry her, but there were moments when he needed her friendship very much. He needed it now. And she was going to marry Major Prime, and go out to some God-forsaken place, and get fat and lose her beauty.

He wished that she would not talk about such things—it made him feel old, and worried about his waist-line.

Even Oscar was failing him. "When Flora gets well," the little man kept telling him, "we are going to do some good with our money. We have done nothing but think of ourselves—"

"Oh, for Heaven's sake, don't preach," George exploded. It seemed to him that the world had gone mad on the subject of reforms. Man was no longer master of his fate. The time would come when the world would be a dry desert, without a cocktail or a highball for a thirsty soul, and all because a lot of people had been feeling for some time as Flora and Oscar felt at this moment.

"I shall take Flora up to the Crossing in a few days," Oscar was saying; "the doctor thinks the sea air will do her good. I wish you would come with us."

George had no idea of going with Oscar and Flora. He had been marooned long enough with a sick woman and her depressed spouse. When Flora was better and she and Oscar got over their mood of piety and repentance, he would be glad to join them. In the meantime he searched his mind for some reasonable excuse.

"Look here," he said, "I'll join you later, Oscar. I've promised some friends at Nantucket that I'll come down for the hunting."

"I didn't know that you had friends in Nantucket," Oscar told him moodily.

"The Merediths," George remembered in the nick of time the name of Becky's grandfather. Oscar would not know the difference.

Having committed himself, his spirits soared. It had, he felt, been an inspiration to put it over on Oscar like that. Subconsciously he had known that some day he would follow Becky, and when the moment came, he had spoken out of his thoughts.

In the two or three days that elapsed between his decision and the date that he had set for his departure, he found himself enjoying the city—its clear skies, its hurrying crowds, its color and glow, the tingle of its rush and hurry, its light-hearted acceptance of the pleasure of the moment.

He telegraphed for a room at a hotel in Nantucket. Once there, he was confident that he could find Becky. Everybody would know Admiral Meredith.

He went by boat from New York to New Bedford, and enjoyed the trip. Later on the little steamer, *Sankaty*, plying between New Bedford and Nantucket, he was so shining and splendid that he was much observed by the other passengers. His Jap servant, trotting after him, was perhaps less martial in bearing than the ubiquitous Kemp, but he was none the less an ornament.

Thus George came, at last, to Nantucket, and to his hotel. Having dined, he asked the way to the Admiral's house. He did not of course plan to storm the citadel after dark, but a walk would not hurt him, and he could view from the outside the cage which held his white dove. For he had come to that, sentimentally, that Becky was the white dove that he would shelter against his heart.

The clerk at the hotel desk, directing him, thought that the Admiral was not in his house on Main Street. He was apt at this season to spend his time in Siasconset.

"'Sconset? Where's 'Sconset?"

"Across the island."

"How can I get there?"

"You can motor over. There's a bus, or you can get a car."

So the next morning, George took the bus. He saw little beauty in the moor. He thought it low and flat. His heart leaped with the thought that every mile brought him nearer Becky—his white dove—whom he had—hurt!

He was set down by the bus at the post-office. He asked his way, and was directed to a low huddle of gray houses on a grassy street. "It is the 'Whistling Sally,'" the driver of the bus had told him.

When George reached "The Whistling Sally," he felt that there must be some mistake. Here was no proper home for an Admiral or an heiress. His eyes were blind to the charms of the wooden young woman with the puffed-out cheeks, to the beauty of silver-gray shingles, of late flowers blooming bravely in the little garden.

He kept well on the other side of the street. It might perhaps be embarrassing if he met Becky while she was with her grandfather. He wanted to see her alone. With no one to interfere, he would be, he was sure, master of the situation.

He passed the house. The windows were open, and the white curtains blew out. But there was no one in sight. At the next corner, he accosted a tall man in work clothes, with bronzed skin and fair hair.

"Can you tell me," George asked, "whether Admiral Meredith lives in that cottage—'The Whistling Sally'?"

"Yes. But he isn't there. He's gone to Boston."

George was conscious of a sense of shock.

"Boston?"

"Yes. He wasn't very well and he wanted to see his doctor."

"Has his—granddaughter gone with him?"

"Miss Becky? Yes."

"But—the windows of the house are open—"

"I open them every morning. The housekeeper is in Nantucket. But they are all coming back at the end of the week."

"Coming back?" eagerly; "the Admiral, and Miss Bannister?"

"Yes."

George drew a long breath. He walked back with Tristram to the low gray house. "Queer little place," he said.

Tristram eyed him with easy tolerance. "Of course it seems queer if you aren't used to it—"

"I thought the Admiral had money."

"Well, he has. But he forgets it out here—"

"Is there a good hotel?"

"Yes. It is usually closed by now. But they are keeping it open for some guests who are up for the hunting."

The hotel was a pleasant rambling structure, and overlooked the sea. George engaged a room for Saturday—and said that his man would bring his bags. He would have his lunch and take the afternoon bus back to Nantucket.

As he waited for the dining-room doors to open, a girl wrapped in a yellow cape crossed the porch and descended the steps which led to the beach. She wore a yellow bathing cap and yellow shoes. George walked to the top of the bluff and watched her. She threw off the cape, and stood slim and striking for a moment before she dived into the sea. She swam splendidly. It was very cold, and George wondered how she endured it. When she came running back up the steps and across the porch, she was wrapped in the cape. She was rather handsome in a queer dark way. "It was cold," she said, as she passed George.

He took a step forward. "You were brave—"

She stopped and shrugged her shoulders. "One gets warm," she said, "in a moment."

She left him, and he went in to lunch. He stopped at the desk on the way out. "I have changed my mind. My man will bring my bags to-morrow."

It was still too early for the bus, so George walked back up the bluff, turning at last towards the left. Crossing a grassy space, there was ahead of him a ridge which marked the edge of the moor. A little fog was blowing in, and mistily through the fog he saw a figure which moved as light as smoke above the eminence. It was a woman dancing.

As he came nearer, he saw that she wore gray with a yellow

sash. Her yellow cape lay on the ground. "I am not sure," George said, as he stopped beside her, "whether you are a pixie or a mermaid."

"Look," she said, smiling, "I'll show you what I am—"

She began with a light swaying motion, like a leaf stirred by a breeze. Then, whipped into action, she ran before the pursuing elements. She cowered, and registered defiance. Her loosened hair hung heavy about her shoulders, then wound itself about her, as she whirled in a cyclone of movement. Beaten to the ground, she rose languidly, swayed again to that light step and stopped.

Then she came close to George. "You see," she said, "I am not a pixie or a mermaid. I am the spirit of the storm."

CHAPTER XV

THE TRUMPETER SWAN

I

The Admiral's rheumatism had taken Becky to Boston. "There'll be treatments every morning," he said, "and we'll invite the Copes to visit us, and they will look after you while I am away."

The Copes were delighted. "Only it seems like an imposition—"

"The house is big enough for an army," the Admiral told them; "that's what we built houses for in the old days. To have our friends. Charles, my butler, and his wife, Miriam, who cooks, stay in the house the year round, so it is always open and ready."

"And you and I shall see Boston together," Archibald told Becky, triumphantly. "I wonder if you have ever seen Boston as I shall show it to you."

"Well, I've been to all the historic places."

"Bunker Hill and the embattled farmers, of course," said Archibald; "but have you seen them since the war?"

"No. Are they different?"

"They aren't, but you are. All of us are."

Louise was not quite sure that her brother ought to leave the island. "You are down here for the air, Arch, and the quiet."

He was impatient. "Do you think I am going to miss this?"

She frowned and shook her head. "I don't want you to miss it. But it will be going against the doctor's orders."

"Oh, hang the doctor, Louise. Being in Boston with Becky will be like—wine—"

But she was not satisfied. "You always throw yourself into things so—desperately—"

"Well, when I lose my enthusiasm I want to—die."

"No, you don't, Arch. Don't say things like that." Her voice was sharp.

He patted her hand. "I won't. But don't curb me too much, old girl. Let me play—while I can—"

They arrived in Boston to find a city under martial law, a city whose streets were patrolled by khaki-clad figures with guns, whose traffic was regulated by soldierly semaphores, who linked intelligence with military training, and picturesqueness with both.

For a short season Boston had been in the hands of the mob. All of her traditions of law and order had not saved her. It had been her punishment perhaps for leaving law and order in the hands of those who cared nothing for them. People with consciences had preferred to keep out of politics. So for a time demagogues had gotten the ear of the people, and chaos had resulted until a quiet governor had proved himself as firm as steel, and soldiers had replaced the policemen who had for a moment followed false gods.

"It all proves what I brought you here to see," Cope told Becky eagerly.

Coffee was being served in the library of the Meredith mansion on Beacon Street. The Admiral's library was as ruddy and twinkling as the little man himself. He had furnished it to suit his own taste. A great davenport of puffy red velvet was set squarely in front of a fireplace with shining brasses. The couch was balanced by a heavy gilt chair also in puffy red. The mantel was in white marble, and over the mantel was an oil portrait of the Admiral's wife painted in '76. She wore red velvet with a train, and with the pearls which had come down to Becky. The room had been keyed up to her portrait, and had then been toned down with certain heavy pieces of ebony, a cabinet of black lacquer, the dark books which lined the wall to the ceiling. The room was distinctly nineteenth-century. If it lacked the eighteenth-century exquisiteness of the house at Nantucket, with its reminder of austere Quaker prejudices, it was none the less appropriate as a glowing background for the gay old Admiral.

Becky and Cope sat on the red davenport. It was so wide that Becky was almost lost in a corner of it. The old butler, Charles, served the coffee. The coffee service was of repoussé silver. The Admiral would have no other. It had been given him by a body of seamen when he had retired from active duty.

"It all proves what I brought you here to see," Archibald emphasized, "how the gods of yesterday are going to balance the gods of to-day."

The Admiral chuckled. "There aren't any gods of to-day."

"The gods of to-day are our young men," Cope flung out, glowingly; "the war has left them with their dreams, and they have got to find a way to make their dreams come true. And that's where the old gods will help. Those fine old men who dreamed, backed their dreams with deeds. Then for a time we were so busy making money that we forgot their dreams. And when foreigners came crowding to our shores, we didn't care whether they were good Americans or not. All we cared was to have them work in our mills and factories and in our kitchens, and let us alone in our pride of ancestry and pomp of circumstance. We forgot to show them Bunker Hill and to tell them about the old North Church and Paul Revere and the shot heard 'round the world, and what liberty meant and democracy, and now we've got to show them. I am going to take you around to-morrow, Becky, and pretend you are Olga from Petrograd, and that you are seeing America for the first time."

Archibald Cope was kindled by fires which gave color to his pale cheeks. "Will you be—Olga from Petrograd?"

"I'd love it."

But the next morning it rained. "And you can't, of course, be Olga of Petrograd in the rain. Bunker Hill must have the sun on it, and the waves of the harbor must be sparkling when I tell you about the tea."

They decided, therefore, to read aloud "The Autocrat of the Breakfast Table."

"Then if it stops raining," said Archibald, "we'll step straight out from its pages into the Boston that I want to show you."

He read well. Louise sat at a little table sewing a pattern of beads on a green bag. Becky had some rose-colored knitting. The Admiral was in his big chair by the fire with his hands folded across his waistcoat and his eyes shut. The colorful work of the two women, the light of the fire, the glow of the little lamp at Cope's elbow, the warmth of the red furniture saved the room from dreariness in spite of the rain outside.

"'It was on the Common,'" read Cope, "'that we were walking. The mall, or boulevard of our Common, you know, has various branches leading from it in different directions. One of these runs down from opposite Joy Street southward across the whole length of the Common to Boylston Street. We called it the long path, and were fond of it.

"'I felt very weak indeed (though of a tolerably robust habit) as we came opposite the head of this path on that morning. I think I tried to speak twice without making myself distinctly audible. At last I got out the question, "Will you take the long path with me?" "Certainly," said the schoolmistress, "with much pleasure." "Think," I said, "before you answer: if you take the long path with me now, I shall interpret it that we are to part no more!" The schoolmistress stepped back with a sudden movement, as if an arrow had struck her.

"'One of the long granite blocks used as seats was hard by— the one you may still see close by the Gingko-tree. "Pray sit down," I said. "No, no," she answered, softly, "I will walk the *long path* with you!"

"'—The old gentleman who sits opposite met us walking arm in arm about the middle of the long path, and said, very charmingly,—"Good-morning, my dears!"'"

The reading stopped at luncheon time, and it was still raining. On the table were letters for Becky forwarded from Siasconset. An interesting account from Aunt Claudia of the wedding of Major Prime and Madge MacVeigh.

"They were married in the old orchard at the Flippins', and it was beautiful. The bride wore simple clothes like the rest of us. It was cool and we kept on our wraps, and she was in white linen with a loose little coat of mauve wool, and a hat to match. The only bride-y thing about her was a great bunch of lilacs that the Major ordered from a Fifth Avenue florist. They are to stay in New York for a day or two, and then visit the Watermans on the North Shore. After that they will go at once to the West, where they are to live on the Major's ranch. He has been relieved from duty at Washington, and will have all of his time to give to his own affairs.

"There has been an epidemic of weddings. Flippins' Daisy waited just long enough to help Mrs. Flippin get Miss MacVeigh married; then she and young John had an imposing ceremony in their church, with Daisy in a train and white veil, and four bridesmaids, and Mandy and Calvin in front seats, and Calvin giving the bride away. I think the elaborateness of it all really reconciled Mandy to her daughter-in-law."

There was also, from Randy, a long envelope enclosing a thick manuscript and very short note.

"I want you to read this, Becky. It belongs in a way to you. I don't know what I think about it. Sometimes it seems as if I had done a rather big thing, and as if it had been done without me at all. I wonder if you understand what I mean—as if I had held the pen, and it had—come—I have sent it to the editor of one of the big magazines. Perhaps he will send it back, and it may not seem as good to me as it does at this moment. Let me know what you think."

Becky, finishing the letter, felt a bit forlorn. Randy, as a rule, wrote at length about herself and her affairs. But, of course, he had other things now to think of. She must not expect too much.

There was no time, however, in which to read the manuscript, for Cope was saying, wistfully, "Do you think you'd mind a walk in the rain?"

"No." She gathered up her letters.

"Then we'll walk across the Common."

They shared one umbrella. And they played that it was over fifty years ago when the Autocrat had walked with the young Schoolmistress. They even walked arm in arm under the umbrella. They took the long path to Boylston Street. And Cope said, "Will you take the long path with me?"

And Becky said, "Certainly."

And they both laughed. But there was no laughter in Cope's heart.

"Becky," he said, "I wish that you and I had lived a century ago in Louisberg Square."

"If we had lived then, we shouldn't be living now."

"But we should have had our—happiness—"

"And I should have worn lovely flowing silk skirts. Not short things like this, and little bonnets with flowers inside, and velvet mantles—"

"And you would have walked on my arm to church. And we would have owned one of those old big houses—and your smile would have greeted me across the candles every day at dinner—" He was making it rather personal, but she humored his fancy.

"And you would have worn a blue coat, and a bunch of big seals, and a furry high hat—"

"You are thinking all the time about what we would wear," he complained; "you haven't any sense of romance, Becky—"

"Well, of course, it is all make-believe."

"Yes, it is all—make-believe," he said, and walked in silence after that.

The wind blew cold and they stopped in a pastry shop on Boylston Street and had a cup of tea.

Becky ate little cream cakes with fluted crusts, and drank Orange Pekoe.

"I am glad you don't wear flowing silks and velvet mantles," said Archibald, suddenly; "I shall always remember you like this, Becky, in your rough brown coat and your close little hat, and that your hand was on my arm when we walked across the Common. Do you like me as a playmate, Becky?"

"Yes."

"Do you—love me—as a playmate?" He leaned forward.

"Please—don't."

"I beg your—pardon—" he flushed. "I am not going to say such things to you, Becky, and spoil things for both of us—I know you don't want to hear them—"

"Make-believe is much nicer," she reminded him steadily.

"But I am not a make-believe friend, am I? Our friendship—

that at least is—real?"

Her clear eyes met his. "Yes. We shall always be friends—forever—"

"How long is forever, Becky?"

She could not answer that. But she was sure that friendship was like love and lived beyond the grave. They were very serious about it, these two young people drinking tea.

II

It was when the four of them were gathered together that night in the library that Becky asked Archibald Cope to read "The Trumpeter Swan."

"Randy wrote it," she said, "and he sent the manuscript to me this morning."

The Admiral was at once interested. "He got the name from the swan in the Judge's Bird Room?"

"Yes."

"Has he ever written anything before?" Louise asked.

"Lots of little things. Lovely things—"

"Have they been published?"

"I don't think he has tried."

Becky had the manuscript in her work-bag. She brought it out and handed it to Archibald. "You are sure you aren't too tired?"

Louise glanced up from her beaded bag. "You've had a hard day, Arch. You mustn't do too much."

"I won't, Louise," impatiently.

She went back to her work. "It will be on your own head if you don't sleep to-night, not on mine."

"The Trumpeter Swan" was a story of many pages. Randy had confined himself to no conventional limits. He had a story to tell, and he did not bring it to an end until the end came naturally. In it he had asked all of the questions which had torn his soul. What of the men who had fought? What of their futures? What of their high courage? Their high vision? Was it all now to be wasted? All of that aroused emotion? All of that disciplined endeavor? Would they still "carry on" in the spirit of that crusade, or would they sink back, and forget?

His hero was a simple lad. He had fought for his country. He had found when he came back that other men had made money while he fought for them. He loved a girl. And in his absence she had loved someone else. For a time he was overthrown.

Yet he had been one of a glorious company. One of that great flock which had winged its exalted flight to France. Throughout the story Randy wove the theme of the big white bird in the glass case. His hero felt himself likewise on the shelf, shut-in, stuffed, dead—his trumpet silent.

"Am I, too, in a glass case?" he asked himself; "will my trumpet never sound again?"

The first part of the story ended there. "Jove," Cope said, as he looked up, "that boy can write—"

Louise had stopped working. "It is rather—tremendous, don't you think?"

Archibald nodded. "In a quiet way it thrills. He hasn't used a word too much. But he carries one with him to a sort of—upper sky—"

Becky, flushing and paling with the thought of such praise as this for Randy, said, "I always thought he could do it."

But even she had not known that Randy could do what he did in the second part of the story.

For in it Randy answered his own questions. There was no limit to a man's powers, no limits to his patriotism, if only he believed in himself. He must strive, of course, to achieve. But striving made him strong. His task might be simple, but its very simplicity demanded that he put his best into it. He must not measure himself by the rule of little men. If other men had made money while he fought, then let them be weighed down by their bags of gold. He would not for one moment set against their greed those sacred months of self-sacrifice.

And as for the woman he loved. If his love meant anything it must burn with a pure flame. What he might have been for her, he would be because of her. He would not be less a man because he had loved her.

And so the boy came in the end of the story to the knowledge that it was the brave souls who sounded their trumpets—One did not strive for happiness. One strove for—victory. One strove, at least, for one clear note of courage, amid the clamor of the world.

Louise, listening, forgot her beads. The Admiral blew his nose and wiped his eyes. Becky felt herself engulfed by a wave of surging memories.

"That's corking stuff, do you know it?" Archibald was asking.

Louise asked, "How old is he?"

"Twenty-three."

"He is young to have learned all that—"

"All what, Louise?" Archibald asked.

"Renunciation," said Louise, slowly, "that's what it is in the final analysis," she went back to her beads and her green bag.

"Randy ought to do great things," said Becky; "the men of his family have all done great things, haven't they, Grandfather?"

"Randolph blood is Randolph blood," said the Admiral; "fine old Southerners; proud old stock."

"If I could write like that," said Archibald, and stopped and looked into the fire.

Louise rose and came and stood back of him. "You can paint," she said, "why should you want to write?"

"I can't paint," he reached up and caught her hand in his; "you think I can, but I can't. And I am not wonderful—Yet here I must sit and listen while you and Becky sing young Paine's praises."

He flung out his complaint with his air of not being in earnest.

The Admiral got up stiffly. "I've a letter to write before I go to bed. Don't let me hurry the rest of you."

"Please take Louise with you," Archibald begged; "I want to talk to Becky."

His sister rumpled his hair. "So you want to get rid of me. Becky, he is going to ask questions about that boy who wrote the story."

"Are you?" Becky demanded.

"Louise is a mind reader. That's why I want her out of the way—"

"You can stay until the Admiral finishes his letter." Louise bent and kissed him, picked up her beaded bag, and left them together.

When she reached the threshold, she stopped and looked back. Archibald had piled up two red cushions and was sitting at Becky's feet.

"Tell me about him."

"Randy?"

"Yes. He's in love with you, of course."

"What makes you think that?"

"He sent you the story."

"Well, he is," she admitted, "but I am not sure that we ought to talk about it."

"Why not?"

"Is it quite fair, to him?"

"Then we'll talk about his story. It gripped me—Oh, let's have it out, Becky. He loves you and you don't love him. Why don't you?"

"I can't—tell you—"

There was silence for a moment, then Archibald Cope said gently, "Look here, girl dear, you aren't happy. Don't I know it?

There's something that's awfully on your mind and heart. Can't you think of me as a sort of—father confessor—and let me—help—?"

She clasped her hands tensely on her knees; the knuckles showed white. "Nobody can help."

"Is it as bad as that?"

"Yes." She looked away from him. "There is somebody else—not Randy. Somebody that I shouldn't think about. But I—do—"

She was dry-eyed. But he felt that here was something too deep for tears.

"Does Randy know?"

"Yes. I told him. We have always talked about things—"

"I see," he sat staring into the fire, "and of course it is Randy that you ought to marry—"

"I don't want to marry anyone. I shall never marry—"

"Tut-tut, my dear." He laid his hand over hers. "Do you know what I was thinking, Becky, to-day, as we walked the Boston streets? I was thinking of why those big houses were built, rows upon rows of them, and of the people who lived in them. Those old houses speak of homes, Becky, of people who wanted house-hold gods, and neighborly gatherings, and community interests. They weren't the kind of people who ran around Europe with a paint box, as I have been doing. They had home-keeping hearts and they built for the future."

He was very much in earnest. She had, indeed, never seen him so much in earnest.

"It is all very well," he went on, "to talk of a tent in a desert or a hut on a mountain top, but when we walked across the Common this morning, it seemed to me that if I could really have lived the game we played—that life could have held nothing better in the world for me than that, my dear."

She tried to withdraw her hand, but he held it. "Let me speak to-night, Becky—and then forever, we'll forget it. I love you—very much. You don't love me, and I should thank the stars for that, although I am not sure that I do. I am not a man to deal in—futures. I'll tell you why some day." He drew a long breath and went on in a lighter tone: "But you, Becky—you've got to find a man whose face you will want to see at the other end of the table—for life. It sounds like a prisoner's sentence, doesn't it?"

But he couldn't carry it off like that, and presently he hid his face against her hands. "Oh, Becky, Becky," she heard him whisper.

Then there was the Admiral's step in the hall and Archibald

was on his feet, staring in the fire when the little man came in.

"Any letters for Charles to mail?"

"No, Grandfather."

The Admiral limped away. Becky stood up. Cope turned from the fire.

"If it doesn't rain to-morrow, I'll show America to Olga of Petrograd."

They smiled at each other, and Becky held out her hand. He bent and kissed it. "I shall sleep well to-night because of—to-morrow."

III

But when to-morrow came there was a telephone message for Becky that Major Prime and his wife were in town. They had messages for her from Huntersfield, and from King's Crest.

"And so our day is spoiled," said Archibald.

"We can come again," said the Admiral, "but we must be getting back to Siasconset to-morrow. I wrote to Tristram. We'll have Prime and his wife here for dinner to-night, and drive them out somewhere this afternoon. I remember Mark Prime well. I played golf with him one season at Del Monte. How did you happen to know him, Becky?"

Becky told of the Major's sojourn to King's Crest.

The Copes made separate plans for the afternoon. "If I can't have you to myself, Becky," Cope complained, "I won't have you at all—"

Madge, sitting later next to Becky in the Admiral's big car, was lovely in a great cape of pale wisteria, with a turban of the same color set low on her burnt-gold hair.

"I have brought you wonderful news of Randy Paine," she said to Becky. "He has sold his story, 'The Trumpeter Swan.' To one of the big magazines. And they have asked for more. He is by way of being rather—famous. He came on to New York the day after we arrived. They had telegraphed for him. We wanted him to come up here with us, but he wouldn't."

"Why wouldn't he?"

"He had some engagements, and after that—"

"He will never write another story like 'The Trumpeter Swan,'" said Becky.

"Why not?"

"It—it doesn't seem as if he could—It is—wonderful, Mrs. Prime—"

"Well, Randy—is wonderful," said Madge.

A silence fell between them, and when Madge spoke again it

was of the Watermans. "We go to the Crossing to-morrow. I must see Flora before I go West."

The blood ran up into Becky's heart. She wondered if George Dalton was with the Watermans. But she did not dare ask.

So she asked about California instead. "You will live out there?"

"Yes, on a ranch. There will be chickens and cows and hogs. It sounds unromantic, doesn't it? But it is really frightfully interesting. It is what I have always dreamed about. Mark says this is to be my—reincarnation."

She laughed a little as she explained what she meant. "And when I was in New York, I bought the duckiest lilac linens and ginghams, and white aprons, frilly ones. Mark says I shall look like a dairy maid in 'Robin Hood.'"

The Major, who was in front of them with the Admiral, turned and spoke.

"Tell her about Kemp."

"Oh, he is going with us. It develops that there is a girl in Scotland who is waiting for him. And he is going to send for her—and they are to have a cottage on the ranch, and come into the house to help us, and there is an old Chinese cook that Mark has had for years."

Becky spoke sharply. "You don't mean Mr.—Dalton's Kemp?"

"Yes. He came to Mark. Didn't you know?"

Becky had not known.

"Why did he leave Mr.—Dalton?"

"He and Georgie had a falling out about an omelette. I fancy it was a sort of comic opera climax. So Mark got a treasure and Georgie-Porgie lost one—"

"Georgie-Porgie?"

"Oh, I always call him that, and he hates it," Madge laughed at the memory.

"You did it to—tease him?" slowly.

"I did it because it was—true. You know the old nursery rhyme? Well, George is like that. There were always so many girls to be—kissed, and it was so easy to—run away—"

She said it lightly, with shrugged shoulders, but she did not look at Becky.

And that night when she was dressing for dinner, Madge said to her husband, "It sounded—catty—Mark. But I had to do it. There's that darling boy down there eating his heart out. And she is nursing a dream—"

The Major was standing by his wife's door, and she was in front of her mirror. It reflected her gold brocade, her amethysts linked with diamonds in a long chain that ended in a jeweled locket. Her jewel case was open and she brought out the pendant that George had sent her and held it against her throat. "It matches the others," she said.

He arched his eyebrows in inquiry.

"I wouldn't wear it," she said with a sudden quick force, "if there was not another jewel in the world. I wish he hadn't sent it. Oh, Mark, I wish I hadn't known him before I found—you," she came up to him swiftly; "such men as you," she said, "if women could only meet them—*first*—"

His arm went around her. "It is enough that we—met—"

Becky was also at her mirror at that moment. She had dressed carefully in silver and white with her pearls and silver slippers. Louise came in and looked at her. "I haven't any grand and gorgeous things, you know. And I fancy your Mrs. Prime will be rather gorgeous."

"It suits her," said Becky, "but after this she is going to be different." She told Louise about the ranch and the linen frocks and the frilled aprons. "She is going to make herself over. I wonder if it will be a success."

"It doesn't fit in with my theories," said Louise. "I think it is much better if people marry each other ready-made."

Becky turned from her mirror. "Louise," she said, "does anything ever fit in with a woman's theories when she falls in love?"

"One shouldn't fall in love," Louise said, serenely, "they should walk squarely into it. That's what I shall do, when I get ready to marry—But I shall love Archibald as long as the good Lord will let me—"

She was trying to say it lightly, but a quiver of her voice betrayed her.

"Louise," Becky said, "what's the matter with Archibald? Is anything really the matter?"

Louise began to cry. "Archie saw the doctor to-day, and he won't promise anything—I made Arch tell me—"

"Oh, Louise." Becky's lips were white.

"Of course if he takes good care of himself, it may not be for years. You mustn't let him know that I told you, Becky. But I had to tell somebody. I've kept it all bottled up as if I were a stone image. And I'm not a stone image, and he's all I have."

She dabbed her eyes with a futile handkerchief. The tears dripped. "I must stop," she kept saying, "I shall look like a fright for dinner—"

But at dinner she showed no signs of her agitation. She had used powder and rouge with deft touches. She had followed Becky's example and wore white, a crisp organdie, with a high blue sash. With her bobbed hair and pink cheeks she was not unlike a painted doll. She carried a little blue fan with lacquered sticks, and she tapped the table as she talked to Major Prime. The tapping was the only sign of her inner agitation.

The Admiral's table that night seemed to Becky a circle of sinister meaning. There was Archibald, condemned to die—while youth still beat in his veins—There was Louise, who must go on without him. There was the Admiral—the last of a vanished company; there was the Major, whose life for four years had held— horrors. There was Madge, radiant to-night in the love of her husband, as she had perhaps once been radiant for Dalton.

Georgie-Porgie!

It was a horrid name. *"There were always so many girls to be kissed—and it was so easy to run away—"*

She had always hated the nursery rhyme. But now it seemed to sing itself in her brain.

> *"Georgie-Porgie,*
> *Pudding and pie,*
> *Kissed the girls,*
> *And made them cry—"*

Cope was at Becky's right. "Aren't you going to talk to me? You haven't said a word since the soup."

"Well, everybody else is talking."

"What do I care for anybody else?"

Becky wondered how Archibald did it. How he kept that light manner for a world which he was not long to know. And there was Louise with rouge and powder on her cheeks to cover her tears— That was courage—She thought suddenly of "The Trumpeter Swan."

She spoke out of her thoughts. "Randy has sold his story."

He wanted to know all about it, and she repeated what Madge had said. Yet even as she talked that hateful rhyme persisted,

> *"When the girls*
> *Came out to play,*
> *Georgie-Porgie*
> *Ran away—"*

After dinner they went into the drawing-room so that Louise could play for them. A great mirror which hung at the end of the room reflected Louise on the piano bench in her baby frock. It reflected Madge, slim and gold, with a huge fan of lilac feathers. It reflected Becky—in a rose-colored damask chair, it reflected the three men in black. Years ago there had been other men and women—the Admiral's wife in red velvet and the same pearls that were now on Becky's neck—She shuddered.

As they drove home that night, the Major spoke to his wife of Becky. "The child looks unhappy."

"She will be unhappy until some day her heart rests in her husband, as mine does in you. Shall I spoil you, Mark, if I talk like this?"

When they reached their hotel there were letters. One was from Flora: "You asked about George. He is not with us. He has gone to Nantucket to visit some friends of his—the Merediths. He will be back next week."

"The Merediths?" Madge said. "George doesn't know any—Merediths. Mark—he is following Becky."

"Well, she's safe in Boston."

"She is going back. On Wednesday. And he'll be there." Her eyes were troubled.

"Mark," she said, abruptly, "I wonder if Randy has left New York. Call him up, please, long distance. I want to talk to him."

"My darling girl, do you know what time it is?"

"Nearly midnight. But that's nothing in New York. And, anyhow, if he is asleep, we will wake him up. I am going to tell him that George is at Siasconset."

"But, my dear, what good will it do?"

"He's got to save Becky. I know Dalton's tricks and his manners. He can cast a glamour over anything. And Randy's the man for her. Oh, Mark, just think of her money and his genius—"

"What have money and genius to do with it?"

"Nothing, unless they love each other. But—she cares—You should have seen her eyes when I said he had sold his story. But she doesn't know that she cares, and he's got to make her know."

"How can he make her know?"

"Let her see him—now. She has never seen him as he was in New York with us, sure of himself, knowing that he has found the thing that he can do. He was beautiful with that radiant boy-look. You know he was, Mark, wasn't he?"

"Yes, my darling, yes."

"And I want him to be happy, don't you?"

"Of course, dear heart."

"Then get him on the phone. I'll do the rest."

IV

Randy, in New York, acclaimed by a crowd of enthusiasts who had read his story as a gold nugget picked up from a desert of literary mediocrity. Randy, not knowing himself. Randy, modest beyond belief. Randy, in his hotel at midnight, walking the floor with his head held high, and saying to himself, "I've done it."

It seemed to him that, of course, it could not be true. The young editor who had eyed him through shell-rimmed glasses had said, "There's going to be a lot of hard work ahead—to keep up to this—"

Randy, in his room, laughed at the thought of work. What did hardness matter? The thing that really mattered was that he had treasure to lay at the feet of Becky.

He sat down at the desk to write to her, cheeks flushed, eyes bright, a hand that shook with excitement.

"I am to meet a lot of big fellows to-morrow—I shall feel like an ugly duckling among the swans—oh, the *swans*, Becky, did we ever think that the Trumpeter in his old glass case—"

The telephone rang. Randy, answering it, found Madge at the other end. There was an exchange of eager question and eager answer.

Then Randy hung up the receiver, tore up his note to Becky, asked the office about trains, packed his bag, and went swift in a taxi to the station.

It was not until he was safe in his sleeper, and racketing through the night, that he remembered the meeting with the literary swans and the editor with the shell-rimmed glasses. A telegram would convey his regrets. He was sorry that he could not meet them, but he had on hand a more important matter.

CHAPTER XVI

THE CONQUEROR

I

If Randy's train had not missed a connection, he would have caught the same boat that took the Admiral and his party back to the island. They motored down to Wood's Hole, and boarded the *Sankaty*, while Randy, stranded at New Bedford, was told there would not be another steamer out until the next day.

The Admiral was the only gay and apparently care-free member of his quartette. Becky felt unaccountably depressed. Louise sat in the cabin and worked on her green bag. There was a heavy sky and signs of a storm. It was not pleasant outside.

Archibald was nursing a grievance. "If your grandfather had only stayed over another day."

"He had written Tristram that we would come. He is very exact in his engagements."

"And he feels that fifty years in 'Sconset is better than a cycle anywhere else."

"Yes. It will be nice to get back to our little gray house, and the moor, don't you think?"

"Yes. But I wanted to show you Boston as if you had never seen it, and now I shall never show it."

They were on deck, wrapped up to their chins. "Tell me what you would have shown me," Becky said; "play that I am Olga and that you are telling me about it."

He looked down at her. "Well, you've just arrived. You aren't dressed in a silver-toned cloak with gray furs and a blue turban with a silver edge. That's a heavenly outfit, Becky. But what made you wear it on a day like this?"

"It is the silver lining to my—cloud," demurely; "dull clothes are dreadful when the sky is dark."

"I am not sure but I liked you better in your brown—in the rain with your hand on my arm—That is—unforgettable—"

She brought him back to Olga. "I have just arrived—"

"Yes, and you have a shawl over your head, and a queer old coat and funny shoes. I should have to speak to you through an interpreter, and you would look at me with eager eyes or perhaps frightened ones."

"And first we should have gone to Bunker Hill, and I should have said, 'Here we fought. Not of hatred of our enemy, but for love of liberty. The thing had to be done, and we did it. We had a just cause.' And then I should have taken you to Concord and

Lexington, and I would have said, 'These farmers were clean-hearted men. They believed in law and order, they hated anarchy, and upon that belief and upon that hatred they built up a great nation.' And thus ends the first lesson."

He paused. "Lesson the second would have to do with the old churches."

They had stopped by the rail; the wind buffeted them, but they did not heed it. "It was in the churches that the ideals of the new nation were crystallized. No country prospers which forgets its God."

"Lesson number three," he went on, "would have had to do with the bookshops."

"The bookshops?"

He nodded. "The old bookshops and the new of Boston. I would have taken you to them, and I would have said, 'Here, Olga, is the voice of the nation speaking to you through the printed page. Learn to read in the language of your new country.' Oh, Becky," he broke off, "I wanted to show you the bookshops. It's a perfect pilgrimage—"

The Admiral, swaying to the wind, came up to them. "Hadn't you better go inside?" he shouted. "Becky will freeze out here."

They followed him. The cabin was comparatively quiet after the tumult. Louise was still working on the green bag. "What have you two been doing?" she asked.

"Playing Olga of Petrograd," said Archibald, moodily, "but Becky was cold and came in."

"Grandfather brought me in," said Becky.

"If you had cared to stay, you would have stayed," he told her, rather unreasonably. "Perhaps, after all, Boston to Olga simply means baked beans which she doesn't like, and codfish which she prefers—raw—"

"Now you have spoiled it all," said Becky. "I loved the things that you said about the churches and the bookshops and Bunker Hill."

"Did you? Well, it is all true, Becky, the part they have played in making us a nation. And it is all going to be true again. We Americans aren't going to sell our birthright for a mess of pottage!"

And now the island once more rose out of the sea. The little steamer had some difficulty in making a landing. But at last they were on shore, and the bus was waiting, and it was after dark when they reached "The Whistling Sally."

The storm was by that time upon them—the wind blew a wild

gale, but the little gray cottage was snug and warm. Jane in her white apron went unruffled about her pleasant tasks—storms might come and storms might go—she had no fear of them now, since none of her men went down to the sea in ships.

Tristram in shining oilskins brought up their bags. He stood in the hall and talked to them, and before he went away, he said casually over his shoulder, "There's a gentleman at the hotel that has asked for you once or twice."

"For me?" the Admiral questioned.

"You and Miss Becky."

"Do you know his name?"

"It's Dalton. George Dalton—"

"I don't know any Daltons. Do you, Becky?"

Becky stood by the table with her back to them. She did not turn. "Yes," she said in a steady voice. "There was a George Dalton whom I met this summer—in Virginia."

II

There was little sleep for Becky that night. The storm tore around the tiny house, but its foundations were firm, and it did not shake. The wind whistled as if the wooden figure in the front yard had suddenly come to life and was madly making up for the silence of a half century.

So George had followed her. He had found her out, and there was no way of escape. She would have to see him, hear him. She would have to set herself against the charm of that quick voice, those sparkling eyes. There would be no one to save her now. Randy was far away. She must make her fight alone.

She turned restlessly. Why should she fight? What, after all, did George mean to her? A chain of broken dreams? A husk of golden armor? *Georgie-Porgie*—who had kissed and run away.

She was listless at breakfast. The storm was over, and the Admiral was making plans for a picnic the next day to Altar Rock. "Hot coffee and lobster sandwiches, and a view of the sea on a day like this."

Becky smiled. "Grandfather," she said, "I believe you are happy because you keep your head in the stars and your feet on the ground."

"What's the connection, my dear?"

"Well, lobster sandwiches and a view of the sea. So many people can't enjoy both. They are either lobster-sandwich people, or view-of-the-sea people."

"Which shows their limitations," said the Admiral, promptly; "the people of Pepys' time were eloquent over a pigeon pie or a poem. The good Lord gave us both of them. Why not?"

It was after breakfast that a note was brought to Becky. The boy would wait.

"I am here," George wrote, "and I shall stay until I see you. Don't put me off. Don't shut your heart against me. I am very unhappy. May I come?"

She wrote an immediate answer. She would see him in the afternoon. The Admiral would be riding over to Nantucket. He had some business affairs to attend to—a meeting at the bank. Jane would be busy in her kitchen with the baking. The coast would be clear. There would be no need, if George came in the afternoon, to explain his presence.

Having dispatched her note, and with the morning before her, she was assailed by restlessness. She welcomed Archibald Cope's invitation from the adjoining porch. He sang it in the words of the old song,

> *"Madam, will you walk!*
> *Madam, will you talk?*
> *Madam, will you walk and talk*
> *With me—"*

"Where shall we go?"

"To Sankaty—"

She loved the walk to the lighthouse. In the spring there was Scotch broom on the bluffs—yellow as gold, with the blue beyond. In summer wild roses, deep pink, scenting the air with their fresh fragrance. But, perhaps, she loved it best on a day like this, with the breakers on the beach below, racing in like white horses, and with the winter gulls, dark against the brightness of the morning.

"Why aren't you painting?" she asked Archibald.

"Because," he said, "I am not going to paint the moor any more. It gets away from me—it is too vast—It has a primal human quality, and yet it is not alive."

"It sometimes seems alive to me," she said, "when I look off over it—it seems to rise and fall as if it—breathed."

"That's the uncanny part of it," Archibald agreed, "and I am going to give it up. I am not going to paint it—I want to paint you, Becky."

"Me? Why do you want to do that?"

He flashed a glance at her. "Because you are nice to look at."

"That isn't the reason."

"Why should you question my motives?" he demanded. "But

since you must have the truth—it is because of a fancy of mine that I might do it well—"

"I should like it very much," she said, simply.

"Would you?" eagerly.

"Yes."

She had on her red cape, and a black velvet tam pulled over her shining hair.

"I shall not paint you like this," he said, "although the color is—superlative—Ever since you read to me that story of Randy Paine's, I have had a feeling that the real story ought to have a happy ending, and that I should like to make the illustration."

"I don't know what you mean?"

"Why shouldn't the girl care for the boy after he came back? Why shouldn't she, Becky Bannister?"

Her startled gaze met his. "Let's sit down here," he said, "and have it out."

There was a bench on the edge of the bluff, set so that one might have a wider view of the sea.

"There ought to be a happy ending, Becky."

"How could there be?"

"Why not you—and Randy Paine? I haven't met him, but somehow that story tells me that he is the right sort. And think of it, Becky, you and that boy—in that big house down there, going to church, smiling across the table at each other," his breath came quickly, "your love for him, his for you, making a background for his—genius."

She tried to stop him. "Why should you say such things?"

"Because I have thought them. Last night in the storm—I couldn't sleep. I—I wanted to be a dog in the manger. I couldn't have you, and I'd be darned if I'd help anyone else to get you. You—you see, I'm a sort of broken reed, Becky. It   it isn't a sure thing that I am going to get well. And if what I feel for you is worth anything, it ought to mean that I must put your happiness—first. And that's why I want to make the picture for the—happy ending."

Her hand went out to him. "It is a beautiful thing for you to do. But I am not sure that there will be a—happy ending."

"Why not?"

She could not tell him. She could not tell—that between her and her thought of Randy was the barrier of all that George Dalton had meant to her.

"If you paint the picture," she evaded, "you must finish it at Huntersfield. Why can't you and Louise come down this winter?

It would be heavenly."

"It would be Heaven for me. Do you mean it, Becky?"

She did mean it, and she told him so.

"I shall paint you," he planned, "as a little white slip of a girl, with pearls about your neck, and dreams in your eyes, and back of you a flight of shadowy swans—"

They rose and walked on. "I thought you were to be with the Admiral in Boston this winter."

"I stay until Thanksgiving. I always go back to Huntersfield for Christmas."

After that it was decided that she should sit for him each morning. They did not speak again of Randy. There had been something in Becky's manner which kept Archibald from saying more.

When they reached the lighthouse, the wind was blowing strongly. Before them was the sweep of the Nantucket Shoals— not a ship in sight, not a line of smoke, the vast emptiness of heaving waters.

Becky stood at the edge of the bluff, her red cape billowing out into a scarlet banner, her hair streaming back from her face, the velvet tam flattened by the force of the wind.

Archibald glanced at her. "Are you cold?"

"No, I love it."

He was chilled to the bone, yet there she stood, warm with life, bright with beating blood—

"What a beastly lot of tumbling water," he said with sudden overmastering irritation. "Let's get away from it, Becky. Let's get away."

Going back they took the road which led across the moor. The clear day gave to the low hills the Persian carpet coloring which Cope had despaired of painting. Becky, in her red cape, was almost lost against the brilliant background.

But she was not the only one who challenged nature. For as she and Archibald approached the outskirts of the town, they discerned, at some distance, at the top of a slight eminence, two figures—a man and a woman. The woman was dancing, with waving arms and flying feet.

"She calls that dance 'Morning on the Moor,'" Cope told Becky; "she has a lot of them—'The Spirit of the Storm,' 'The Wraith of the Fog.'"

"Do you know her?"

"No. But Tristram says she dances every morning. She is getting ready for an act in one of the big musical shows."

The man sat on the ground and watched the woman dance. Her primrose cape was across his knee. He was a big man and wore a cap. Becky, surveying him from afar, saw nothing to command closer scrutiny. Yet had she known, she might have found him worthy of another look. For the man with the primrose cape was Dalton!

III

George Dalton, entering the little sitting-room of "The Whistling Sally," had to bend his head. He was so shining and splendid that he seemed to fill the empty spaces. It seemed, indeed, to Becky, as if he were too shining and splendid, as if he bulked too big, like a giant, top-heavy.

But she was not unmoved. He had been the radiant knight of her girlish dreams—some of the glamour still remained. Her cheeks were touched with pink as she greeted him.

He took both of her hands in his. "Oh, you lovely, lovely little thing," he said, and stood looking down at her.

They were the words he had said to her in the music-room. They revived memories. Flushing a deeper pink, she drew away from him. "Why did you come?"

"I could not stay away."

"How long have you been here?"

"Five days—"

"Please—sit down"—she indicated a chair on the other side of the hearth. She had seated herself in the Admiral's winged chair. It came up over her head, and she looked very slight and childish.

George, surveying the room, said, "This is some contrast to Huntersfield."

"Yes."

"Do you like it?"

"Oh, yes. I have spent months here, you know, and Sally, who whistles out there in the yard, is an old friend of mine. I played with her as a child."

"I should think the Admiral would rather have one of those big houses on the bluff."

"Would you?"

"Yes."

"But he has so many big houses. And this is his play-house. It belonged to his grandfather, and that ship up there is one on which our Sally was the figure-head."

He forced himself to listen while she told him something of the history of the old ship. He knew that she was making conversation, that there were things more important to speak of, and that she knew it. Yet she was putting off the moment when they must speak.

There came a pause, however. "And now," he said, leaning forward, "let's talk about ourselves, I have been here five days, Becky—waiting—"

"Waiting? For what?"

"To ask you to—forgive me."

Her steady glance met his. "If I say that I forgive you, will that be—enough?"

"You know it will not," his sparkling eyes challenged her. "Not if you say it coldly—"

"How else can I say it?"

"As if—oh, Becky, don't keep me at long distance—like this. Don't tell me that you are engaged to Randy Paine. Don't—. Let this be our day—" He seemed to shine and sparkle in a perfect blaze of gallantry.

"I am not engaged to Randy."

He gave an exclamation of triumph. "You broke it off?"

"No," she said, "he broke it."

"What?"

She folded her hands in her lap. "You see," she said, "he felt that I did not love him. And he would not take me that way—unloving."

"He seemed to want to take you any way, the day he talked to me. I asked him what he had to offer you—" He gave a light laugh—seemed to brush Randy away with a gesture.

Her cheeks flamed. "He has a great deal to offer."

"For example?" lazily, with a lift of the eyebrows.

"He is a gentleman—and a genius—"

His face darkened. "I'll pass over the first part of that until later. But why call him a 'genius'?"

"He has written a story," breathlessly, "oh, all the world will know it soon. The people who have read it, in New York, are crazy about it—"

"Is that all? A story? So many people write nowadays."

"Well," she asked quietly, "what more have you to offer?"

"Love, Becky. You intimated a moment ago that I was not—a gentleman—because I failed—once. Is that fair? How do you know that Paine has not failed—how do you know—? And love hasn't anything to do with genius, Becky, it has to do with that night in the music-room, when you sang and when I—kissed you. It has to do with nights like those in the old garden, with the new moon and the stars, and the old goddesses."

"And with words which meant—nothing—"

"*Becky*," he protested.

"Yes," she said, "you know it is true—they meant nothing. Perhaps you have changed since then. I don't know. But I know this, that I have changed."

He felt back of her words the force which had always baffled him.

"You mean that you don't love me?"

"Yes."

"I—I don't believe it—"

"You must—"

"But—" he rose and went towards her.

"Please—we won't argue it. And—Jane is going to give us some tea." She left him for a moment and came back to sit behind the little table. Jane brought tea and fresh little cakes.

"For Heaven's sake, Becky," George complained, when the old woman had returned to her kitchen, "can you eat at a moment like this?"

"Yes," she said, "I can eat and the cakes are very nice."

She did not let him see that her hand trembled as she poured the tea.

George had had five days in the company of the dancer in yellow. He had found her amusing. She played the game at which he had proved himself so expert rather better than the average woman. She served for the moment, but no sane man would ever think of spending his life with her. But here was the real thing— this slip of a child in a blue velvet smock, with bows on her slippers, and a wave of bronze hair across her forehead. He felt that Becky's charms would last for a lifetime. When she was old, and sat like that on the other side of the hearth, with silver hair and bent figure, she would still retain her loveliness of spirit, the steadfast gaze, the vivid warmth of word and gesture.

For the first time in his life George knew the kind of love that projects itself forward into the future, that sees a woman as friend and as companion. And this woman whom he loved had just said that she did not love him.

"I won't give you up," he said doggedly.

"How can you keep me?" she asked quietly, and suddenly the structure of hope which he had built for himself tumbled.

"Then this is the—end?"

"I am afraid it is," and she offered him a cup.

His face grew suddenly gray. "I don't want any tea. I want

you," his hands went over his face. "I want you, Becky."

"Don't," she said, shakily, "I am sorry."

She was sorry to see him no longer shining, no longer splendid, but she was glad that the spell was broken—the charm of sparkling eyes and quick voice gone—forever.

She said again, as she gave him her hand at parting, "I'm sorry."

His laugh was not pleasant. "You'll be sorrier if you marry Paine."

"No," she said, and he carried away with him the look which came into her eyes as she said it, "No, if I marry Randy I shall not be sorry."

IV

Randy, arriving on the evening boat, caught the bus, and found the Admiral in it.

"It's Randy Paine," he said, as he climbed in and sat beside the old gentleman.

"My dear boy, God bless you. Becky will be delighted."

"I was in New York," was Randy's easy explanation, "and I couldn't resist coming up."

"We read your story, and Mrs. Prime told us how the editor received it. You are by way of being famous, my boy."

"Well, it's mighty interesting, sir," said young Randy.

It was late when they reached the little town, but the west was blood-red above the ridge, with the moor all darkling purple.

Becky was not in the house. "I saw her go down to the beach," Jane told them.

"In what direction?" Randy asked; "I'll go after her."

"She sometimes sits back of the blue boat," said Jane, "when there's a wind. But if you don't find her, Mr. Paine, she'll be back in time for supper. I told her not to be late. I am having raised rolls and broiled fish, and Mr. and Miss Cope are coming."

"I'll find her," said Randy, and was off.

The moon was making a path of gold across the purple waters, and casting sharp shadows on the sand. The blue boat, high on the beach, had lost its color in the pale light. But there was no other boat, so Randy went towards it. And as he went, he gave the old Indian cry.

Becky, wrapped in her red cape, deep in thoughts of the thing that had happened in the afternoon, heard the cry and doubted her ears.

It came again.

"Randy," she breathed, and stood up and saw him coming.

She ran towards him. "Oh, Randy, Randy."

She came into his arms as if she belonged there. And he, amazed but rapturous, received her, held her close.

"Oh, oh," she whispered, "you don't know how I have wanted you, Randy."

"It is nothing to the way that I have wanted you, my dear."

"Really, Randy?"

"Really, my sweet."

The moon was very big and bright. It showed her face white as a rose-leaf against his coat. He scarcely dared to breathe, lest he should frighten her. They stood for a moment in silence, then she said, simply, "You see, it was you, after all, Randy."

"Yes," he said, "I see. But when did you find it out?"

"This afternoon. Let's sit down here out of the wind behind the boat, and I'll tell you about it—"

But he was not ready yet to let her go. "To have you here—like this."

He stopped. He could not go on. He lifted her up to him, and their lips met. Years ago he had kissed her under the mistletoe; the kiss that he gave her now was a pledge for all the years to come.

They were late for supper. Jane relieved her mind to the Admiral and his guests. "She had a gentleman here this afternoon for tea, and neither of them ate anything. And now there's another gentleman, and the rolls are spoiling."

"You can serve supper, Jane," the Admiral told her; "they can eat when they come."

When they came, Becky's cheeks were as red as her cape. As she swept within the radius of the candle-light, Archibald Cope, who had risen at her entrance, knew what had happened. Her eyes were like stars. "Did Jane scold about us?" she asked, with a quick catch of her breath; "it was so lovely—with the moon."

Back of her was young Randy—Randy of the black locks, of the high-held head and Indian profile, Randy, with his air of Conqueror.

"I've told them all about you," Becky said, "and they have read your story. Will you please present him properly, Grandfather, while I go and fix my hair?"

She came back very soon, slim and childish in her blue velvet smock, her hair in that bronze wave across her forehead, her eyes still lighted.

She sat between her grandfather and Archibald.

"So," said Cope softly, under cover of the conversation, "it has happened?"

"What has happened?"

"The happy ending."

"Oh—how did you know?"

"As if the whole world wouldn't know just to look at you."

The Randy of the supper table at "The Whistling Sally" was a Randy that Becky had never seen. Success had come to him and love. There was the ring of it in his young voice, the flush of it on his cheeks. He was a man, with a man's future.

He talked of his work. "If I am a bore, please tell me," he said, "but it is rather a fairy-tale, you know, when you've made up your mind to a hum-drum law career to find a thing like this opening out."

Becky sat and listened. Her eyes were all for her lover. Already she thought of him at King's Crest, writing for the world, with her money making things easy for him, but not spoiling the simplicity of their tastes. If she thought at all of George Dalton, it was to find the sparkle and shine of his splendid presence dimmed by Randy's radiance.

"I hate to say that he is—charming," Cope complained.

He was a good sport, and he wanted Becky to be happy. But it was not easy to sit there and see those two—with the pendulum swinging between them of joy and dreams, and the knowledge of a long life together.

"Why should it be?" he asked Louise, as he stood beside her, later, on their own little porch which overlooked the sea; "those two—did you see them? While I—"

Louise laid her hand on his shoulder. "Yes. I think it is something like this, Arch. They've got to live it out, and life isn't always going to be just to-night for them. And perhaps in the years together they may lose some of their dreams. They've got to grow old, and you, you'll go out—with all—your dreams—"

He reached up and took the kind hand.

"'They all go out like this—into the night—but what a fleet of—stars.' Is that it, Louise?"

"Yes."

The clearness of the moonlight was broken by long fingers of fog stretched up from the horizon.

"I'll wrap up and sit here, Louise," Archibald said; "I shan't sleep if I go in."

"Don't stay too long. Good-night, my dear, good-night."

Archibald, watching the fog shut out the moonlight, had still upon him that sense of revolt. Fame had never come to him, and love had come too late.

Yet for Randy there was to be fulfillment—the wife of his heart, the applause of the world. What did it all mean? Why should one man have all, and the other—nothing?

Yet he had had his dreams. And the dreams of men lived. That which died was the least of them. The great old gods of democracy—Washington, Jefferson, Adams—had seen visions, and the visions had endured. Only yesterday Roosevelt had proclaimed his gallant doctrines. He had died proclaiming them, and the world held its head higher, because of his belief in its essential rightness.

The mists enveloped Archibald in a sort of woolly dampness. He saw for a moment a dim and distant moon. If he could have painted a moon like that—with fingers of fog reaching up to it—!

His own dreams of beauty? What of them? His pictures would not live. He knew that now. But he had given more than pictures to the world. He had given himself in a crusade which had been born of high idealism and a sense of brotherhood. Day after day, night after night, his plane had hung, poised like an eagle, above the enemy. He had been one of the young gods who had set their strength and courage against the greed and grossness of gray-coated hordes.

And these dreams must live—the dreams of the young gods— as the dreams of the old gods had endured. Because men had died to make others free, freedom must be the song on the lips of all men.

He thought of Randy's story. The Trumpeter Swan was only a stuffed bird in a glass case. But once he had spread his wings— flown high in the upper air. There had been strength in his pinions—joy in his heart—thrilling life in every feather of him. Some lovely lines drifted through Archibald's consciousness—

> "Upon the brimming water, among the stones
> Are nine and fifty swans.
> Unwearied still, lover by lover,
> They paddle in the cold
> Companionable streams or climb the air;
> Their hearts have not grown old;
> Passion and conquest, wander where they will.
> Attend upon them still—"

From the frozen north the swan had come to the sheltered bay and some one had shot him. He had not been asked if he wanted to live; they had taken his life, and had set him up there on the shelf—and that had been the end of him.

But was it the end? Stuffed and quiet in his glass case, he had looked down on a little boy. And the little boy had seen him not dead, but sounding his trumpet. And now the whole world would hear of him. In Randy's story, the Trumpeter would live again in the hearts of men.

The wind was rising—the fog blown back before it showed the golden track of the sea—light stretching to infinity!

He rose and stood by the rail. Then suddenly he felt a hand upon his, and looking down, he saw Becky.

"I ran away from Randy," she said, breathlessly, "just for a moment. I was afraid you might be alone, and unhappy."

His hand held hers. "Just for this moment you are mine?"

"Yes."

"Then let me tell you this—that I shall never be alone as long as I may have your friendship—I shall always be happy because I have—loved you."

He kissed her hand. "Run back to your Randy. Good-night, my dear, good-night."

Her lover received her rapturously at the door of the little house. They went in together. And Archibald looked out, smiling, over a golden sea.

THE END

www.ingramcontent.com/pod-product-compliance
Lightning Source LLC
Chambersburg PA
CBHW030523020726
47494CB00004B/1208